WANDMAKER'S
APPRENTICE

ED MASESSA

SCHOLASTIC PRESS
NEW YORK

Library of Congress Cataloging-in-Publication Data available

ISBN 978-0-545-86177-9

10 9 8 7 6 5 4 3 2 1   17 18 19 20 21

Printed in the U.S.A.   23

First edition, August 2017

Book design by Carol Ly

For Lorenzo and Milo—
may your futures
be bright and your
imaginations run wild

PROLOGUE

M alachai sat hunched over a table, where he had arranged a dozen elements in the order he was to use them. It had taken centuries of research and every bit of his expertise as a Wand Master to identify and locate them. One he'd found in Mexico at the bottom of a cenote—a water-filled sinkhole once used by the Maya for sacrificial offerings. Another he'd located in Burma, in a lost and abandoned temple after months of searching. He smiled as he recalled the tragic deaths of his exploration team in that unforgiving rain forest. If the jungle hadn't killed them, he would have. There could be no witnesses.

The rarest of the elements was an almost-mythical metal he'd located in a coral reef near an uncharted island in the South Pacific Ocean. For all he knew, this was the last specimen on Earth. Diffluonium was not on the periodic table of elements. Its properties were a mystery . . . except for one.

For the sixth time that morning, Malachai started, then stopped. Each of the elements needed to be combined in the proper sequence, using a technique that required extreme precision. He knew of only two other times this procedure had been successfully accomplished, and both times it had required the skill of three Wand Masters working in unison.

He was determined to do it alone.

Malachai took a deep breath and plunged into his work. The first six elements combined quickly and flawlessly, as he knew they would. He doubled his concentration. The minutes became hours. The stress caused him to sweat, and he quickly wiped the moisture on a sleeve to prevent it from contaminating the process. He doubled his concentration once more and took a deep breath that he would have to hold throughout the final step. Even the tiniest molecule of dust could make the wand he was crafting worthless. Finally, using every ounce of his power, he fused the diffluonium into the wand. His fingers, where they held it, began to tingle. He gently placed it on the table, where it began to glow with a dim, dark crimson light. A tiny wisp of smoke escaped from the tip.

Malachai smiled.

Ten minutes later, he took a breath.

PART ONE

"**B**ahtzen bizzle!"

Henry cringed. He knew he had made a mistake the second he squeezed a drop of the yellow fluid into an Erlenmeyer flask. A bright flash and a puff of smoke was a pretty strong clue. Serena and Brianna stifled giggles across the room.

"Sorry," Henry said.

"SORRY?" Coralis exploded. "Tell that to the small village you just eradicated due to your carelessness. Or to the forest you just turned to stone. Or to the caverns you just collapsed—" The old Wand Master's rant stopped abruptly as his next words caught in his throat. His forehead creased with lines of sorrow and pain. Silence filled the room for several uncomfortable seconds. Henry held his breath, and he knew Serena was doing the same.

The tails of Coralis's long black coat snapped as he spun and exited the room at a brisk pace. Henry had seen this reaction enough times over the past year to know their lessons were through for the day.

"Not again," Brianna moaned. She gazed at the half-finished

experiment in her hands. "What's the use? I'm pretty sure I don't have any talent anyway. At least he yelled at *you* this time."

Serena watched Henry's pout spread to his shoulders. "It's not your fault." She offered a one-armed hug. "How long is it going to take before he's himself again?"

Henry shrugged. He had no answer to that, because he understood there was no timetable for grief. When they'd defeated Dai She in the Arizona desert fourteen months earlier, Randall had been killed in the process. Once Coralis's finest apprentice, Randall was the main reason the world was still in one piece.

Coralis had not forgiven himself for what had happened, and occasionally something would come up in casual conversation that would trigger another painful memory. They never knew what would set Coralis off or how long it would take him to recover.

"Help me clean this mess up and we'll get an early start on the gardens," said Henry. "Gretchen will appreciate the extra time we can give her."

"Isn't today when she plans to try her new fertilizer?" asked Serena as she gave Henry a light jab with her elbow.

"Yes. She's going to try *your* fertilizer, which *you* created, totally by accident." Henry acted jealous, but they both knew how proud he was of her. He smiled broadly and she turned away as her olive skin turned a slight shade of pink.

Brianna rolled her eyes. "I'm outta here. Enjoy your 'garden time.'" She signaled air quotes with her fingers and smiled mischievously . . . then squinted in pain. "Ow!"

"Another headache?" Henry started toward her.

She held a hand up to stop him. "I'm okay. Like Gretchen said, it's probably just growing pains." Brianna smiled weakly and waved good-bye.

"I hope Gretchen's right." Serena took Henry's hand. "But in the meantime, there's 'gardening' to do."

Henry laughed. If there was an upside to Coralis's frequent absences, it was that the time he spent with Serena had been good for them. Aside from having the common link of being uprooted from their homes and sent to a foreign country, they seemed to learn more about their abilities when left alone to figure things out. Serena had once commented how it was just as important to know what would happen when they did something wrong, through trial and error, as it was to learn through careful study. As long as they didn't blow anything up—which was something Henry was more apt to do.

At times the results even gave Coralis a rare chuckle—like the time one of Henry's missteps caused a large piece of rose quartz to sprout eight legs and chase Gretchen through the courtyard. The quartztopus was all the ammunition Serena needed for days of relentless teasing.

"Wait a minute! Gardening can wait. Isn't today Thursday?" Henry asked brightly.

"Detour day!" exclaimed Serena. She took Henry's hand and pulled him from the classroom.

Castle Coralis was nestled into an area of the Carpathian Mountains so remote that weekly supplies had to be delivered by horse-drawn carriages. Lush forest thick with flora and fauna extended for kilometers in every direction. And this forest had one other characteristic that others didn't—a personality. Henry and Serena even went so far as to call it Forest, as if it were a person.

Forest seemed to enjoy toying with them. Each excursion presented a challenge. A footpath would be there one day and gone the next; occasionally, a path would close behind them as they walked, sealing them off from the castle and any sign of civilization.

Such was the case today.

They exited through an opening in the courtyard wall that hadn't been there the previous day. It immediately closed, blocking any hope of reentry. These were the trips Serena enjoyed the most. It was as if the castle and its surroundings were as much an instructor as Coralis was, sending them on journeys of discovery, directing them to explore new, unknown areas. She giggled with the delight of a five-year-old getting her first princess tiara.

Henry forged ahead so she wouldn't see him smiling at her reaction.

They walked an unfamiliar path for long minutes. Finally, they came upon an open field filled with wildflowers and herbs. On their walks, it wasn't unusual for them to stumble upon unfamiliar plants, which they would bring back for Gretchen. Her knowledge of botany was limitless and she willingly shared every detail—which plants could be used for healing wounds and ailments, which could be used to add potency to spells, and which were so poisonous that simply touching them to their lips could have devastating results.

The botanical bounty in the open field before them was unprecedented. Nearly every plant was new to them. As the forest path closed at their backs, inviting them to step forward, Serena suggested there would be far too many to bring back this time.

Henry came to an abrupt stop, deeply suspicious. He felt the tiny hairs on the back of his neck rise with a tingling that he called his "Spidey-Sense."

Serena noticed his mood and immediately switched from exhilaration to caution. "What is it, Henry?"

"I don't know." He rubbed the top of his head nervously and focused on the tree line surrounding the field. The entire setting was so calm that he could have easily imagined families enjoying peaceful picnics among the flowers. Yet something wasn't right. "I don't think we should go out there."

"Forest has never led us into danger before," Serena said. But his worry was infectious. She turned as if to leave—then remembered the path had already closed behind them. "We don't have many choices."

It suddenly struck him what was amiss. "There's no path through the field. We've never been given free rein before."

"Maybe it's finally up to us to make a choice," Serena said. "Maybe it's a gift from Forest." She seemed to like the sound of that and took several steps into the field.

Henry's Spidey-Sense flared up in warning. "Get back!" he yelled.

Too late. In the blink of an eye the field disappeared from his view, replaced by a wall of vegetation—and Serena was on the other side of it. "Serena!" he shouted. "Where are you?"

If she replied, he couldn't hear her. In fact, all was deadly silent—no insects chirping, no wind rustling. He thrashed wildly through the underbrush. But instead of moving forward, he found himself repelled backward by the plant life. The more effort he made, the harder it fought against him; he was losing ground.

Almost comically, Henry thought, *This is the angriest vegetation I've ever seen.* And it was *definitely* angry. When he finally gave up and turned around, the path had reopened behind him.

He shouted her name again and again. Nothing. Desperation hit him like a wave. He yelled "Serena!" at the top of his lungs. There was no training for this, no spells. Even if he thought of one, he worried it would only make Forest angrier.

He threw a tantrum, attempted to rip a branch from a shrub, and came away with nothing but a handful of leaves. The stripped branch immediately sprouted more leaves, showing no signs of damage. "Fine! Be that way!"

He turned toward the path, shoulders slumped, and began making his way back to the castle.

The walk was much longer than it should have been. Whereas the path into the forest had been fairly straight, the one leading back almost seemed to go in circles. It narrowed every few hundred meters, forcing Henry to duck or squeeze to avoid being scratched. Forest was teaching him a lesson— don't mess with Mother Nature.

The tree line ended abruptly, much closer to the castle walls than he'd expected. Henry looked up and gasped, nearly stumbling onto his rump before righting himself.

"Where have you been?" Coralis growled from eight meters up. "Well? Answer me!"

Henry recoiled from Coralis's anger. He was attempting to come up with a response when a thought struck him. "With all due respect, sir, you obviously knew precisely where to find me."

He thought he detected the briefest of smiles, which was quickly masked. "Watch your tongue," Coralis said darkly. "Where's the girl?"

Henry narrowed his eyes. Coralis knew Henry hated it when he referred to Serena as "the girl." The old man was deliberately trying to provoke him. "In there," he said, nodding toward the trees.

"Humpf. About time." Which wasn't the response Henry expected. "Never mind that now. Get in here. We have visitors."

Coralis quickly disappeared, leaving Henry with a dilemma. The openings in the castle wall were never in the same place, but Forest always led him straight to one. Not today. As far as he could see in either direction, there were no doorways. "How do I get back in?" he shouted up at the wall.

"You're the smart one," Coralis answered from farther down the ramparts. "You figure it out. And don't upset the castle like you did the poor trees!"

Poor trees, my foot, thought Henry. *They pushed me around worse than a bully.*

He decided to go in the opposite direction of Coralis, running his hands along the massive gray bricklike boulders that made up the outer surface of the wall. He arrived at the corner and hesitated. Given the events of the day, he wanted to be prepared for more surprises.

He tentatively took a step forward. Then two. On the third, he leapt forward and turned the corner. He thought he had steeled himself for any surprise. He was wrong.

Three meters away, a falcon stood its ground, blocking his path. Henry raised his head to shout to Coralis. The falcon moved its head from side to side as if to say no.

It was the same thing Randall had done in Henry's garage at the very start of his adventure.

But Randall was . . .

Henry swallowed hard. It wasn't possible. He slapped his hand against the stone wall, hoping one of two things would happen. Either he'd spook the falcon and make it leave, or he'd wake up from a strange dream.

His palm made direct contact with a sharp outcropping on the stone surface. "Ouch!" He rubbed it vigorously while watching the falcon slowly shake its head—this time in disgust.

Henry stopped rubbing, suddenly feeling humiliated. He nervously cleared his throat. "I can't imagine how you could be, but I should probably ask. Are . . . are you Ran—"

The falcon screeched as it leapt into the air, and with a giant flap of its wings, it almost cleared Henry's head. Almost. The tip of a talon scraped against his scalp. Henry would look at it later, but he instinctively knew it was the exact same spot where Randall had nicked him in the garage.

He threw his arms up in self-defense, stumbling into . . . and *through* the wall, landing unceremoniously at the feet of Coralis.

"Are you quite through playing?" growled the Wand Master. "Get up and dust yourself off. We're keeping them waiting."

Henry stared at the wall. The opening, if there indeed had been an opening, had disappeared so quickly that he wondered if he had magically passed through solid stone. Coralis walked rapidly through the courtyard, leaving Henry no option but to run to catch up.

He knew he'd eventually have to tell Coralis about the falcon, but he also knew the old man's moods, and now was not the time.

Serena's fate at the hands of Forest weighed heavily on Henry's mind. He chastised himself for not trying harder to reach her, yet he strongly suspected it would have done no good. And if Forest wanted to separate them, he had to believe it was for a good reason and that Serena was safe. Certainly Coralis didn't seem concerned.

He followed on the Wand Master's heels through the courtyard. One of the first things Henry had done when he arrived over a year ago was to pace off the courtyard's interior, which was an almost-perfect square, roughly two hundred meters on each side. Surrounding the courtyard on three sides were three perfectly level walls, eight meters high and three meters thick, with a walkway along the top that allowed someone to walk the entire perimeter.

The only two structures within the courtyard were a small chicken coop and an even smaller shed for garden supplies. The rest was soft, feathery grass with landscaped patches of fragrant flowers—and, of course, Gretchen's expansive garden. She grew all the vegetables and herbs they needed.

On its fourth side, which was set with multiple doorways, the courtyard ran up against the main castle. The Wand Master referred to it as Castle Coralis, but it reminded Henry more of a medieval fortress than any castle from a storybook. He had studied designs of grand buildings with turrets, towers and spires, drawbridges and keeps. This one, though it loomed huge and imposing above the courtyard and its walls, was as simple as something a small child would construct on a sandy beach.

It was as if the word *round* was not in the architect's vocabulary. The facade stood four stories tall, with each level set slightly back from the previous one—like the levels of a pyramid. In contrast, the rear of the castle was a sheer wall—as if the builders had either run out of materials or imagination.

Inside, the angular theme continued. There were no rounded archways between rooms, no grandiose paintings or sculptures, no massive chandeliers. The only room of any majesty was the foyer, which rose to ten meters, supported by six solid wooden columns, though not the kind with ornate carvings or molding. These columns were covered in tree bark and were very much alive.

No amount of poking or prodding could get Coralis to reveal any secrets about the castle. Henry anxiously awaited a behind-the-scenes tour, which Coralis said would come only when he learned to be patient. A year was a long time to be patient.

There wasn't a shred of doubt in Henry's mind that the castle contained secrets beyond his wildest dreams. He had seen doors with complex locking mechanisms, and they teased his imagination. He hoped that what was behind them lived up to his expectations.

Coralis led Henry into the rear of the castle through a large teakwood door swinging on well-oiled hinges. Within moments, Henry was hopelessly lost. It had taken weeks before he was able to navigate his way through the mazelike hallways to arrive at dinner on time. At one point, he'd resorted to dropping bread crumbs, but only succeeded in doubling back over the crumbs he had already deposited, apparently having walked in one big circle. There was nothing magic about it. It was just that Henry's internal compass wasn't quite level.

Serena, on the other hand, had no such problem. She had an uncanny knack for navigating the halls with ease. "I had excellent teachers who were experts in tracking both animals and humans," she had told him with a sly smile.

He worried again about her encounter with Forest and hoped her tracking skills were as good as she said they were.

Three left turns and two right turns later, they emerged onto what Henry called the den. It was the closest thing he had seen to an office, although there was no desk to speak of. Two of the walls were lined with shelves that housed numerous volumes of leather-bound books and hundreds of artifacts ranging from misshapen skulls to odd pieces of driftwood to the mummified remains of creatures Henry could not identify.

Currently, however, and much to his surprise, there were two additional items—both human.

"Henry, allow me to introduce our two new guests, Luis Saenz and Katelyn O'Neill." Coralis then turned to Henry and raised an expectant eyebrow.

"Oh . . . I'm . . . my name is Henry Leach." He stumbled over his words.

A short laugh, more like a snort, came from Luis, who quickly covered his mouth.

Henry immediately took a dislike to him. "What's so funny?" He meant to be firm and confident but his voice betrayed him and cracked—something that had been happening more and more frequently.

"Where I come from, a leech is a bloodsucking worm," Luis said defiantly, accepting Henry's challenge with a tone of disdain.

Henry had become better at reading a person's aura. He could sense anger seeping from every pore of the boy's body, and he suspected there was much more to it than Henry's presence. The boy was slightly taller than him, with shoulder-length jet-black hair and skin a shade or two lighter than Serena's but darker than Henry's. He wore a dark green button-down shirt and black cargo shorts that came to his knees. His many pockets bulged in shapes that Henry could not identify, but about which he was mildly curious.

Well-worn, thick-soled shoes that had seen many months of hiking completed the jungle explorer look.

"Luis is from Ecuador." Coralis mercifully spared Henry the humiliation of having to come up with a retort. He hadn't been bullied in a long time, and his comebacks were a little rusty.

Henry knew three things about Ecuador. He knew it was located on the equator, that it contained part of the Amazon rain forest, and that the Galápagos Islands (one of his favorite places to read about) were about nine hundred kilometers off its coast. He decided to start over, and this time he'd take a friendly approach. "Have you been to the rain forest?"

"Ha!" Luis laughed incredulously. "I *live* in the rain forest." He spoke perfect, if accented, English, and his mockery came across loud and clear. He even went so far as to stand taller and puff his chest out.

This time it was the girl's turn to snicker as she took in Luis's posturing with a sidelong glance. Henry immediately liked her.

Luis turned to her with his lip curled in a sneer. Henry prepared himself to come to her defense, but she gave Luis a disarming look that sapped all the bravado out of the air.

Henry had not seen a look like that since his encounter with Bella, also known as "the Amazing Zeppo," who many months ago he'd witnessed holding an entire crowd under her command. He knew there must be much more to Katelyn than her diminutive appearance implied. Her skin was very pale, as if never touched by the sun, and her face was framed by curling locks of auburn hair that fell halfway down her back. In complete contrast to Luis, she wore a simple white blouse and light khaki trousers.

"And where are you from?" Luis asked. There was still a snide undertone, but none of the anger he had projected toward Henry a moment earlier.

"I hail from County Clare in Ireland." If her look was mesmerizing, her voice was captivating. Her delicate Irish accent perfectly complemented her small features, which were highlighted by a button nose speckled in tiny freckles.

Henry felt a blush coming on for no apparent reason and was once again rescued by Coralis. "You can do better than that, Katelyn."

"Aye. I grew up on the Aran Islands, a wee bit off the coast." Her brow wrinkled as she stopped abruptly, unwilling to share any more.

"Hm," Coralis mumbled. "Since none of you wish to elaborate, and Serena has been momentarily detained, perhaps we should save the rest of the introductions for later."

"Who's Serena?" Luis asked, suddenly interested.

"She's an apprentice, like me." Henry was surprised by his forceful venom. There was something about Luis that instinctively irritated him and made him feel that he had to prove himself superior.

Unfortunately, Luis seemed to pick up on Henry's insecurity. "Maybe I should take a hot bath before those introductions. It's been a long trip and I'd like to look my best for the apprentices." He winked knowingly at Henry.

"We wouldn't want to have any odors at the dinner table that would ruin our appetite," Henry snapped.

Coralis watched the exchange with growing confusion. "Gretchen!" he yelled.

"Yes, Coralis." She appeared instantly at his side.

The Wand Master flinched at her sudden appearance. "Have you been eavesdropping?" he growled.

"Oh, no, sir. I was just passing by," she said with a broad smile.

"Well. Please show our guests to their rooms." And he added with a mischievous smile of his own: "Take the long way."

Serena's muscles ached, her arms were covered in shallow cuts, and sweat dripped down her body. Despite years of outdoor activity in the Navajo Nation and her rigorous training at Castle Coralis, nothing had prepared her for an afternoon at the mercy of Forest.

There was no point in fighting it. Every time she stopped to protest, it quickly grew in around her, forcing her forward. In one particularly stubborn moment she had held her ground and allowed Forest to consume her. It reacted angrily, growing thick brambles that she had to fight past, tearing her clothes and accumulating many cuts and scrapes in the process. From that point on, she'd obediently moved forward.

Several hours later, she encountered a steep incline covered in rocks and boulders, with only a few sparsely spaced shrubs to assist her climb. When the vegetation ran out, she was reduced to a difficult crawl.

Serena paused to catch her breath. She sat heavily, cursing the fact that Henry had their only water supply. Her lips were parched and her clothes were drenched with sweat despite the cool mountain temperature.

But when she finally looked up, back in the direction she'd come from, the beauty of her surroundings took her breath away all over again. She slowly stood to take it all in. The steep slope blocked the view at her back, but for 180 degrees in front of her, the forest spread out in a canopy of rich greens of every shade imaginable. As much as she loved her native desert, she could easily imagine herself staying in Romania for a very long time.

The air was crisp and clean. A sudden breeze wafted up from the trees, filling her with wonder and purpose. She had been forging ahead blindly, and it occurred to her that without Forest to provide a path, she had no idea where to go—but she knew that she must continue climbing.

A soft snort at her back startled her. She slid precariously down the incline before regaining her balance and crouching in a defensive stance. Less than five meters away, an animal that appeared to be a cross between an antelope and a goat stared at her, motionless. About the size of a Rottweiler, it had rich brown hair and two horns that grew out straight before ending in small hooks.

Serena noted the white markings on the sides of its head and recalled its name from Coralis's nature lessons—this was a chamois. Of all the species native to Romania that she might stumble upon alone, she was glad to encounter this one. While the bear, wolf, and lynx were powerful totems back home, she wouldn't have wanted to meet one in the wild.

It snorted again and jerked its head for her to follow. "So much for not knowing where to go," she murmured.

The chamois had a distinct climbing advantage but seemed to recognize her limitations, and carefully selected a route that allowed her to walk without stumbling. It approached one of the few remaining shrubs, used its mouth to grab it by the base, and yanked it out of the ground.

A small pool of water bubbled up. Serena dove for it and drank greedily, cupping it with her hands. Because of the natural filter provided by the rocky base, the water was clear and cold. She had never tasted anything so good. The chamois gave her a gentle nudge, reminding her of her manners. "Sorry," she said, allowing it to take its fill as well.

As their journey continued, Serena's thighs and calves burned from the effort. At last, they approached the crest of the mountain. The chamois was a dozen meters ahead of her. It dropped from sight over the ridge. When she finally caught up and looked down the other side, it had disappeared completely.

There was no time to wonder where it had gone, for a short distance away was a small stand of medium-growth trees. In the center of the stand was a pool of water, and surrounding the pool was a group of colorfully clad people. One of them motioned her forward . . . as if she had a choice.

She laughed to herself, wishing Henry were there with her. She could imagine the look on his face. It would light up with surprise at every new thing. In moments like this, his blue eyes would grow large and round and he'd rub his hair nervously. She couldn't wait to tell him about it.

She carefully picked her path down to the trees. Another of Coralis's lessons came to her. These were Hutsuls, a group of people native to Ukraine and Romania who called the Carpathian Mountains their home. This gathering consisted of four women and six men, one of whom was no taller than a child. He was the one who stepped forward to greet her.

"You have been chosen," he said. His voice was rich and deep, and he spoke with great gravitas, as if leading some ceremony. "But are you ready to pay the price?"

"Chosen?" she said, taking a single step back. "Price?"

The man broke character and laughed then, as did the rest of the group. She had a feeling that this wasn't the first time they had orchestrated this scene.

"I apologize," he said in clipped English. "We took bets on how . . . surprised you would be. I think Lesya wins." Hearing her name, a woman curtsied.

Serena nodded. "My name is—"

"Serena," he finished. "Yes, we know. The old man told us."

Well, at least Coralis knows where I am, she thought.

"Come." He motioned her forward. The men rolled up their pants and the women hiked up their skirts. They sat at the edge of the pool and put their feet in the water. Serena took this as a cue to join them and did the same. Her reaction to the water gave them another hearty laugh.

"It is hot spring, yes?" The small man chuckled.

"Yes!" She laughed back. "Quite hot." The water was clear and warm enough to be a hot bath, yet not uncomfortable.

Her toes tingled. The pain in her calves subsided. She was tempted to jump in to relieve the rest of her muscles.

"It is for you," he said.

Her brow creased in confusion. "What do you mean?"

"In you must go." Gone was the jovial bantering. The group looked at her expectantly. Something in their manner told her they wanted her to go in all the way.

"Um . . ." The moment became awkward. Did they really expect her to go for a swim while they all sat there and watched her?

The small man acknowledged her discomfort with a tilt of his head. "Just step in. You will see."

She stood and took a tentative step forward. The sunlight upon the water made it difficult to tell how deep it was. Which was why one second she was knee-deep and the next she was grasping for the surface. She popped up and laughed joyously, then gasped. She spun in a circle, treading water.

The Hutsuls were gone. They had disappeared as quickly as the chamois had.

The water began to swirl around her, faster and faster. Suddenly she was caught in a whirlpool. She tried desperately to swim to shore, but it was impossible. "Help!" She tried to make a mind connection with Henry. But if she did, what then? It had taken her hours to get there, and Forest had purposely cut him off.

"Help me . . ." She realized the small man had never told her his name, and nearly choked in her panic. The water swirled faster, pulling her under. And though she thrashed wildly with every ounce of effort she had left, the water won.

Her last breath would not last long. She was spinning in a tight circle, going farther and farther down. The surface was unreachable—just a hazy vision of light and shadow so far away. How could she be raised in a dry desert only to drown in a mountain hot spring?

She said one last prayer and gave up. She stopped fighting her burning lungs and took in a watery breath.

That's when she realized she could still breathe!

Despair gave way to wonder. Panic gave way to something she could only describe as liberation. Her fear of drowning transformed into a sensation of euphoria. She quickly touched her neck and checked her feet, then laughed at her foolishness. If she had sprouted gills and a tail, she might have panicked all over again—although she found the idea of becoming a mermaid intriguing. What would Henry have thought about that!

Henry. She needed to attempt another mind connection. They had secretly been practicing in earnest since discovering they had a natural mind-link. Distance didn't seem to matter—but this was much farther apart than they'd been in any of their experiments.

The process of breathing underwater was identical to breathing air. Her chest rose and fell with each watery gulp. She relaxed, focused, and reached out to Henry's mind. In reply she received a jumble of thoughts that made no sense. It was like hearing a foreign language for the first time.

She closed the link, focused, and tried again. This time, the connection was immediate. She reeled from the impact—not of words, but a cluster of colors and images. They slammed at her in an overwhelming torrent. She felt like her head might actually explode and tried in vain to break the link.

She knew it instinctively: This wasn't Henry's mind.

The sender must have felt her pull back. The connection strengthened. Many images swirled in a brilliant mix of colors, re-forming into a single figure. It was a woman. Her outline was fuzzy—like looking at a 3-D film without wearing the glasses—yet Serena could tell it was the most beautiful woman she had ever laid eyes on. Long raven hair waved around a porcelain face. Eyes like pockets of coal pierced her own. Serena blinked and the image clarified a bit more, but never completely.

"Hello," the woman said. Her voice was a symphony of tones, a combination of birdcalls and whale song and wind chimes. *"I am Gaia."*

Serena knew the name. Gaia, the Earth Mother. It was impossible! Gaia was a myth—the mother goddess, creator of all.

The woman laughed. *"No,"* she said. *"I am as real as the sun and the sea."*

"Nahasdzaan," Serena said, voicing the name given to the Earth Mother by the Navajo.

"Yes, her too," came the reply. *"I am all things to all people. The Earth is mine to care for."*

Serena struggled to maintain any sort of rational thought. If the legends were actually true, and this was indeed the embodiment of the Earth Mother, then she was in the presence of one of the greatest powers in the universe. Even if she could overcome the shock that paralyzed her speech, she wasn't sure what she would say.

"You have been chosen." Gaia repeated the words spoken by the Hutsul man. *"Watch and learn."*

Her image dissipated. In its place an unfamiliar landscape appeared—one covered in rock, snow, and ice. A herd of large animals, possibly musk oxen or yaks, trudged across the frozen surface. Like a video taken from a plane, the landscape moved forward with dizzying speed.

Serena was flying!

Within seconds, she was at the foot of an enormous mountain range that continued as far as the eye could see, the tops of which faded into the clouds high above. The mountain she had just climbed was a small countryside hill in comparison.

Frightfully fast, she soared up the mountain face. She winced and ducked her head as she entered the clouds, then gasped as she broke clear of them. The mountain continued upward. Instinctively, she looked behind her and could imagine angels walking on the soft white blanket of clouds below.

She inhaled sharply as she crested the mountain and went into free fall down the other side, gathering the speed of an out-of-control roller coaster. The vision took a sharp right turn. In the distance, a valley that looked as if it had never been touched by humans came into view. It was so surreal it could have been a mural painted on the mountain wall.

A temple materialized at the far end of the valley, sprawling across the top of a ridge and extending down along the sheer mountain face. Serena recognized the design as Asian, but she didn't know enough about architecture to be more specific. In sharp contrast to the whiteness around it, the temple was a beautiful shade of crimson.

She drew closer, awed by the incredible size of it—the temple might have taken centuries to build. Massive gates provided the only entrance, flanked on either side by enormous sculptures of Tibetan snow lions. Beyond the gates loomed an expansive courtyard with a huge golden Buddha in the center. Kneeling monks in simple red robes were arranged before it in rows of worship.

Without warning, Serena veered sharply left and reflexively threw her arms out to keep her balance. The Earth Mother laughed softly, putting Serena at ease. The ancient goddess was toying with her as only an old friend could.

With the temple behind her, she flew alongside the mountain. Again she extended an arm, thinking she was close enough to touch it. In response, the Earth Mother dipped her in closer. Serena laughed aloud as her hand disappeared inside the rock. The experience was so real she had forgotten her physical presence was still submerged in a small mountain hot spring.

Abruptly, the forward motion stopped. She stood at the mouth of a cave. *"Go,"* said the Earth Mother. All levity was gone. That one word was as much an omen as a command.

Serena walked forward, her feet gliding a dozen meters for each step. Several minutes later, deep inside the mountain, she came upon a pair of intimidating guards. Clothed in the same red robes as the monks, these figures also wore masks. The masks were not decorative, but appeared to provide some sort of biological or chemical protection.

Slung across their chests were dark brown sashes lined with pockets, each one housing a wand—some wood, some crystal. She knew they couldn't see her, but their heads swiveled from side to side as if they sensed her presence.

The Earth Mother took control. She swept Serena past them into a small cavern where the tunnel ended. An ancient, man-made brick wall blocked her path. "What is it you want me to see?" she asked. Her eyes were drawn to a hollowed-out depression in the wall. Something was inside. Something that radiated immense power.

"Pangaea," the Earth Mother replied with such reverence and sadness that Serena's heart felt suddenly heavy.

"Remember."

Serena opened her eyes, tried to breathe, and coughed up a lungful of water. She rolled onto her side as she retched uncontrollably until at last she lay on her back, her chest heaving from exhaustion.

"Are you all right?"

The familiar voice startled her. "Yes. I think so."

"Good." Coralis gazed toward the west, where the sun shone directly through a mountain pass in the distance. He turned to Serena, then looked into the pool.

Serena did the same, almost expecting Gaia to be there. But whatever magic the water had provided was now gone.

"It's getting late. We should hurry." Coralis walked swiftly up the slope.

Serena held back for just a moment and was rewarded with a final wave good-bye from the depths of the pool.

Henry sat on the edge of his bed, reliving the meeting with the new guests over and over, like hitting a replay button on his brain. There was no denying it: Luis had gotten under his skin. The new boy's anger had nothing to do with Henry, yet there was little doubt that he was to be the target. One thing he knew for certain: If Luis was to stay at the castle for any length of time, they were going to have to work through it.

Much to his chagrin, life had just gotten more complicated.

His thoughts drifted to Katelyn. Henry had always been an avid reader. His favorite books were fantasies, and one of his favorite topics was the land of faerie. As far as he was concerned, that land truly existed. His short time with Coralis had taught him that anything was possible. So why not a parallel world or dimension in which mythical creatures thrived?

Many faerie stories took place in Ireland, where Katelyn was from. In fact, with her facial features, she could almost be an elf. Perhaps even a changeling, swapped at birth for a human baby and left to live her life in Henry's world. He smiled at the thought but knew he'd have to keep it to himself. He imagined that if Luis found out, he would use it against him.

A knock at the door interrupted his rambling thoughts, startling him. "Who is it?"

He expected Gretchen but got Coralis. "May I come in?"

Henry was certain the Wand Master was there to reprimand him for his earlier behavior. But time with the old man had taught him he could not postpone the inevitable. Better to apologize and move on. He opened the door. "Look, I'm sorr—Oh!"

Coralis wasn't alone. Serena smiled broadly, then rushed forward and wrapped him in a bear hug. "You are not going to believe what happened!" She bounced lively on her toes, unable to contain her excitement.

"Just a minute, young lady." Coralis ushered them into the room and closed the door. He motioned for them to have a seat on the bed and pulled up a chair to sit across from them.

Henry and Serena glanced at each other. Something was troubling Coralis.

"Serena has brought back some disturbing news." He stopped, as if unsure how to proceed. "I . . . When I saw that Malachai had returned, I knew it would only be a matter of time before he would strike again. Our encounter with his son, Dai She, was bad enough. We lost too much . . . almost lost everything in that struggle. And yet Dai She had the bite of a teething puppy compared to his father."

He stood and began to pace. "Shortly after arriving back here, I put out a call to Wandmaker conclaves around the world. Partly to alert them of the forthcoming danger, and partly to instruct them on what to watch for. I know this enemy well. In all likelihood, he will leave residual traces of wand activity that might help lead us to him. But mostly . . ."

He sat again, demanding their full attention. "Mostly, it was to put out a call for more apprentices."

"Not him!" Henry shouted before he could catch himself. Coralis frowned deeply.

"Who's *him*?" Serena asked, puzzled by the outburst.

Henry slumped back. He'd been hoping Luis was nothing more than a temporary houseguest. To think that they would be in class together, living under the same roof, sharing uncomfortable meals together . . . He felt like Coralis had added a wolf to a kennel full of Chihuahuas.

"You will meet our guests very soon, Serena. And stop brooding, Henry. It doesn't suit you," Coralis growled. "Two of the new recruits arrived earlier today. A third will arrive tomorrow. I am counting on the two of you to make them feel comfortable as quickly as possible."

Henry groaned.

"What's wrong?" Serena asked, concerned over his obvious apprehension.

Henry stopped short of giving an honest reply when he saw a dark cloud settle over Coralis's face. "You'll see soon enough."

"I need to know that I can count on you." Coralis paused, awaiting an answer.

Serena patted Henry lightly on the hand. "Of course you can."

Henry stared at his hand, ignoring the four eyes that applied silent pressure for an answer. But something gnawed at his stomach. Over the course of the last year, he'd begun to think of himself as unique. Capable of doing things others couldn't. For the first time, he was fully in charge of his life, unthreatened by bullies and free to learn and explore and grow. His world had changed for the better and he had found his place in it. But in the span of a few hours, everything had changed once again.

"Well, Henry?" Coralis nudged him, but the words were spoken with kindness and understanding. Perhaps he suspected how Henry felt.

His hand still tingled where Serena had touched him. He smiled. If she was part of his team, there was no way he'd refuse. "I'm in."

"Good!" Coralis smiled at last. And it suddenly occurred to Henry that the old man could have forced Henry to comply, if he'd so chosen. But the Wand Master had not done anything to influence his decision. He never attempted to read Henry's thoughts or coerce him into doing something he didn't want to.

The pit in his stomach vanished. Coralis had shown true respect for him. He knew he had made the right choice and would not let them down. "When do we start?"

Coralis stood. "We meet for dinner in an hour." On his way out the door he glanced back over his shoulder. "The girl can fill you in on her little adventure." He winked slyly at Henry and left.

"The girl?" Serena asked indignantly.

"Let it go." Henry laughed. "Just tell me what happened."

"Serena, would you please pass me that plate of mashed cauliflower?"

From the moment they sat down, Luis had gone into flirt mode. He poured his full attention on Serena as if there was no one else in the room. Several times, Henry looked around the table at the others' faces, but no one seemed bothered by it except him.

Coralis had seated Henry and Katelyn on one side of the broad, weathered table that was meant to accommodate three times as many people. Serena and Luis sat across from them, with Coralis and Gretchen at either end. Brianna, who had a headache, had taken dinner in her room. Henry wished that their mother were near enough to visit, but after she'd left Brianna in Coralis's care, she had returned to her childhood home to fully reconcile with her estranged parents.

The cauliflower was directly in front of Henry. He pushed it—slowly—toward Luis before Serena could reach for it. "Did you eat much cauliflower in the jungle?" He pressed hard on the word *jungle* with a sarcastic tone.

Luis flashed a wicked grin. "No, which is why I asked for more. It's very different from the mashed cassava roots my people eat."

"That sounds yummy," Serena said, then proceeded to ask him about other things he ate in the Amazon.

"Oh, you'd be surprised. Pan-fried piranha is one of my favorites."

"Piranha! Aren't they dangerous?" Serena asked eagerly.

Henry stabbed at his food. No matter what he did to take Luis down a notch, the other boy had a response that enticed Serena to ask more. It bothered him that he couldn't tell if it was her insatiable thirst for knowledge . . . or something else.

"We eat potatoes," Katelyn said.

Henry was so caught up in Luis's antics that he'd almost forgotten she was there. "Excuse me?" he asked politely.

"We eat potatoes," Katelyn repeated. "I know everyone thinks the Irish only eat potatoes, and that's not strictly true, but I can tell you, we eat a *lot* of them." She smiled at Henry and started speaking with a horrible Southern accent. "There's fried potatoes, barbecued potatoes, mashed potatoes, potatoes and gravy, potatoes and shrimp . . ."

"Forrest Gump?" Henry laughed. "Is that your best impression of Forrest Gump?"

"Aye, from the movie. One of my favorites." She giggled. "But it was actually Bubba who said that line."

Henry lost it. "Say that again. Say 'Bubba.'"

She repeated the name. Henry laughed loud and long until Coralis tapped a fork against his plate in reprimand.

"Sorry," Henry said, but could barely contain a chuckle.

"Katelyn, why don't you tell us about yourself," said Gretchen as she popped a piece of baked butternut squash into her mouth.

"There's not much to tell, really." Katelyn moved the food around on her plate.

Henry knew what it was like to be shy and reluctant to talk to a group of strangers, but he was very interested in her homeland and was glad Gretchen had opened that door. "There has to be more to Ireland than potatoes," he prodded. "What town are you from? What's it like there? Have you ever seen faeries?"

As soon as the words came out, he wished he could take them back. Luis snorted from across the table. Even Serena failed to stifle a giggle. But the effect on Katelyn was quite the opposite. Her hand froze in place and her entire body visibly tensed up. The others must have noticed too, as conversation ground to a halt and silence settled like a dead weight.

"Why don't you tell us about Inishmore," said Coralis, using the slightest push of Voice to calm her down.

"Inishmore," she said softly. "An old isle with an older past." She abruptly laughed, startling everyone. "You certainly don't want to hear me talk in riddles now, do ya? Though truth be told, you can learn the most about Ireland through riddles, limericks, and ballads. 'Tis the best way to learn history. Helps you remember things that otherwise might be forgotten."

"Is it pretty?" Serena leaned forward. "Where I'm from is mostly red earth and rock. I'd always imagined lots of green in Ireland."

"Green in every shade." Katelyn smiled and relaxed. "Inishmore is a lovely island off the western coast, with lush green grass and beautiful flowers."

"Like Hawaii?" asked Serena.

"I couldn't say, but probably fewer people. When my friend Trisha and her family moved away, that left eight hundred thirty-seven of us."

"My village had half that," said Luis thoughtfully.

"Aye, then you know, eh? No secrets in small places."

Luis frowned as he nodded. "No secrets."

"Well then." She exhaled deeply. "Let's get to it. I grew up not far from Dun Aengus."

"I only meant for you to tell us more about your home," said Coralis, suddenly concerned.

"No, this is fine. Better I share now than they find out later." The tiniest smile and shrug of her shoulders told him she was okay to continue. "Dun Aengus is an old fort that dates back over three thousand years. How old is America?" she asked Henry.

"A little more than five hundred years."

"By your history books," Serena said, offended.

Henry stuttered, "S-sorry . . . I mean . . ."

"It's okay." Serena winked at him. "That's a story for another day."

"Still," continued Katelyn. "You get my point. There's old, and there's *old*. There are no clever limericks to tell us the history of Dun Aengus. Some think it was built as a fort to defend the island. Others think that perhaps it was used for ancient religious ceremonies. It doesn't really matter what anyone thinks. What matters is what happened."

She paused to collect her thoughts. "It's a popular tourist site, as it sits on a cliff one hundred meters high with a spectacular view of the water. But when the days turned cold and the tourists were gone, Trisha, our friend Liam, and I would sneak over the outer walls and play among the ruins. Sometimes it was just hide-and-seek, but sometimes we fashioned ourselves to be druids, conducting ancient rituals. We'd chant all sorts of silly things that made no sense."

She smiled at the memory, but it disappeared rapidly. "Until the day I found the old book in Mum's closet. It was hidden for a reason, but I was always the curious one. What's the old saying? Curiosity killed the cat? Well . . . the book contained many passages that looked like they could be spells."

"Oh no," said Henry gravely.

"Aye, it gets worse. One particular spell had notes in Mum's handwriting, so I memorized it." She reached into a fold in her skirt and withdrew a stone wand. "Not much to look at, is it?"

Henry and Serena groaned.

"Then you know already. It doesn't matter how innocent it looks. I'd like to take credit for finding it, but about six months ago—"

"You got a visit from a falcon." Luis finished her sentence, then reached into a pants pocket and produced a wand of his own.

Henry glanced worriedly toward Serena. Now was not the time for another Coralis relapse.

Katelyn raised an eyebrow at Luis. "At first I thought it was just a piece of limestone the bird picked up. But there was something about it that spoke to me. I kept it. But I never thought to try and use it until that day at Dun Aengus. There is a very large stone slab that always seemed like a place we druids should conduct our business. Liam stood larger than life, chanting his usual nonsense while Trisha urged him on. I joined in—pointing my wand toward the slab and reciting my mum's spell."

Her bottom lip trembled slightly. "The two of them stared at me, frightened, and backed away. I looked down and saw myself glowing. It spread from me onto the slab. The ground rumbled and began to crack open. You asked if I've ever seen a faerie, Henry? Not until that moment. But they weren't the wee cutesy type. They were large and angry and misshapen and horrible-looking. As you might imagine, I panicked. But I was at a loss for what to do. It was totally beyond my control."

She stopped again, this time to calm herself down. She took a deep breath and let it out slowly. "Fortunately, Mum had found that her book had been opened and tracked me down. She looked like a raving witch as she hurdled the stone wall and tackled me off the slab. She quickly reversed the spell and the cracks slowly closed, trapping the beasties within."

Katelyn picked up her fork and began to eat. Henry glanced at the others, whose mouths were open in shock. All but Coralis. His grim expression was one Henry had not seen since the Wand Master had unsuccessfully tried to remove all the bad moonbeams from his aura. His visible concern worried Henry. Was Katelyn under the sway of an evil similar to the bad moon?

"Katelyn," Coralis said softly. "I am sorry. I did not know the whole story, only that your mother thought it best to send you here for training."

Katelyn put her fork down gently and dabbed the corners of her mouth with a napkin. Tears welled in her eyes. "Why me? Why didn't someone tell me who I was, what I could do? Liam will never speak to me again. Trisha moved away. Because they saw the real me. They saw I am a monster!" She slammed her hands flat against the table, the force of which made it jump a half meter off the ground.

Henry, Luis, and Serena leapt back from the forceful power of her reaction. Coralis stood slowly. "You are nothing of the sort. To be honest, you are quite the opposite. You have enormous talent and potential. I take full responsibility for what happened."

"Ha!" Katelyn's scornful laugh cut him short. "You weren't even there! If it's anyone's fault other than my own, it's Mum's. She should have told me something . . . anything."

Coralis went to her side and touched her lightly on the shoulder. Katelyn immediately relaxed. "I should have been in contact with your mother long ago. You have a very strong Wandmaker bloodline, and it is up to me to nurture that. But I went into seclusion and shut out the world, ignoring all the signs. If it hadn't been for that meddling falcon . . ."

"Randall," Henry said solemnly. "Please call him by his name."

A range of emotions flashed across Coralis's face before it twitched in a brief smile. "Yes. Well, if not for Randall's interference, we wouldn't be alive to have this discussion. In fact . . ." His words were cut off by a piercing scream from somewhere in the castle.

"Brianna!" Henry shoved his chair back and started for the door.

"Wait!" Gretchen froze Henry in midstride with a powerful burst of Voice. "I will tend to your sister's needs." She brushed brusquely past Henry and moved with remarkable speed up the staircase.

"What's happening?" Henry spun on Coralis. "What's wrong with my sister, and why aren't you helping her?"

"Calm down, Henry," Coralis commanded as he directed everyone back to the table. "Her transformation from hedgehog back to human form has come with some residual side effects that have only recently begun to manifest."

"Wait a minute," Luis interrupted. "You have a sister here in the castle who used to be a hedgehog?"

"It was an accident," Henry mumbled, and blushed.

"*You* did it? You turned your own sister into a rodent?" Luis laughed so hard he was unable to catch his breath.

"Stop it!" Serena scolded. "He said it was an accident."

Henry was about to thank her when Katelyn squeezed his hand gently. "Seems like we have a wee bit in common. My guess is Luis has a story to tell as well."

His face darkened like a storm cloud. "I have nothing to say. Nothing in common with you two. When that creepy falcon gave me that wand, I threw it away!"

"Then what is that in your hand?" Katelyn asked slyly.

Luis stood, his eyes ablaze in defiance. "It's none of your business!" He stabbed his fork into the bowl of mashed cauliflower and stomped angrily out of the room.

Coralis slumped back in his chair and massaged his temples. "Oy," he said softly, then got up and left the room.

"Looks like the Wand Master has bitten off more than he can chew," Katelyn said as she began eating again.

"Indeed he has," Serena said silently to Henry.

But Henry wasn't listening. He was remembering something Katelyn had said—about how the falcon had brought her a wand six months ago.

But Randall had been dead for more than a year.

CHAPTER
FIVE

The following morning, the sun rose in a cloudless sky, streaming through Henry's window with the promise of a better day . . . not that Henry was aware of it. He snored softly on his back, mouth agape. The sun continued to climb until it reached high enough to catch the glass frame of a picture on the wall at just the right angle, deflecting a brilliant ray of sunshine directly onto Henry's face.

He winced, moaned, and rolled over. Yet even in his half-conscious state, he realized something was wrong. It took all of three seconds for his slumber to wear off as he leapt from the bed. "Holy moly, what time is it?" He lunged for his watch. "Nine o'clock? What the . . . How the . . ."

He raced around the room, pulling on whatever clothes he could find. He yanked open the door, hopping on one foot while frantically trying to put a shoe on the other. Running down hallways and skidding around corners, he arrived at the kitchen in record time.

"Good morning, *Liebchen*," Gretchen sang as she handed him a steaming bowl of oatmeal.

"No time for breakfast," Henry said breathlessly. "Where is everyone? Why didn't someone wake me?"

"Oh, that," she said sheepishly. "Well, the others are at lessons, and I asked Coralis if I could borrow you for a bit."

"Borrow?" He rubbed the top of his head vigorously. "I don't understand. Coralis is teaching. I need to be there."

"There is more to life than what Coralis can teach," she said, stern yet pleasant. "Now eat."

"Good morning." Brianna shuffled into the room, stifling a yawn. She took the oatmeal from Henry's hands, sat heavily, and began chowing down. "Mmmm . . . food. Oh, hi, Henry."

"You just took my breakfast. What do you mean 'oh, hi, Henry'? Didn't you see me here?" *This is just like the old days. Good old annoying Brianna,* he thought.

"I am not annoying. Just very hungry," she said with her mouth full. "Can you please pass me a banana?"

"Sure. Wait . . . How did you know what I was thinking?" He passed the banana, eyeing her suspiciously.

"Really? I'm gulping down boiling-hot oatmeal like a bowl of pudding and that's the question you ask?" Brianna rolled her eyes at Gretchen. "I am trying to be patient."

"What did I tell you, young lady? No reading the brains." Gretchen took the empty bowl from Brianna and ladled another scoop of oatmeal.

"I told you I can't help it. Your brains are screaming at me." She attacked the second bowl with as much vigor as the first. "Fine!" She put the spoon down. "I'll slow down."

Henry's mind swirled with questions. "Um, okay. Let's start with the obvious. How can you eat boiling-hot oatmeal without scalding your mouth?"

"Good question," Brianna said. "I don't have an answer. Two days ago, my stomach became a bottomless pit, and I'm not going to let a bit of heat stop me from filling it. Next?"

"How long have you been able to read minds?" Henry wasn't sure he wanted to know the answer to that one.

"You mean, how long have I known you have a crush on Serena?" She smiled mischievously.

"What? No! I mean . . ."

She laughed. "Relax, Henry. Nobody has to read your mind to guess that. It's plain as day." Gretchen turned to cough, attempting to hide her laugh. Brianna continued. "To answer your question, it happened shortly after my appetite flared up. But on the bright side, I can only hear thoughts that are directed at me. Weird, huh?"

"How do you know?" he asked.

"Because I've been practicing. I was eavesdropping on your dinner last night. And I gotta tell ya, the smell of all that food was hard to ignore. Nobody knew I was out in the hall, so nobody thought to think anything about me. Everything was quiet." She suddenly got serious. "But then I heard . . . *other* voices."

"What others?" He turned to Gretchen, assuming more guests had arrived, but she simply shrugged.

"Voices in the walls," Brianna said. "All jabbering non-sense. I ran back to my room in a panic. I thought maybe I was going crazy. Until the mouse appeared." Her body shook as she recalled the memory. "That's when I screamed. When I heard the mouse speak."

"Talking mice?" he asked incredulously. "You *are* crazy."

"I wish," she said glumly. "It wasn't talking to me. Just squeaking like ordinary mice do, but I understood it."

"What did it say?"

"Ha! Does it matter? Some nonsense about food and string and babies." Brianna waved her hands helplessly. "He wasn't the only one. Apparently this place is overrun with mice, and I could hear all of them. It was deafening." She pushed the bowl away and leaned forward, gently banging her forehead against the table. "Coralis can't explain it. Gretchen can't explain it. And I'm going nuts." She sat up quickly. "Speaking of nuts, is there any more oatmeal?"

"Peanut butter," Henry thought at her.

"I love peanut butter! Do you have any?" she asked.

"Guacamole," he thought.

"With corn chips? Excellent idea, Henry!"

"All right already." He laughed. "I get it. You can hear mice, read minds—sometimes—and want to eat everything in sight. Is there anything else?"

Brianna hesitated for only a second. "No. That's all."

"Ahem." Gretchen drummed her fingers on the tabletop.

Brianna's shoulders slumped. "Okay . . . I have to clip my fingernails every day."

"Every day?" Henry exclaimed.

"But not my toenails—only my fingers."

"What happens if you don't?"

"I'm afraid to find out."

"Is this why Coralis kept me out of today's lessons? Do the others know?" Henry asked Gretchen.

"Ja und nein." She smiled warmly. "Sometimes brothers *und* sisters can help each other in ways no one else can." She stepped into the large walk-in pantry, came out with a fully stuffed World War II vintage backpack, and thrust it at Henry. "For your hike."

Brianna clapped her hands excitedly, but Henry's thoughts went immediately to his last encounter with Forest. "I don't think that's such a good idea."

"I beg to differ," said someone behind them.

Henry and Brianna whipped their heads toward the new voice—one they immediately recognized. "Molly!" They nearly tripped over each other as they ran to wrap her in a hug.

"When did you get here?" Henry asked happily.

Molly yawned. "About an hour ago. Coralis sent for me, so I closed up the shop and caught the first plane out of JFK. Looks like I arrived just in time, too."

Henry couldn't believe it. Molly had been the first person they'd turned to when their mother suddenly disappeared and Brianna transformed into a hedgehog. She operated a small tavern on the Lower East Side of Manhattan that was a local refuge for the Wandmakers' Guild. And she had an amazing collection of oddities in her basement workshop.

Then something occurred to him. "Molly, this is Brianna."

"Aye, I know. 'Tis my little hedgehog all grown up." She ran her hand through the permanent blue streak in Brianna's hair, a remnant of their last adventure. "Though she's a wee bit older than I thought she'd be."

Brianna giggled.

"I have a feeling we have a lot of catching up to do." Molly laughed. "So when do we start that hike?"

"Here's the list so far." Henry and Molly sat in the shade of a tall pine tree and waited for Brianna to catch up. It hadn't taken long for her to realize that a hike was not the same as a casual stroll. Forest allowed them fairly easy passage, but the terrain was much more hilly and rugged than anything Brianna was accustomed to.

Their goal was to find out what kind of animals Brianna could connect with. Molly read from the list. "To varying degrees, she can hear red squirrels, wood mice, marmots, voles, and shrews. All are rodents, except the shrew, so . . . I don't know what to make of that." She scratched her head, puzzled. "Then there are the ones that were blank—a red fox, a brown bear, a hare, and, most intriguing, a hedgehog. I had a theory that she was somehow connecting to rodents because of her time as a hedgehog."

"But hedgehogs aren't actually rodents," said Henry, equally puzzled.

"Which leaves us with—I have no idea." Molly leaned back, staring up at nothing, trying to make some sense of it.

"Phew! That was some hill." Brianna wiped beads of sweat from her forehead and plopped down to join them. "Can we eat now?"

"You've already eaten everything," Henry complained. "Have you considered the rest of us might be hungry, too?"

"Not as hungry as I am," she moaned as Molly handed her the list of animals. "So what does any of this mean? Henry is the animal expert, not me. And what's a marmot?" She passed the list to Henry and rummaged through the backpack. "I thought we had some apples in here."

"The marmot was that oversize squirrel you fed the apple slices to," said Molly. "You said it wanted them."

"Oh yeah." She tossed the bag aside. "I probably should have waited. It was either apples or wood chips, and we didn't have wood chips."

"What exactly do you hear?" Molly asked.

"It's hard to explain." Brianna stood and gazed up into the trees. "They aren't words or symbols or even pictures. They're just chirps and squeals that mean things to them, and somehow I can translate them . . . . Well, almost. I think if I practice, I'll get better at it."

Henry shook his head. In a way, it made sense to him. His own connection with nature had gotten stronger since he began studying with Coralis. There was a subtle power he could feel in just about everything, especially in animals and minerals. He thought back to the revelations at dinner the previous night. Katelyn's experience had been horrifying. And while he didn't know why Luis's reaction was so violent, he suspected the boy's first experiences might have been pretty bad as well. Henry was glad that Coralis had been there to guide him before he did anything destructive . . . not that changing his sister into a hedgehog was anything to sneeze at.

Suddenly he turned to Molly. "Why did Coralis send for you? There are only five of us. Coralis shouldn't really need an assistant. Unless . . . Is he going somewhere?"

Molly laughed. "Oh, he can handle the training all right. It's the teenage hormones he's not so good with." She stood and brushed the pine needles from her pants. "Don't look so confused, Henry. Lock a few boys and girls your age in a castle and nature takes its course. Coralis tells me Luis bothers you."

"No, he doesn't." His response was too defensive and he immediately knew it. "It's not that he bothers me; he's just so angry. He seems to hate me and I just met him. Although he's fine with Serena." Then it dawned on him. Luis's hostility toward him was only part of the problem. He'd told Coralis he'd work through it. But that was before he saw Luis and Serena together.

He was jealous.

"Hormones," Brianna teased.

"You're not immune, young lady," Molly chided. "You went through a physical growth spurt, but soon your hormones will catch up as well."

"Ew!" Brianna wrinkled her nose. "Boys will always be yucky."

Henry laughed. "For a second, you looked like your old hedgehog self."

Brianna appeared to be thinking of a comeback, but Molly stepped in. "We'd best be moving along. And I can use the exercise. I must confess, I'm a wee bit out of shape. And to answer your other question, Henry, yes, Coralis will soon be taking a short trip. He won't tell me where, but I can tell you he's worried." She motioned for them to follow, then set off at a brisk pace.

Henry directed a thought at Brianna. *"What do you think that means?"*

"Who cares? We'll get to spend more time with Molly!" She smiled broadly and jogged to catch up.

Henry was about to follow when he suddenly felt as if someone was watching him. He scanned the forest until the feeling passed, then ran after the others.

He missed a falcon taking flight.

Clouds thickened overhead, blocking the remaining sunlight. The darkness of twilight settled long before they returned to the castle walls, circling the perimeter twice before an opening finally appeared to let them in.

"This place still has the same sense of humor I remember from long ago," Molly said.

"Yeah, it's a real barrel of laughs," Henry said sarcastically, recalling the time he'd fallen through the wall.

Gretchen waved to them from across the courtyard and beckoned them into the castle, where they found the kitchen table set for the four of them. "The others have already eaten," she said happily as she handed out generous bowls of vegetable stew. Brianna was on her second bowl before the stew had cooled enough for Henry and Molly to start eating. "I see your little walk has given one of you an appetite." Gretchen chuckled.

"Where are the others?" Henry asked.

"In the Kunstkammer. We have a new arrival. A young girl, Bryndis, from Greenland. An interesting addition, if I do say so."

"Another apprentice? In the Kunstkammer? But even we haven't been allowed in there yet!" Henry whined.

"*Ja. Und* she put that other young man right in his place." She laughed. "Uff! There were fireworks for sure. I think that is why they went to the Kunstkammer so soon. It is good you came when you did," she said to Molly. "I've never seen Coralis so flustered."

"Hormones?" Molly winked at Henry.

When they arrived at Coralis's Kunstkammer—his innermost private workspace—Luis was trapped in one corner by a grayish-brown snake with dark brown blotches. And the girl who could only be Bryndis was trapped in the opposite corner by a nasty-looking olive-brown snake. It hissed at her, the insides of its mouth black as coal.

"It's about time you got back," Coralis growled at Molly.

"Now, is that any way to treat an old friend?" She gave him a light pat on the back and faced the new apprentices. "How about we start with some introductions. My name is Molly."

"Luis." His voice trembled as he stared at the deadly viper, which whipped threateningly.

"Bryndis," the new girl said gruffly. Henry studied her briefly, trying not to stare. She was nearly as tall as Molly but stockier, with short, dark brown hair and skin a few shades darker than Serena's. She wore thick boots that appeared to be made of animal skin. Her heavy, knitted sweater was red, with an intricate geometric pattern of many bright colors.

She looked as though she was ready for a harsh winter, and Henry was instantly curious about her. Yet her most noteworthy feature was the raw power that emanated from her in waves. She stood very still but did not appear frightened by the snake. Henry thought she either wasn't aware of its deadly venom or simply didn't care—and it was probably the latter. His instincts told him she could probably make the snake go away if she wanted to.

With a quick jerk of her head, she delivered a wave of frosty air in his direction. "Stop look," she said in choppy English.

"Sorry." He turned to Serena for help.

"I am Serena." She introduced herself and extended a hand toward Molly.

"Ah, yes, the Navajo girl. So good to finally meet you." Molly raised an approving eyebrow in Henry's direction.

"And I am Katelyn."

Molly spoke to her in a foreign language for nearly a minute. It must have been about something funny because by the end they were both laughing.

"What so funny?" said Bryndis, her eyes ablaze.

"My apologies." Katelyn dipped her head. " 'Tis nice to know someone else here speaks Gaelic, my native language. And rest assured, the joke was not at your expense."

"Away!" Coralis's sudden, sharp command sent the snakes slithering toward a tall bucket. They slinked inside and instantly went rigid, joining another dozen that Henry had initially assumed were canes.

"Okay, that's pretty amazing." Serena took a step toward the petrified snakes, but Coralis stopped her.

"You will have time to look around later—if I'm feeling generous," he growled. "Right now, I'm not. Luis, I understand your issues, but you are a part of this group and need to control your irrational anger toward those who are not your enemy. There will be a time—very soon, I'm afraid— for you to release that anger at a more acceptable target. And you." He pointed at Bryndis. "I will make an exception this one time because you just arrived—and who knows what kind of baggage you brought to this motley crew—but if I ever see another outburst like that, I will send you back from whence you came. Understood?"

Her facial features cycled through a range of emotions in the span of a second—anger, fear, resignation. She inhaled, then exhaled deeply. "Understood."

"Good." Clearly feeling in control again, he gave terse commands. "Molly, they're all yours. Run them through some basic wand-control drills. Gretchen, you'll know where to find me."

"You could have at least said please," Molly joked once Coralis was out of earshot.

"Ja," Gretchen agreed. "The grouchy side is my least favorite."

The tension in the room instantly dissipated and everyone relaxed with a nervous chuckle. Everyone but Bryndis. "Bryndis," said Molly. "May I call you Bryn?"

"No."

"And you thought I was bad." Luis had crept behind Henry and whispered the line, but not soft enough.

Bryndis lunged toward him. Molly whipped a wand from a small side pocket in her pants and froze the new girl in her tracks. Her face turned a deep shade of crimson as she fought against whatever was holding her in place. "You need to calm down," Molly said sternly. "He didn't mean anything by it. Did you, Luis?"

"No!" Luis slid farther behind Henry for protection, obviously afraid of the new girl.

"Wow!" said Brianna. "What did she do to you?"

Bryndis's eyes blazed at Brianna as she struggled to speak. Only a garbled croak came out.

Henry thought her eyes were going to pop right out of her head from the strain of trying to break free. "Bryndis, you have to know that we are your friends," he offered. She twitched and jerked but he could see her back off slightly. "None of us asked to be here. And some of us probably don't want to stay here any longer than we have to, but right now we need to find out more about ourselves and how to use the power we were given."

Bryndis listened and relaxed. Her head was locked in place but her eyes shifted from one apprentice to the next, resting a shade too long on Luis, who ducked behind Henry again.

"What exactly did she do to you?" Henry asked.

"She had just arrived," Luis started hesitantly. "We were in the main entrance—the one with the live tree columns. All I said was 'nice boots.' "

Bryndis garbled meanly and strained to lunge at him.

"I wasn't making fun!" he said defensively. "I think they are really nice boots. But she went crazy. She pulled out a wand and pointed it at a tree. The roots burst through the floor, wrapped around my ankles, and slammed me to the floor." He rubbed his butt. Brianna giggled.

"Fortunately, Coralis reversed whatever she did. But then she got mad at him and swung her wand at him."

"Oh, snap!" said Brianna.

Molly whistled softly. "That's playing with fire."

Luis nodded vigorously. "I know, right? I mean, like, I just got here too, but I'm not *loco* enough to attack a Wand Master."

"So what did he do?" Brianna asked.

"He made her wand disappear. Poof! Then he marched us all down here. When she came after me again, Coralis made those sticks come alive. That one is a yarará snake. I've seen people die from their bite and wasn't going to be one of them. So I stood as still as I could. Why would he do that to me?" he asked Molly. "I did nothing and he tried to kill me."

"It's been a long time since he's trained several young apprentices at once," said Molly. "He's rusty, and I don't think he's ever dealt with such a diverse group. Bryndis, you are from Greenland?"

Bryndis strained to speak. "Sorry." Molly released her from her frozen state. "Promise to behave or I will encase you in a block of ice."

"Ha! That would be welcome," she scoffed. "I am from Qaanaaq, northern city in Kalaallit Nunaat—what you call Greenland. Small town, not many people but much ice."

She finally smiled, more or less. Her mouth twitched at the corners and her eyes crinkled ever so slightly. But from Henry's perspective it transformed her from a snarling Doberman to a Labrador retriever. He almost laughed when Luis got up the nerve to step from behind him and offer a hand to her.

"Friends?" he asked hopefully.

"Not yet." The Doberman returned. She pointed to her boots. "Kamiks—made from caribou . . . um, reindeer—like Rudolph." Her left eyebrow wiggled a short dance and her eyes twinkled with amusement. "When I hunt seal, I use sealskin kamik. Does not get feet wet."

"You hunt seal? That's amazing!" Katelyn exclaimed.

"How else we eat?" Bryndis placed her hands on her hips and thrust out her chin.

"You *eat* seal?" Henry winced at the thought.

"I just said so."

Bryndis stated it so matter-of-factly that Henry felt foolish for asking. "What is that around your neck?" he asked to change the subject.

"Tupilaq—means soul of ancestor. I carved from walrus tusk," she said proudly.

"You made that yourself?" Serena asked.

"Everyone in Qaanaaq make tupilaq. Very powerful." Bryndis eyed Serena curiously. "You know this—call it totem."

She pointed to either end of the fifteen-centimeter carved figure. "Polar bear here, dog here. Make strong protection."

Suddenly Gretchen burst out laughing. "Please stop. I can't take it anymore. *Qallunaatituusuunguviit?*"

Bryndis paled. "Where did you learn that?" Her broken English vanished as if she had flipped a switch. Her entire demeanor changed from defiant warrior to suspicious teenager.

"I spent several years in Kalaallit Nunaat. The schools there teach the English language from the first year." Gretchen placed her arm on Bryndis's shoulder. "There will be no fakery here, dear." She turned to the others. "I asked her if she spoke English in her native tongue of Kalaallisut."

"Sounds like a pretty complicated language," Henry remarked. Katelyn, Luis, and Bryndis all laughed. "What's so funny?"

"When you grow up speaking your native language, English is the most difficult second language to learn," said Bryndis.

"Really?" Brianna asked.

"Really," Luis answered. He glanced nervously at Bryndis, who twitched a smile.

Molly sighed in relief. "So now that we've crossed that bump in the road, let's have a look around."

Once they began to explore, any tension that remained vanished as quickly as Bryndis's wand—which, coincidentally, was found on a shelf behind a bottle of giant leeches.

"No one can make something actually disappear," said Molly. "Magicians use misdirection and sleight of hand to make things *seem* to vanish. Coralis's technique is much more complex than that and is something only Wand Masters can do."

"Is it teleportation?" asked Katelyn.

"Impressive word," Luis commented as he held the leeches up for closer inspection.

"I happen to like *Star Trek*," she answered as she poked the stick-snakes.

"Not teleporting, more like sucking something through a high-speed wind tunnel. He manipulates the air molecules to pull or push an object at a velocity that is too fast for the untrained eye to see." Molly leaned against a bench as she assumed the role of instructor. "A Wand Master, as the title implies, has mastered all four elements—air, fire, water, and earth."

"The symbols on the front of the *Guidebook*," Henry said as he examined a unique chair with the hooves of a large animal. He rubbed a hand gently over the rawhide surface and felt it respond with a rippling sigh. He grinned, suddenly aware of the fact that he was inside Coralis's private work space—his inner sanctum.

When he had first gone to New York, he and Brianna stayed in the basement of Molly's tavern. She had a fascinating collection of oddities, but nothing like this. Coralis's room was not only quite large, but as Henry walked past certain bookcases and shelves, he felt that there was something beyond them he couldn't see—other rooms, perhaps even more Kunstkammers. He thought of the way Coralis had taught him to store information in his mind. Drawers full of compartments and subcompartments. It would make sense that a well-developed Kunstkammer would have the same, if not a more intricate, level of depth.

"So what is this place?" Luis asked.

"*Ein Kunstkammer*," Gretchen answered. "The translation from my native German is 'art room,' but it has also been called a cabinet of curiosities."

Molly took over. "Every Wandmaker will begin collecting their own special objects soon after they begin their apprenticeship. This particular collection is the result of hundreds of years of scientific study by dozens of Wand Masters who date back almost four thousand years. You will never see another one like it."

Katelyn whistled softly in amazement. She turned to Henry and Serena. "You two have been at the castle awhile, but from your reaction, I'll guess this is your first time in here."

They nodded and Serena asked the obvious question. "Why now? We've been here for over a year and Coralis never thought to reveal it before."

"Perhaps because he can't wait any longer." Molly's brow creased.

Henry eyed her warily. "What do you mean?"

Instead of answering immediately, Molly walked over to a built-in shelf unit. It was as tall as the room and about two meters wide. There were ten shelves, each lined with skulls— some human, but mostly animal. She ran her hand lightly along the edge of a center shelf, stopping midway at a small bronze plate.

Henry recalled reading a section of the *Guidebook* about skulls. He had studied the book in meticulous detail, which was how he was able to guess what the bronze plate had engraved on it before he read it. "From the collection of Ole Worm." He pronounced it *Olay Vorm*.

"Do you know the story?" Molly asked.

"Not much of it," Henry replied. "Only the short paragraphs from the *Guidebook*."

"What guidebook?" Luis and Bryndis asked simultaneously.

"*The Wandmaker's Guidebook,*" Brianna answered. "Our dad gave it to Henry as a Christmas gift. From the way he treated it, you'd think it was some valuable treasure."

"It is," Henry said defensively. "Coralis wrote it himself, trying to attract people who might be worthwhile apprentices. It's how he found me," he said proudly.

"Randall found you," Brianna corrected.

"That name came up last night," said Luis. "Coralis said it was the falcon's name."

"*Ja,* but so much more than a falcon." A pained expression crossed Gretchen's face. "A young man like yourself. One of the best and brightest. He transformed himself into a falcon and set all of this into motion." She waved a hand at the group, then dabbed at a tear with her handkerchief.

"We'll get back to Randall later." Molly nodded to Gretchen with a terse smile. "Henry, what can you tell us about Ole?"

He could have recited the entire section from memory. "I don't know what rank of Wandmaker he was, but in his lifetime, he had assembled one of the most astounding workrooms Coralis had ever seen. One of his hobbies was collecting skulls."

"That's a pretty morbid hobby, if you ask me," said Serena.

Henry scanned the shelves, looking for a particular specimen. He stopped at the center of the top one. "The unicorn goat."

"There is no such thing as a unicorn," Serena said adamantly.

"Maybe not in this world." Katelyn's eyes sparkled with mischief.

Serena involuntarily shivered as she recalled Katelyn's story from the previous night.

"What does this have to do with Coralis?" Luis shifted impatiently. "Is there a point to all of this . . . history?"

Henry frowned—not so much at Luis's reaction but because of something else he remembered. "I thought that when Ole died, his collection was taken by the king of Denmark."

Molly grinned like the Cheshire cat. "Only the items out in the open."

Henry's face lit up. "He had a secret room?"

In response, Molly placed one finger on either side of the nameplate and pressed. With a soft click, the shelf unit moved ever so slightly. "He wasn't the only one. Welcome to the *real* Kunstkammer." She pushed on one side and the unit swung inward. Seven pairs of eyes stared on in wonder.

"Ach, the secrets that man keeps from me." Gretchen led the way, entering the hidden room for her first time as well. "I suppose there is a magic lamp to give us light?"

Henry felt along the wall, recalling his brief time at the New York Marble Cemetery. With some satisfaction, he flipped a light switch. His smugness evaporated when he saw the room in its entirety. He was at a loss to come up with an adjective that could adequately describe it. The room was at least quadruple the size of the previous one. Earlier, he'd thought he had felt something was hidden, but he did not expect this. "Is this the only secret room?"

Molly smiled and shook her head. "Smart lad. You must have sensed them, and that's something that cannot be taught."

There was a time when Henry would have been proud of himself. But standing in the presence of all the ancient artifacts left him awestruck. The group slowly made their way around the room, as if moving too quickly would somehow show disrespect. Enormous cabinets and row upon row of skulls, mummies, and fossils filled the room. Henry gingerly opened one of the cabinets that looked like an armoire to reveal hundreds of drawers—each three fingers in height and the length of his hand.

"That's as far as you should go, Henry," Molly warned.

"I know. I can feel it," he said.

Serena came to his side. "I do, too."

One by one, the others joined them. Each drawer had a nameplate. Henry scanned the names, most of which were unfamiliar, until he came to one he had learned about in his studies—Marcel Denard. One of the Guild's most infamous failures. The Wand Master to Napoléon Bonaparte, emperor of France.

"Each of these compartments contains the wand of a deceased Wandmaker," Molly told them. "Each wand still possesses the power that its owner amassed, for once a wand has power, it never goes away. Which is why it is essential that none of you ever let your wands out of your possession. If you were to pick up one of the wands in this cabinet, horrible things would happen to you."

"Then why aren't they locked up?" Bryndis asked in a whisper.

The group was still and quiet, awaiting Molly's response.

"Because no one but Coralis knows where it is. And now that you know"—she turned to the group for dramatic effect—"I have to kill you."

As one they jumped back in shock. Molly laughed. "Just kidding. You should see the looks on your faces."

"Not funny." Katelyn was the first to recover.

"Was that just some story meant to scare us? Because it did," Luis said angrily.

"Only the killing part." Molly shrugged. "Seriously. I know about it and I'm still here. The rest is true. Scout's honor. Recognize any other names, Henry?"

He studied the names, pointing to ones he knew. Sus Akai from the Ming dynasty. Cormac the Skald, the Viking warrior.

"Laars Thornkill." Bryndis leaned in for a closer look. "I am a descendant of this man." Awestruck, she reached out but pulled her hand back just before touching the drawer. "He died a very mysterious death. I think perhaps you can remove the mystery for me some day."

"There's Tecumseh's wand!" Serena nearly shouted, seeing the name of the great Shawnee chief.

"And Merlin," Katelyn whispered in awe.

Bryndis scoffed. "Merlin? Another joke?"

"No joke," Molly said sternly. "Many legends are derived from truth. Granted, some have been embellished a bit too much over the years, but Merlin is as real as you or I."

"You said 'is,'" Henry remarked.

Molly closed the cabinet, smiling cagily. "Someday. But let's talk about why we are here." She motioned them to be seated around a small, innocuous table in the center of the room. "Coralis brought you here because he is out of time. It takes many years to train an apprentice. Unfortunately, the six of you must be given a crash course."

"Six?" asked Henry. "You mean . . ."

"Yes, Brianna has talents as well and will be trained as an apprentice."

"Um, I think Coralis made a mistake," Brianna said. "I mean, Henry's the one with all the ability. I'm just, like, his sidekick."

"Not from what Coralis has told me." Molly grinned. "If not for you, Henry would not have succeeded in defeating Dai She. And while your power might not be that of a typical Wandbearer, you are nonetheless an important element."

"An Enabler." Gretchen stood and placed a hand on Brianna's shoulder. "One who has the ability to amplify the power of a Wandbearer. It's been hundreds of years since the last one—who just happened to be my great-great-great-grandmother. She died well before I was born, but the details of her life have been passed down through the generations. It is a privilege to be in the presence of one and a rare honor to be given the opportunity to pass my knowledge on to you. It looks like you and I will be spending some time together."

"Thank you," Brianna said.

Henry knew she was relieved that it wouldn't be Coralis. He smiled at her relief, then saw something move out of the corner of his eye. A long, waist-high cabinet topped with a glass hutch was filled with tall glass jars, each containing specimens of exotic arthropods. He approached the table, drawn by the rippling of a giant centipede's legs. The top of its jar was secured with a tight lid. He cautiously lifted it for a closer look. He gasped as the insect twisted around and stared at him.

Brianna had snuck up behind him. "Don't let it get you!"

"Gaa!" Completely startled, Henry bobbled the jar in his hands and watched helplessly as it dropped and shattered on the floor.

The centipede literally hit the ground running . . . right toward Luis, who screamed and performed a meter-high vertical leap onto a table. Molly whipped her wand and froze the centipede in its tracks, just as she had done to Bryndis. "You need to be more careful," she scolded. "Now let's get this cleaned up and . . ."

All eyes turned toward Luis. The color had drained from his face and he panted rapidly through his open mouth. Molly saw that he was about to hyperventilate. "Gretchen, talk to him, quickly!"

Gretchen gave him reassurance that everything was okay. But even with her very persuasive use of Voice, it took several minutes to calm him down.

"Are you all right?" Molly asked tenderly.

Luis nodded. "Yes . . . I mean, no." He looked into the faces of the concerned apprentices. "I have a story, too." He smiled tersely at Katelyn.

Luis sat heavily, pressing the heels of his palms to his forehead as if trying to suppress a headache. "It was shortly after the falcon delivered the wand. The jungle has thick vines that wind their way through the trees—monkey ladder vines. Fun to climb. I was practicing a new technique, trying to copy something I had seen a howler monkey do, when one of *those* ran over my hand and startled me." He pointed to the centipede.

"Yikes!" said Henry.

"It's a giant Amazon centipede. Like everything else where I live, they are much bigger than you'd think. That one isn't an adult. They grow up to thirty centimeters long and bite with a painful venom. They eat mice, and frogs, and lizards." He closed his eyes.

"I was at least seven meters off the ground and nearly lost my grip. Had I fallen, I would have been badly hurt—or dead. I don't know what possessed me. In a flash of anger, I whipped out the wand and struck the centipede in the head." He lowered his voice to a fear-filled whisper. "Something happened to it. It lifted its body into the air with only its hind pair of legs anchoring it to the vine and faced me head-on." He pointed at the immobile insect. "Those legs near its head are shaped like claws. It began to rub them together. Slowly at first, then faster. They began to make a sound like a cricket does when it rubs its wings together. Except that it got so loud that it hurt my ears and soon took on the tone of an animal being eaten alive—or like an infant wailing in intense pain. An unbearable screeching sound."

He stopped as his hands began to quiver. He sat on them quickly and squeezed his eyes shut again as if he were trying to block the image. "Suddenly, it stopped. A stillness came over the jungle and I knew something bad was about to happen. Then it lunged at me, and this time I did fall, banging against branches on the way down. They slowed my fall enough that I was not seriously hurt—not yet."

He looked at Katelyn, pain and fear etched on his face. "I understand how you felt. I heard them before I saw them. Like armored soldiers marching into battle. I don't know where they all came from—didn't think there were that many in all of the Amazon. Thousands upon thousands of giant centipedes. They looked like a column of army ants. I was nearly paralyzed with fear but somehow managed to run. I thought I heard them screaming, but realized it was me. When I finally stopped to catch my breath, the jungle had gone silent. They had disappeared."

Gretchen handed him a glass of water. The room was as quiet as the jungle must have been. "That's when it got bad. They hadn't disappeared after all. They simply took to the trees. I wasn't aware of where they had gone until the bats began to fall—by the hundreds. Each in the deadly grasp of a centipede. They are relentless killers that feed until their victims are sucked dry. The bats continued to fall until the ground was a carpet of squirming death. And still more fell—each one attacked in their daytime sleep, never to wake up again."

He addressed Serena. "You've seen bats in the desert. You know what they eat."

She nodded. "Insects."

"Yes. In the jungle it's mostly mosquitoes. They will eat almost their body weight every night."

"That's a lot of mosquitoes," said Henry.

"Millions." Luis scowled at him. "Millions of bloodthirsty bugs that fell upon my village that night like sharks in a feeding frenzy. It was as if they knew we had lost the protection of the bats. I will never forget the screams of every man, woman, and child that night." His voice was firm, yet a tear rolled down his cheek.

"They attacked us all night long. When the sun finally came up, they were gone. And the crying replaced the screams."

"It wasn't your fault." Serena reached for his hand but he jerked it away.

"Yes, it was! And they all knew it was, because I was the only one without a single bite mark. Nature got its revenge on me and made sure everyone knew it was my fault. Three children had to be rushed to a hospital that night! And it *was—my—fault!*"

"That's enough," Molly said softly.

"No." The tears came freely but his voice refused to falter. "It will never be enough. They took me from the village and banished me here—not to be some apprentice. But because I was dangerous and they were afraid of me."

"There was nothing you could have done." Molly rested a hand on his shoulder. "Nature is as strange as it is unpredictable. Just as you think you've figured something out, chaos will erupt and prove you wrong. But even chaos has a way of providing us with opportunities. If that hadn't happened, you might not be here with us. And we need you."

Luis scoffed. "Don't lie to me to make me feel better."

"No lies," Molly said. "What you did required incredible power. Power you didn't know you had. It was an accident, and you cannot dwell on it. As of this moment, you will all receive the training you need to become masters of your craft. Together we will become an invincible team united against a common enemy. Coralis will not let you fail."

Luis's face was shrouded in doubt, but he finally nodded and stood. "Okay. But one of these days I want to hear the details of the hedgehog story." He glanced at Brianna with a hint of a grin.

Molly smiled. "Good. Gretchen will assist in your training, Brianna. The rest of you are mine until Coralis returns. So I suggest we get started. Bwa-ha-ha-ha-ha!" She rubbed her hands together like a mad scientist as the apprentices rolled their eyes.

CHAPTER

EIGHT

"This is exhausting," Luis complained. "Tell me again why mixing this herb with this liquid will save the world."

Serena and Katelyn groaned. In the nine days since Molly had begun teaching, Luis proved to be a fast learner—and a constant whiner.

Despite the complaints, Henry found it hard to believe how much Luis had learned in such a short time. He and Serena should have had a significant advantage over the rest of the group, having spent over a year at the castle. But there was a distinct difference between Coralis's passive tutorial methods and Molly's aggressive ones. Coralis had given them plenty of material to read along with weekly hands-on instruction in the laboratory. But much of the time he was absent, leaving them on their own to learn through discovery.

In contrast, Molly was like a drill sergeant. The first day, she taught them how to store information in their heads the way Coralis had taught Henry on the train. Her drills were so tight and thorough that by the end of the day they were compartmentalizing lessons in geology and physics.

At first, Henry was invigorated, eager to absorb every bit of knowledge, and excited that he was the best of the group. By the end of day two, he was as exhausted as the rest of them. By day three, Bryndis had surpassed him in some areas and Katelyn in others. By day four, he felt like he was treading water while the rest of them swam laps around him.

Brianna showed up on day five looking every bit as tired as he felt. But she had learned her lessons well. Something about her had changed. She exuded confidence. Grasping Henry's upper arm, she sent a thought: *"Can you feel it?"*

A surge of power coursed through him, giving him a momentary feeling of invincibility. *"Awesome!"*

She turned her attention to Luis next, but for him she used a different approach. Gretchen had taught her that an Enabler could affect someone mentally as well as physically.

Luis was undoubtedly talented and intelligent, but his attention span was short and he was easily distracted. He constantly questioned the value of facts he was forced to memorize. At one point, Molly asked him flat out if he had a problem with authority figures.

"No," he answered humbly. "But I've always had a problem learning something if I didn't understand *why* I had to learn it. I like solving math problems. There are rules to follow and reasons for every rule. But the rest doesn't make sense."

Brianna grasped what needed to be done and set to work on him. She answered all of his questions with questions and prodded him with key words that stimulated his thoughts. Before long, he had stopped challenging Molly's instructions and begun offering explanations that helped them all comprehend better. His question about the importance of mixing herbs and liquids stemmed more from exhaustion than anything else, and in his own way, he spoke for the group. Even Bryndis, Katelyn, and Serena had gone from fanatical attention to slumping in their chairs and occasionally doodling.

Molly had just finished a lesson on the laws of thermodynamics when Henry asked, "When is Coralis coming back?"

Molly's eyes narrowed to mere slits.

"Sorry, I mean . . ." Henry hesitated. "It's just that Coralis has been gone for a while, and I was wondering if you might know if he's coming back soon."

Molly smiled. "As a matter of fact . . ." She motioned for them to follow her. As they filed out of Ole Worm's room, Luis almost stepped in Bryndis's path, then took a quick step back to allow her to go first. She twitched her hands in his direction, making him flinch, and then casually ignored him. But a half minute later she was giggling with Katelyn and Serena at his expense.

"Very funny," he grumbled.

They continued through the maze of corridors and out the front door of the castle to walk along the exterior perimeter of the compound in single file like ducklings following their mother. On their third lap, Molly suddenly stopped and addressed the wall. "Any time now!"

Henry was the first to snicker, realizing the castle was toying with her. Brianna joined in until Molly couldn't help but crack a smile. The others looked at them as if they were crazy.

Molly stepped away from the wall and yelled, "Coralis!"

"Confound it, woman!" Coralis's head popped through a hole in the wall that had not been there a second ago—right next to Bryndis, who shrieked. "Stop your tomfoolery and get in here. We have work to do."

His head disappeared with a POP and a narrow doorway appeared. One by one, they entered, appearing apprehensive about what was in store for them. But Henry had seen the humorous twinkle in Coralis's eyes.

"Where are we?" Luis asked, his gaze darting nervously as the doorway sealed silently behind them.

Henry was about to reply with a snarky comment. But after a quick look around, he saw why Luis was puzzled. They were in a courtyard, but it wasn't the courtyard they knew. This one was smaller—much smaller, and Gretchen's familiar garden was missing.

Another secret of Castle Coralis stood revealed.

The ground of this hidden rectangular courtyard was firmly packed red earth. The walls were lined with a mineral Henry had not seen before, teal and shimmering in the sunlight.

"What I am about to show you has only been seen by Wand Masters."

Henry examined the enclosure as Coralis spoke, eventually settling his eyes on the old man. Henry could sense he was tired, and it was more than simply a lack of sleep.

"This entryway is lined with alternating layers of quartz and extremely rare luminescent labradorite. Can any of you tell me why?" He stood with his hands clasped behind his back. The silence grew long, and it became clear that he would not proceed without an answer.

Henry thought back to all the hours he had spent studying his book about minerals and their properties. Suddenly he recalled something, but it was from a different book. It was from one of the secret books he had found in his attic and painstakingly translated with ulexite last year. "Atlantis," he mumbled, deep in thought.

"What was that, Henry?" Coralis prodded.

"It's the same combination that keeps Atlantis hidden." He closed his eyes, picturing the page in the book. "It repels negative energy while sealing in positive energy."

"First Merlin, now Atlantis?" Bryndis sounded doubtful. "What next . . . the Loch Ness monster?"

Coralis's eyes burned like hot coals in her direction. "Sorry." She stepped back and bumped up against the wall, withering before his gaze.

Katelyn inched closer to her and whispered, "Even I know Nessie isn't real."

"Do not dismiss that which you cannot see as something that does not exist," he admonished, squinting in Katelyn's direction. "Though in this case you are correct. There is no Nessie." He shrugged with a brief grin and continued. "These minerals keep this castle protected from the prying eyes of the outside world. It will never show up on satellite imagery as more than an empty field. And only Wand Masters know how to use an Argus Wand properly to locate it."

"What about the villagers who brought us here?" Luis asked.

"Descendants of the Hutsuls who built this place. They have pledged undying loyalty and are trusted beyond a doubt." Coralis waved a wand at one of the shorter walls. The teal mineral dissipated into a mist, revealing a door that was both ancient and intimidating. Weathered planks ran vertically and were fastened with horizontal straps of riveted metal. Iron hinges in the shape of lion claws held the door in place, and along its left side hung five padlocks, evenly spaced from top to bottom. Each padlock displayed an identical geometric pattern.

To Henry, it looked like the door to a medieval torture chamber.

Coralis approached the door and casually flipped over a palm-sized rock with the toe of his boot. Beneath the rock, among the various scurrying insects, lay a small stone the size of a dime. Plain and unremarkable on one side, he turned it over to reveal an intricate geometric pattern—a pattern that matched the design upon the locks.

Coralis studied the group's reaction out of the corner of his eye as he grabbed the center padlock and inserted the stone into a perfectly sized indentation in its back. Immediately, light raced throughout the pattern on the lock, illuminating sections of the design in a dazzling display. Coralis then tapped his wand against each lock in sequence. With a loud snap, the center lock popped open, followed in quick succession by the other four.

They jumped, as he knew they would. Henry caught the cagey grin on the old man's face. He'd once overheard Coralis tell Gretchen that the surprises he could spring on the unsuspecting were among the few true joys of his life.

The Wand Master chuckled to himself as he removed each lock from the lion-clawed hinges.

"Are you sure about this?" Molly asked softly.

"No," Coralis replied. "But we have no choice."

The room was black as pitch. Molly was the first to step through the doorway and was immediately swallowed by the darkness. The rest of the group followed tentatively, not knowing what to expect.

Coralis was last and closed the door behind him, plunging them into an abyss totally devoid of light. A set of interior locks snapped briskly into place. Ten seconds went by. Then twenty.

Luis was the first to break the silence. "Um . . ."

"Quiet!" Coralis barked. "I need to test something." A full minute later, he grunted with satisfaction. "It would appear, Henry, that all residual traces of exposure to the bad moonbeams have left you."

"What does that mean?" Katelyn asked from a dark space to Coralis's left.

"It means Henry used to glow in the dark," Brianna said lightly.

"Man," Luis said. "When you have accidents, they are whoppers!"

Serena giggled.

"Henry, would you do us the honor of providing some sunshine?" Coralis asked.

Henry was steaming over how easily Luis could make Serena laugh; he nearly missed the request. "But I . . . ," he began to object.

"Sunshine, Henry," Coralis prodded.

Henry nodded, forgetting no one could see, and took out his wand. The first time he'd attempted this, he'd nearly blinded Coralis and caused an accident. But he had practiced since then. He envisioned the sun just peeking over the edge of the horizon, slowly rising in the morning sky. His wand began to glow like a low-wattage bulb.

"Brighter," Coralis encouraged.

Henry urged his wand until it was so bright the entire chamber was lit. They had entered an enormous circular room with a domed ceiling that stretched far beyond what should have been the height of the castle.

"That ceiling has to be over twenty meters away!" Luis gasped.

"From the outside, you would not think a room of this magnitude could exist. And yet, here it is. The right combination of natural elements can accomplish many things," Coralis explained. "This entire vault is constructed of rare elements that account for its exterior invisibility." The room was impressive by anyone's standards. There was awe even in Coralis's voice, and Henry noticed the Wand Master glance sideways at the group to see how far their jaws had dropped.

"That's enough, Henry," Coralis said. "Now put it out."

Henry switched his thoughts to darkness and his light went out.

"Wow!" Serena said in awe, but it wasn't directed at Henry.

"Double wow!" said Bryndis. As one the group gawked at the ceiling, which was aglow in a soft blue light.

"The labradorite again?" asked Henry.

"Very good." Coralis raised his arms as if offering homage to the heavens. "As I said outside, it has luminescent qualities." He abruptly turned and strode to the far side of the vault, disappearing into a darkened doorway. Moments later he reemerged. "Well! Are you coming or not?" he yelled, and immediately turned back into the darkness without waiting for a reply.

"Let's go, kids," Molly said as she hurried them across the room. They arrived at the doorway, where Henry expected Coralis to be waiting, but instead he heard his distant footsteps down a long, sloping tunnel. His eyes adjusted rapidly to the darkness, getting just enough light from well-placed crystals to make out the twists and turns.

They had followed the tunnel for a short distance when suddenly the floor seemed to disappear.

"Watch out for the staircase." Coralis's voice sounded very close, though Henry could still hear his footsteps far away.

The walls must have qualities that reflect sound, he thought. Pressing a hand against the smooth, hard walls, he descended a long staircase that doubled back on itself every thirteen steps. "Come along," a voice whispered in his ear. "I don't have all day."

"*This is soooo cool!*" Brianna directed at Henry.

"How is he doing that?" Serena asked.

They continued down several more levels until at last a brighter light emerged. The group entered a room that was spacious yet much smaller than the enormous vault far above. But what it lacked in size it made up for in intensity. Instead of luminous rock, torches burned brightly in wall sconces.

Again, the room was circular. In the center was an enormous round slab of wood that served as a table. Coralis stood at its far side, and using his height for perspective, Henry estimated the table to be approximately half a meter thick and six or seven meters' diameter. He could not even begin to guess how it got down there.

Around the perimeter of the room, scale models of buildings and monuments and even cities were on display. "Is that the Colossus of Rhodes?" Katelyn asked incredulously as she recognized a small-scale replica of one of the Seven Wonders of the Ancient World.

Coralis ignored the question. "Welcome to the Cryptoporticus. It is one of the oldest man-made rooms on Earth. For centuries this room has been used by Wand Masters like me to experiment and develop ways to use the power of nature—not just for the betterment of the human race, but also to protect mankind from the Scorax—the followers of Malachai.

"You thought Atlantis was nothing but a myth. Look here!" He directed Bryndis to an intricate model of a city about half the size of the large wooden table and encased beneath a glass dome.

"Atlantis thrives today, as it has for several thousand years, yet it is extremely well hidden. The unique layering of crystals that form its foundation provides a stealth cover that cannot be penetrated."

"Do you know where it is?" she asked.

"Yes," he said with a slight smile, but offered nothing further.

Henry walked from one display to the next, examining the models with profound interest until he came upon an empty table. Daggerlike shards of glass still reached upward, the only remnants of a dome that had failed to protect what had lain beneath it. On the surface of the table, there was a rectangular discoloration. A feeling of dread crept up on him. "Is this what I think it is?" he asked.

"Indeed it is," Coralis said grimly. "This was the repository of the Corsini Mappaemundi. The map was developed thousands of years ago by an exceptional Wand Master who was on the very first High Council of Aratta. His name was Epifanio Corsini." Suddenly his eyes widened and his face lit up. "I could ask Henry to give you a boring history lesson." He winked knowingly at Henry, who smiled back. "But since it's show-and-tell time, why don't you witness it yourself?"

"I suppose you have a time machine," Bryndis said.

"Even better!" he said, ignoring her sarcasm. He hurried to the far wall and tapped it with a wand.

Henry could not contain his curiosity and edged closer to see what Coralis was up to. A section of the rock wall rotated on silent hinges to reveal a large display cabinet that contained hundreds of wands, each identified by a label written in a language that looked alien. He'd edged in for a closer look when Coralis suddenly exclaimed, "Aha!" and spun so quickly he nearly stepped on Henry's foot.

The wand Coralis had selected was slightly shorter than the length of his own forearm. It was bloodred, and carved into the shape of a long, slender dragon. "This wand dates back to Corsini's time—over four thousand years ago." He rushed quickly toward the large wooden table. "This slab is known as the Sugi, which is a reference to the Japanese name for the tree from which it was cut—the Japanese cedar, or *Cryptomeria japonica*. There are only twenty-five slabs like this in the world, one for each member of the original High Council," he said excitedly. "Now watch!"

He whispered something to the wand and it began to pulse. He placed it down on the table, and the second it came in contact with the wood, it transformed into a live miniature dragon. The dragon blinked twice and shook its head as if waking from a long sleep. It crept slowly toward Luis and sniffed, then snorted a flaming sneeze.

He jumped back in alarm. "Does it bite?"

"Don't be ridiculous," Coralis chided. He tapped the Sugi. The dragon ran to the center of the slab and disappeared into a tiny hole with a puff of smoke.

Coralis smiled broadly as he directed them all to step back. A loud crack punctuated the silence. Then, groaning as if it were on gears that hadn't been oiled in a lifetime, the Sugi began to rise.

The entire group gasped, unable to contain their astonishment. When it had risen just over a meter, the table came to a grinding halt. Luis slowly bent down to look beneath it and nearly fainted as the dragon, now standing half a meter tall, held it aloft over its head . . . and winked at him.

"To use one of your horrid colloquialisms: You ain't seen nothing yet." Coralis bent under the slab and whispered to the dragon, which purred in response. He tapped the underside of the slab with his wand and row upon row of small panels rotated downward, each one etched with symbols similar to those Henry had just seen in the wand case. Finding the one he was looking for, he tapped it again and a drawer slid open.

Tucked into the drawer were rows of tightly rolled scrolls of ancient papyrus. Coralis selected one and smiled. But the smile quickly vanished into a frown as he stared at the scroll. Pain etched his face as if he recalled a terrible memory. He stood and walked to the far side of the Sugi and did something with the scroll the group could not see. But the effect was astounding.

The entire surface of the slab came to life like a 3-D

hologram. The walls of an ancient city appeared in incredible detail. And as Coralis began to speak, the image zoomed in, showing an old man hunched over a map. "Behold Epifanio Corsini and his greatest achievement."

They watched together as the surface of the map rippled.

"Did that map just move by itself?" Serena moved closer to Henry. She started to extend her hand.

"Stop!" Coralis said sharply. "Do not disturb the scroll." Coralis began to pace around the table. "The Corsini Mappaemundi," he began as if instructing a class, then hesitated. "You saw the map move. It can adjust itself. Coastlines, mountains, forests—all constantly changing on the map as they change in the physical world.

"Naturally the only explanation could be the metaphysical link between the materials he used and the life-force of the planet itself!" he exclaimed, his excitement about the story beginning to build.

"Naturally," Molly whispered sarcastically.

"I heard that," he growled. "When Malachai stole the map, I could not understand why. Up until then, the map had served a good purpose. To heal wounds in the earth and prevent catastrophic disasters.

"About a year later I learned of a landslide that buried a troop of Genghis Khan's fiercest warriors—the same troop that had stolen the map under Malachai's direction. But landslides were common and I did not make the connection. In fact, things were so quiet for a time that I thought Malachai might also have died in the landslide."

The holographic image continued to unfold a scene that could easily have been mistaken for an old black-and-white movie. Epifanio worked with great haste scribbling notes on an ancient papyrus.

"Is that the scroll you just took from the drawer?" asked Molly.

"Good observation," Coralis said warmly. "All the scrolls in this table are the equivalent of what would now be video recordings. It's how we kept accurate records so that blow-hards like Wand Master Androcles could not lay false claims to accomplishments they did not achieve." The dragon snorted a puff of flame in reaction to the name. Coralis bent down. "I agree," he said to the dragon.

He stood and continued his story. "A century or so later, I was summoned to Bangkok by an old friend. He was a wise Buddhist monk and a great Wand Master. He told me about one of his apprentices who had been approached by another Wand Master—one whose aura had been tainted with shades of deep purple and black, and tinged in vivid red. His power was great, as was his rage.

"When the young man refused to join him, the evil Wand Master scorched him with a powerful beam of light. Physically, he recovered with a few lingering burns, but mentally, the poor man was never able to reconnect with reality. It was as if sections of his brain had been surgically separated. His speech was limited, but through intensive healing and patient questioning, the monk was able to piece together the disturb-ing details of the encounter. I had my suspicions that the culprit was Malachai, but there was no proof and he was never heard from again . . . until a year ago."

Coralis stopped, and motioned them over to a wall where a pool of rippling water lay nestled in a small alcove. He handed each of them a small wooden bowl and told them to fill it. "A freshwater stream runs through the mountain. Some of the finest water on Earth!" He smacked his lips in approval.

Henry sipped from the bowl. While cool on the tongue, the water spread warmth and energy down his throat. He hadn't realized how parched he was. "Can I have a refill?"

"Of course." Coralis nodded and smiled cagily. "So that you can tell everyone your story."

Henry hesitated as all eyes turned toward him. "From the beginning?" Coralis's silent stare was all the confirmation he needed. "Right, well . . ." He launched into an account of everything that had happened to him and Brianna. Luis and Katelyn smiled when he got to the part about Randall, and how Henry had accidentally knocked the bird unconscious. Brianna added an occasional detail—like nipping at Coralis's foot. And Serena helped with details about their time in Monument Valley.

He gained confidence as he spoke, though he knew better than to embellish the story. When he finally finished, they could hear the water ripple softly against the sides of the pool. "What?" He wasn't sure what to expect, but he'd thought he'd get a bigger reaction.

Bryndis broke the silence. "So your father is Malachai?"

"No!" Henry shouted. "He would never do the things Malachai has done. It isn't possible!"

Coralis raised a hand to calm him. "Malachai used Henry's father as he has so many others in the past. He uses deception and manipulation with the same ease a conductor would lead an orchestra."

"Then where is he?" Brianna croaked as a tear slid down her cheek. "What happened to our father?"

"That is what we must discuss." Coralis tapped his wand on the table. The image flickered out and the table lowered to its original height. The miniature dragon popped out of the center and scampered to Coralis. He petted it softly on the head before it changed back into its wand form. "I believe Gretchen has prepared some delicious stew for us. But first, a confession and an apology. Randall was not just an apprentice; he was my adopted son."

Henry and Serena looked at each other in shock as the mystery of Coralis's behavior came into glaring focus.

"His death . . . troubled me greatly. But more than that, it distracted me from my duties. And for that I am sorry. I will not allow it to happen again. You have my word. Now then. Dinner is ready."

Coralis ushered them up the stairs but Henry held him back. "I'm sorry about Randall. But my dad . . . He's okay, isn't he?"

"*Okay* is a relative term," Coralis answered grimly. "But not to worry. We are the cavalry."

TEN

"And so we have come to the crux of your apprenticeship." Coralis gathered the apprentices and Molly back into the space they now referred to as the Worm Room since so many of Ole Worm's artifacts occupied it. One corner of it was set up much like a classroom, but with a notable exception. There were no desks. Instead, thick, round logs of wood standing on end served as seats. Each log was topped with a dark green mineral that had been honed and polished. "Your seats might not be the most comfortable, but they will serve to keep your postures upright—as many young men and women such as yourselves are prone to slouching."

"The rich green and the swirls." Katelyn ran her hand over one. "They remind me of Ireland."

"Perhaps, but they originated in copper mines in Russia," Coralis explained. "And with that hint, who can tell me what kind of mineral it is?"

"Malachite!" Serena, Henry, and Bryndis shouted quickly.

"Excellent! And why will you be sitting on them?"

"Because green is Katelyn's favorite color," Luis quipped. "And because it helps to amplify positive energy—or, in this case, brain power."

"Lucky save," Henry whispered.

Luis smirked. "Luck had nothing to do with it."

As they each took a seat, Henry took in more details of the room. There were a dozen more seats than there were occupants, which suggested a lot of apprentices had passed through over the millennia. He wondered who might have occupied the one he chose.

Coralis interrupted his thoughts. "As members of the Wandmakers' Guild, you will be required to MAKE wands. Each wand will serve a specific purpose."

Bryndis's hand shot up. "What about the wands the falcon gave us?"

Henry was about to tell her to call it Randall, but Coralis flashed a stern look of warning in his direction. They'd had a discussion—more like a heated argument—over whether the bird could indeed be the boy who had supposedly died. Henry insisted that it was simply too big a coincidence for another falcon to appear and suddenly start delivering wands to random people.

Coralis, on the other hand, knew what he had felt the moment Randall died. And while he admitted nothing was impossible, he insisted the probability was so infinitesimally small as to be virtually impossible.

To Henry, that meant there was a chance—one that he

would cling to. But Coralis also made it clear that Henry was to keep those thoughts to himself.

"By now you should know what type of wood your wand is made from. In each case, you were given a wand made from a tree that is native to your country. Luis: the Tabebuia Rosa, which has excellent healing properties. Katelyn: the Sorbus Aucuparia, a source of great stability. Bryndis: the Betula Pubescens, a source of great tenacity. This is important, as where you come from defines who you are."

Henry twirled the wand Randall had given him between his fingers—not wood, but rather a black mineral he could not identify that was laced with vertical veins of clear quartz.

Coralis saw his confusion. "Henry, knowing your heritage, I selected that specific wand for you. But why don't you explain to your fellow apprentices the steps you took to construct your own personal wand."

Henry swallowed hard as the entire class turned toward him. "Well . . . the wood is oak, a symbol of strength and wisdom. It was important that I prepare it with things that were very personal to me." He held the wand up, explaining how he stained it purple using berries that blue jays (his favorite bird) would eat. And how he used water from the tank where his tadpoles changed into frogs. And how he rubbed it down with a piece of blanket that his mother had wrapped him in as an infant.

"Thank you." Coralis nodded. "What is important to note is that Henry was able to use this wand to call a flock of blue jays to his aid, and now that its use has been defined, it can forever be used to summon birds as he needs them. It's that personal connection to nature that gives you power. And it is always essential to use it wisely. Serena, what about your wand?"

"I chose this piece of quaking aspen from the Coconino National Forest because of these." Serena pointed to two vertical black scars on the wand. "I was tracking animals with Joseph when we stopped to watch an elk strip the bark off a tree with its front teeth, leaving these scars."

"Sounds like you have some competition," Luis joked to Henry.

"Joseph is our chief and my grandfather," Serena said with a laugh. "The elk is my totem. It symbolizes stamina, strength, and agility."

"And like Henry, did you apply any special treatment to it?" Coralis leaned forward, showing keen interest.

Serena blushed. "Well . . . to amplify the totem's power, Joseph had me . . . um . . . cure it in elk urine."

"Eww." Katelyn wrinkled her nose.

"Elk is a good totem." Bryndis nodded. "How long did you track it before it peed?"

"Seriously?" Luis laughed. "That's the first question that pops into your head?"

"Tracking takes skill," Bryndis said scornfully. "Hers must be a powerful wand. When do we start on ours?"

"Excuse me," Brianna interrupted. "One of us doesn't have a wand."

Coralis smiled broadly. "What a perfect way to start! Did you bring what I asked?"

Brianna nodded and pulled a mason jar out of a bag.

"Are those what I think they are?" asked Henry.

Serena leaned in for a closer look. "They appear to be nail clippings . . . a lot of them."

"Correct!" Coralis exclaimed happily. "Brianna has been experiencing certain physical anomalies, among which has been abnormal fingernail growth. At first I attributed it to being a side effect of spending time as a hedgehog. But after careful research, I discovered they are her body's reaction to her emergence as an Enabler. And here's the best part." Coralis paused, giddy with excitement. "Making her wand from these clippings will increase her power tenfold! Now then, we will need a few items from the other room. Talk among yourselves. I'll be back in a moment." Coralis nearly skipped out of the classroom.

Luis grimaced. "How long have you been saving them?"

"Only about ten weeks," Brianna replied meekly. "I had to clip them once a day, but the good news is they've slowed down a lot, so it's only about every third day now."

"I'm not sure what's worse," Luis said. "The number of clippings you produce in ten weeks or the fact that you save them."

Henry was fascinated by Brianna's condition, and a quick look around confirmed he wasn't alone. Only Luis seemed to have a problem with it, but Henry had a suspicion that the boy was exaggerating his reaction in order to bring attention to himself.

Coralis returned in full-blown instruction mode. "Gather 'round, apprentices. Nails are made of keratin, which cannot be melted into another shape. Many mammalian body parts are also made of keratin, like horns, scales, and quills, so this knowledge will become useful as you hone your wand-making skills and begin to experiment. Since we cannot melt the nails, we will have to transform them."

Over the course of the next hour, Coralis amazed the group with a display of finesse and power. By the time he was through, they knew they were in the presence of a master.

And Brianna had received her first wand. The beauty of it was that the final product looked very much like phantom quartz, which would allow her to go undetected as an Enabler. They dubbed the wand the "Nailinator," and as they admired it, Katelyn drifted away from the group.

Henry saw that she was worried about something. "Are you okay?" he asked.

"Aye, nothing wrong. But I just took to wonderin'. How did the falcon know what wands to give us, and why did they make such a mess of things?"

Coralis overheard and answered before Henry could respond. "I believe I can answer part of that, though I don't wholly understand the other. The falcon that was Randall died and the blame rests squarely on my shoulders. I did not witness the event, and others might have different theories." He raised an eyebrow at Henry. "However, I felt his demise as strongly as if someone had pulled off an arm. And yet shortly after, another falcon appears, delivering wands around the globe. There can be no natural explanation—which leaves us with the supernatural.

"The universe is filled with phenomena we don't understand. So when someone's essence is released into the cosmos, there may indeed be forces that can bring it back in a kind of reincarnation. This is something we may never know for certain. But Randall was an extraordinarily talented young man, capable of performing exceptional deeds, so mine is not to doubt, but to accept."

"This is all very interesting, but you haven't answered Katelyn's question," Bryndis grumbled.

Coralis folded his arms in front of him and sat on one of the unoccupied logs, scanning the group and holding eye contact with each of them in turn. "There are things I cannot answer with certainty, and this is one of them. Suffice it to say that regardless of how the falcon found you, it is clearly your destiny that you have been brought together."

"Then why did the wands backfire?" Luis looked toward Bryndis for confirmation.

"Yes. Mine, too." But she did not offer any details.

"That was only because you did not understand the extent of your powers and how to control them. Your wand is an extension of you," Coralis said softly. "Which is why you are here—to learn the craft of the Wandmakers' Guild.

"But there is one more thing we should do before we proceed any further. Molly, will you please give me a hand?" Coralis tugged on a thick, ornate rope that hung from the rafters, where it was supported by several pulleys. As he released the rope, a series of grinding, clanking, banging sounds filled the room.

"Is that a sound effects machine?" Luis asked.

"Wait for it . . ." Molly smiled.

The noise stopped. A pocket door on the opposite side of the room slid open to reveal a long walk-in closet full of coats.

"Why all the dramatic effects?" Serena asked.

"Aye, seems a bit Willy Wonka for a Wand Master," Katelyn added.

Coralis laughed. "I agree, but Randall felt that opening this particular door deserved more fanfare than normal. I present to you—your Wandmaker coats!"

Each coat hung on a hook with a name tag stuck to the wall above it. Henry still had the coat Coralis had given him in New York, but this one was different.

Coralis held the coat open for him and he slid his arms into it. He did the same for Luis as Molly fitted the girls with their coats. Coralis then lightly tapped them each on the shoulder with his wand. The apprentices giggled as the coats conformed to their body shapes like tailor-made suits. As soon as the coats had settled, a circular insignia wavered into focus on their upper arms near the shoulder. Inside the circle were the letters *WG* in an interlocking script, with a pair of wands in the shape of an X beneath them.

"The Wandmaker's coat is yet another weapon in your arsenal." Coralis brushed a piece of lint from Bryndis's sleeve. "It is made from extremely rare fibers and filaments. It is very much like the synthetic material known as Kevlar in that it is very difficult to penetrate. But these coats are not synthetic plastic. They are one hundred percent natural. And they will offer you a great deal of protection from the elements—though they will not make you indestructible, invincible, or invisible."

"And it has pockets!" Henry exclaimed as he examined the inner lining.

"I prefer to call them sleeves," Coralis corrected. "They are designed to hold your wands securely in place and allow you to function as if you were wearing a second skin."

"Why are they all different colors?" Brianna asked.

All the coats had a dark, earthen tone, but it was possible to detect differences in their shades. Brianna's was green, Bryndis had blue, Luis had brown, Serena's was gray, and Katelyn's was maroon.

"What's wrong with his?" Luis pointed at Henry, whose coat swirled from color to color before settling on a camouflage pattern that incorporated all the colors.

Coralis grinned. "Nothing. Nothing at all."

"This isn't a training exercise," Henry panted. "It's a death march."

"For once, you and I are on the same page," Luis gasped. "These backpacks are too heavy. And I can't even see two meters in front of me in this fog."

"It's not fog," Serena said, her breathing unaffected by the hike. "It's a cloud."

"All of you stop," Bryndis groaned. "Your lip flapping is making me tired."

"No, that's the altitude," said Serena. "I told you before we left that we have to keep drinking water."

"My head hurts," Brianna grumbled.

"Okay, everybody. Stop right now and listen up," Serena commanded. "Coralis sent us on this training exercise for two reasons—to survive on our own and to work as a team."

"As we say in Ireland, *Ní neart go cur le chéile*," said Katelyn. "There's strength in unity."

"Exactly!" said Serena. "Some of you might be experts in other things, but I know about mountain climbing. So if you don't start listening, we are going to fail miserably. Let's take a ten-minute break. DRINK WATER! Vegetarians, eat your nuts. Carnivores, chew on your jerky. We all need protein and hydration."

Henry plunked his backpack on the ground. Water sloshed in its plastic container. He winked at Serena, who smiled back. Since the others had arrived, they had not spent enough time together. Their world had gone into perpetual motion. He missed their time alone, and part of him wished life could go back to the way it was. But there was no going back. He would just have to make the most of their rare private moments.

Henry had also been watching Brianna closely. Despite her instant aging, he still thought of her as his little sister. And while she had been a bit of a brat before growing up so suddenly, he wouldn't trade those early years for anything. He loved her in that unconditional way only siblings would understand. Not for the first time, he worried about her safety. *I'll just have to make sure nothing happens to her,* he thought.

"I'll watch out for you, too, big brother," Brianna answered with a broad smile.

When they set off again, the rest, along with the food and drink, had helped their mood. Yet the mountain trail challenged them at every step. Scree made for treacherous travel. Occasionally, boulders from a previous rockslide blocked their path. Fortunately, the cloud had thinned, improving visibility—which was why they saw the cave. Bryndis had taken the lead, raising a hand to stop the group and motioning for silence.

"I hardly think that's necessary," said Luis. "From the amount of noise we've been making, any animal within a kilometer already knows we're here."

"Good point," Bryndis acknowledged. "Must be an old habit."

"Do you think something is in there?" Brianna asked nervously.

Katelyn moved next to her, giving her hand a gentle squeeze. "Aye. I think it's the home of the killer rabbit. It has large pointy teeth and big bushy ears and it hops its victims to death."

Brianna giggled. Of all the apprentices, she seemed to like Katelyn the most. They usually paired up when it was time for group lessons.

"Who's going in first?" Henry asked, not expecting the entire group to turn in his direction. "Now hold on. I wasn't volunteering."

"I think you're the one who started this mess, so you should lead the way," Luis taunted.

Henry knew he had been backed into a corner. He couldn't stand the thought of Luis getting the better of him— especially in front of Serena. "Fine." He reached for his wand and came up empty, forgetting Coralis had made them leave their wands as well as their Wandmakers' Guild coats behind.

"You must learn to think on your own and not use your wand as a crutch," he'd said.

Henry blew out a lungful of air to steady himself, lit a wooden matchstick, and marched into the mouth of the cave. It wasn't very deep, and as soon as he saw what was waiting for them inside, he decided to play a joke. He screamed, then kicked up loose dirt and rocks as if he were fighting someone.

Brianna was the first to react, running into the cave to save her brother. And when she found him laughing, she gave him a swift punch. Henry noted that Luis was the last one in.

"Are you going to be the boy who cries wolf?" Bryndis asked testily.

"Wow! What is all this?" Serena asked, striking a match of her own.

"I don't get it," Brianna said once they had gathered the contents and moved them outside. "Did some caveman leave all this behind?"

Luis picked up a straight, meter-long stick and held one end up to his eye, aiming it skyward. "Nice!"

"What is it?" Brianna asked.

"It's a blowgun." He pressed the end with a mouthpiece to his lips, puffed his cheeks full of air, whipped it around to face Henry, and blew.

"Hey!" Henry ducked.

"Oops." Luis laughed. "Guess it wasn't loaded."

"Okay, boys, cut it out," Serena said. "How do you know about blowguns?"

"I spent many months among the Achuar people. They use such tools to hunt birds and monkeys. Whoever made this one was very skilled." Luis examined it more closely.

"Definitely from my home. See the type of wood and the bark of the vine that was used to wrap it?"

But the others had turned their attention elsewhere. Bryndis hefted a long spear, testing the weight and balance in her hand. "Good. Strong."

"Why is there a string attached to a spear?" Henry asked.

"This is not a spear. It's a harpoon." She held it up to demonstrate. "You throw it hard. When it connects, you use this cord made from sealskin to pull the animal toward you."

"What if you only wound it and it takes off?" Luis asked.

"Then you are a bad shot." She winked.

Serena picked up a bow and a quiver of arrows. "Nice stereotyping," Henry remarked.

"Maybe," she said warily. "But I am an expert shot. And this is not your typical bow. The wood is backed with animal tendon—sinew—which gives it more spring action." She turned to Katelyn, who had selected a braided leather cord with a wooden ball attached to either end.

"It's a bola." Katelyn smiled. "Not sure why me mum taught me to use one but I'm quite good at it." She demonstrated by swinging it around her head several times before letting it fly at Henry, where the balls spun the cord around his legs and promptly deposited him on his butt.

He untangled the bola and dusted himself off. "Thanks for the warning." Then he looked at what was left—a small patch of leather with a cord wrapped around it.

Katelyn picked it up. " 'Tis a sling—like for hurling rocks." She quickly demonstrated by nesting a rock into the leather patch and whipping it at a tree thirty meters away, nailing it dead center.

"Impressive," said Luis. "But why two weapons for you?"

Katelyn flipped the leather over to reveal the initials *BL* branded into it. She smiled at Brianna. "Looks like I've got some teaching to do."

It became all too obvious that there was nothing for Henry. He couldn't bear to make eye contact with the others, so he didn't notice Serena approach him until she slid her hand into his. "I think this might mean that you're in charge," she said reassuringly.

"No, it doesn't!" Luis yelled. "It just means he doesn't know how to use a weapon."

"Aye." Katelyn had a twinkle in her eye. "I'd say the soldiers have been issued their weapons and the captain has his work cut out for him."

Henry waited to see if anyone else had something to add. When Bryndis finally gave her begrudging consent, Luis caved. "Fine! At least we'll know who to blame when we're all running around as rodents."

"A hedgehog isn't actually a rodent," Brianna said . . . then giggled . . . then laughed as the others joined in and clapped Henry on the back.

"Okay, then, I guess we keep moving." Henry was eager to leave the cave and give himself time to think. "It should be a few more hours until we reach the campsite Coralis showed us on the map."

They walked in single file, Bryndis in the lead, Henry

picking up the rear, deep in thought. Why had Coralis given them weapons when they could be using their wands? What was he preparing them for, and how worried should he be that he didn't know how to use any of the weapons?

Katelyn dropped back alongside Brianna and explained the basics of the rock sling, loading it up and hitting target after target with pinpoint accuracy. Brianna studied her technique, as did Henry. A helpless feeling came over him as he realized once again he had absolutely zero athletic ability.

Serena walked in front of him, her backpack slung over one shoulder and her quiver over the other. He watched the arrows bounce to the rhythm of her steps, but something was odd about them. One of the arrows had a delayed bounce, like one member of a marching band who's out of step from all the rest. He was about to reach for it when the first wolf howled.

It didn't take much outdoor experience to know they needed to find the campground quickly. They broke into a jog but tired quickly from the altitude. Nonetheless, they arrived at their destination with an hour of daylight to spare. The campsite was nothing but a clearing. Henry had hoped to find the shelter of a cabin. Without one, they were exposed to anything nature might throw at them.

The temperature had begun to drop. They all scattered to find enough wood to build a fire. Henry toyed with the idea of leading them back to the cave, but darkness would be upon them well before they could reach it, and one false step on the rocky trail could be disastrous.

Once they got the fire going, they felt much safer. They hadn't heard from the wolf again but weren't naive enough to let their guard down. He suggested they practice with their weapons, which succeeded in taking their minds off any danger.

Luis went off to find something that would make suitable darts for the blowgun. He refused any help, telling the others they wouldn't know what to look for.

Henry walked a short distance into the woods and spotted a plant he thought he recognized. He smiled as he recalled tossing a book into his backpack just before leaving the castle.

"What's that?" Bryndis asked as Henry flipped through the pages. He showed her, and she nodded approvingly. "*Headley's Deadlies: The Book of Harold Headley's All Things Dead and Some Things That Aren't.* Sounds interesting."

"I'm pretty sure I spotted some poison hemlock back there," Henry said. "I think we can use it on the blowgun darts."

"Good thinking, Captain." Her tone was terse, but he suspected it was as close to a compliment as he'd ever get from her.

"Are you sure you know what you're doing?" Serena asked.

"Not a clue." Henry laughed. "But at least I feel useful. What do you think is taking Luis so long?"

Another howl rang out. This time much closer. "You'd better make it quick," Serena urged.

Henry gathered leaves from the plant, protecting his hands by removing his socks and using them as gloves. He used an old can discarded by a previous camper to boil water and let the leaves simmer.

Luis finally returned, a broad smile announcing his success. "Porcupine quills!" He held them aloft like a trophy.

"Good," Bryndis said. "Henry is brewing some poison. We might have a chance at living through the night."

"It's only a wolf," Luis said snidely. "We have more than enough firepower to take him on."

"One wolf, maybe," Bryndis said, watching the tree line. "I have hunted wolves and they have hunted me. When there is one, there are many." As if on cue, the sun set and the campsite was cloaked in ominous darkness. "If anyone has to pee, do it now. We will stand guard in shifts." She looked toward Henry.

It took him a minute to realize she was giving him direction to lead his troops. "Right. We'll do it in pairs, switching off every . . ." Bryndis slyly held up two fingers. "Every two hours. Katelyn and I will take the first watch, then Serena and Luis, then Bryndis and Brianna." Luis grinned. Henry had intentionally paired Brianna with Bryndis to give his sister the best protection, but in the process he had handed Luis an opportunity to spend time alone with Serena—and it was too late to take it back without looking foolish.

"Good plan, matching one skilled with a weapon with one not as skilled." Bryndis winked at Henry, then turned to Luis. "You should practice. Now let's eat. I'm famished."

The attack came at two in the morning. Serena and Luis were nearing the end of their shift. Drowsiness had dulled their senses by the time wolves snarled from three directions. "Wake up!" Serena yelled, and rapidly nocked an arrow. Immediately, they tossed their blankets aside and manned the positions Henry had assigned them, forming a circle with their backs to the fire.

"How many do you think there are?" Henry asked, surprisingly calm.

"Too many," Bryndis answered. "Let them make the first move. Do not panic."

The wolves were nearly invisible, hidden among dark shadows within the trees. Only their eyes gave them away, light from the fire reflecting yellowish-red orbs. Henry counted three wolves, but gradually a fourth appeared. They were spread out, completely surrounding the apprentices.

"They will try to separate us—pick off the weakest," Bryndis said. "We cannot allow that to happen. We must attack first. Remain calm. Breathe as evenly as you can. Try not to show your fear."

Henry picked up on the even pacing of her voice and how she used it to regulate their fear. She was definitely in her element when hunting.

"Here's what we'll do," she instructed. "No sudden moves. Blowgun boy, take that one. Aim for the neck. Serena, take that one. Not a direct hit. Try for an ear. We only want to wound them. Brianna, swing a rock on your sling as fast as you can. Do not release it. Chances are you'll miss. You will do better to threaten it."

Bryndis had Katelyn move closer to her side, the two of them facing the one Bryndis identified as the alpha male. "When I give the word, we attack as one. Ready . . . now!"

Luis and Serena fired, wounding their wolves, while Brianna swung wildly as she yelled. As soon as they attacked, the alpha male charged. Katelyn whipped her bola at its front legs, tripping the large wolf, which sprawled in a tumbling heap. Bryndis quickly pounced on it. While it was dazed, she wrapped the cord of her harpoon around the wolf's snout, then secured the rear legs with loose cord from the bola.

Seeing their leader taken down, the other three slunk back into the tree line. Bryndis held the deadly tip of her harpoon against the wolf's neck. She stared hard into its eyes as she applied more pressure to the tip. Finally, in an act of submission, the wolf looked away.

Bryndis slowly stood. The wolf remained still. "The pack has seen their leader go down." She breathed heavily, the combination of adrenaline and exertion catching up to her. "They need a new leader. Blowgun boy, come here and bite the wolf on the neck as hard as you can."

Luis gulped. "You've got to be kidding."

Bryndis turned on him angrily—then suddenly burst out laughing. "Of course I'm kidding. Not even a crazy wolf would believe you're the boss."

They arrived back at the castle around midmorning. The downhill trek was all the more appreciated considering their lack of sleep. Despite Bryndis's reassurances, they had scarcely closed their eyes all night.

They staggered into the foyer, where Coralis was waiting. "Well, look what the cat dragged in."

Henry rolled his red-rimmed eyes. "Speaking for the group, we respectfully request a day off." That was one of the few things they had talked—more like grumbled—about the entire morning.

"So, our band of merry apprentices has a leader," Coralis said cheerfully.

"More or less." Henry wasn't in the mood. He'd been afraid to put his socks back on, and his feet had sprouted some nasty blisters.

Serena shook her bow angrily. "We could have been killed!"

"Do tell," Coralis taunted. "You could die falling down a flight of stairs on any given day. What made your excursion so dangerous?"

"We were attacked by wolves!" Brianna exclaimed. "And all we had to defend ourselves with were rocks, ropes, and sticks."

"Wolves?" Coralis echoed. "Perhaps you should fill me in."

Henry recounted their adventure, giving the lion's share of the credit to Bryndis.

"Impressive," Coralis admitted.

"We could have been killed," Serena repeated through clenched teeth.

"Nonsense." Coralis snorted. "Henry, as their leader, did you feel as though your lives were in danger?"

"No." He answered immediately, which stunned the group.

"Perhaps you'd like to explain," Coralis prodded.

Henry blew out a deep breath, reached into Serena's quiver, and pulled out a plain wooden stick.

"Is that a wand?" Katelyn asked.

Luis scowled. "You knew we had a wand and didn't think to tell us?"

"I suspected," Henry said defensively. "I noticed something about one of the arrows."

"And kept it to yourself?" Brianna snapped.

"Look, we succeeded without having to rely on a wand. That was the point!" Henry insisted. "We worked as a team—a darn good one—and we found out what we could accomplish using nothing but our wits and some primitive weapons. You guys were amazing! I mean, just think about what we did. We took down a pack of wolves!"

"And we did it without killing them," Bryndis added proudly.

"I have to admit, I feel pretty good about that part," Luis added. "And I can't wait to make some decent darts for this." He held the blowgun up triumphantly.

"Well then," Coralis said, smiling proudly. "I'd say you've earned a day off. Gretchen has prepared an early lunch. The rest of the day is yours."

As they shuffled out, Henry held back. "You knew those wolves were out there. And I'm guessing you knew they wouldn't hurt us."

Coralis looked at him in mock surprise. "Dear boy, I knew nothing of the sort."

"Right." Henry smiled.

As he got to the door, Coralis called out to him. "But we will have to work on your nature skills. That is not the way to prepare poison hemlock."

Henry grinned broadly. He had never mentioned the hemlock.

"Never thought I'd see *that*."

"What do you think he's doing?"

"Are those the legs of a man or an emaciated chicken?"

"Hope his heart can take it."

Since her arrival, Molly had been a stickler about exercise. Every day began with yoga and ended with calisthenics to improve the apprentices' coordination and stamina. Today, they had just finished a few warm-up exercises in the courtyard—stretching, bending, lunging. They were about to start some light soccer drills when Coralis appeared, bringing all motion to a screeching halt. He jogged in place and attempted to bend in ways that his muscles had all but forgotten how to do.

"It hurts me just to look at him." Katelyn winced.

"When was the last time those legs saw daylight?" Luis laughed.

"We're going to need sunglasses to keep them from blinding us," Bryndis added.

"I can hear you!" Coralis shouted. He jogged awkwardly toward the group. "So . . . whose team am I on?"

"You can't be serious." Molly had the ball tucked under an arm. She flipped it at Coralis and it bounced off his chest, startling him.

"What was that for?" He sounded offended.

"No offense, sir, but those aren't even proper shorts." Luis struggled to talk without laughing.

"In my day, we didn't need shorts." He looked down. His lips contorted in an ugly grimace. "There was probably a good reason for that," he said as he unrolled his pants down to their normal length. He straightened up with a broad grin. "So who wants to be on the winning team?"

"Oh, so that's the way it's going to be, is it?" Molly laughed. "I accept your challenge!"

On a scale of athletic talent from zero to ten, the apprentices covered the full range. Henry was the zero, Luis and Bryndis the tens. "How could you not know how to play football?" Luis asked Henry as he tried to give him a few quick pointers.

"In case you haven't noticed, I'm not very athletic." Henry swiped at the ball with his left foot and missed as it rolled between his legs. "And this isn't football; it's soccer."

"Only in America." Luis scooped the ball with his toe, bounced it from knee to knee, then popped it in the air and used his head to pass it back to Henry.

"Show-off!" Serena shouted from the opposite side of the makeshift playing field.

"Give it to me." Bryndis deftly stopped a pass from Serena and popped it in the air as Luis had done. Then, with a powerful sweep of her leg, she kicked the ball straight up into the air. It seemed to go up forever before plummeting directly back to her, where she somehow caught it with her foot. She smiled at Luis, who nodded respectfully.

"Can you do that?" Henry gulped. He had hoped this would be a quick game of casual soccer in which the ball might not even come to him. Now it was looking like he could be carted off the field on a stretcher.

"Don't worry, team." Katelyn stepped up to join Luis and Henry. "Finesse will win more football games than brute strength. Though . . . she is quite good."

"Well then, let's hope Molly is a better goalkeeper than Coralis." Luis fired a shot at her, which she swatted away with one hand as if it were a pesky fly. "Not bad for an old lady!" He laughed and she threw the ball back at him, which he stopped with his chest. An audible "Umph" confirmed the speed and power of the ball's flight.

Luis, Katelyn, and Molly formed a triangle, passing the ball back and forth from knee to knee, foot to foot, head to head. Henry was so far out of his league it was ridiculous. Somehow, though, it didn't really bother him. When he'd played baseball back home, it had felt like the whole world was laughing at him. Here, he felt surrounded by friends . . . even if his athletic efforts remained somewhat laughable.

The past week had been a whirlwind of lessons, assignments, and experiments. Molly had accomplished exactly what she was brought in to do: She got them focused on learning and kept them on track by wearing them out. Each day was surprisingly different from the previous one, with no apparent structure or lesson plan. Their classroom was the whole compound and the entire surrounding forest. And they were learning at such an accelerated rate that Henry thought Coralis must be spiking their water with nanobots.

He grinned, thinking back to when Katelyn had first used that word. She had turned out to be their resident techno geek, mostly due to her love of reading science fiction. She and Henry had similar reading habits—taking copious notes as they read in order to explore terms and concepts more fully.

There was a time when Henry had been reluctant or embarrassed to participate in classroom discussions. More often than not, it led to ridicule. But here, Katelyn led the way, sharing her knowledge with such open willingness that at times, Molly let her take over instructions as she sat and watched. Katelyn's love of sci-fi had led not only to her interest in cutting-edge technology; it had also fostered a fascination with unique and unusual power sources—which included the sun. The ultimate power source was her ultimate obsession.

To Henry's surprise, Luis was equally engaged and helpful. The bully tactics he had employed upon his arrival had mostly dissipated, though he could still get under Henry's skin by flirting with Serena. Growing up in a jungle had subconsciously imprinted an incredible amount of knowledge in his brain. Molly had called it osmosis and said he absorbed knowledge the way a plant absorbed water. Just as a car mechanic understood an engine, Luis knew plants. And that knowledge extended to soil and animal life—because all those elements worked together.

Next was Serena, whose life on the open plains and time spent with Elders gave her an uncanny sense of the universe around her and enabled her to understand systems and patterns on a global and even a cosmic scale. She was absolutely amazing when it came to explaining weather patterns. During a discussion of tornadoes, she spoke with such force and authority that Henry could have sworn a breeze stirred in the closed room.

Bryndis was still a bit of a mystery. She had yet to share the tale of how she'd ended up at the castle, but she was in her glory when telling stories about her prowess on the open seas. Fishing and seal hunting were her life, and to hear her tell it there wasn't a seaworthy craft she couldn't handle. Henry suspected some of it was poppycock, as Coralis would say. But if even half of it were true, she knew her way around water.

And then it hit him. He had just managed to kick the ball more than five meters when he pulled up short and looked back at Coralis. This was no random gathering of apprentices. They each embraced one of the four basic elements. Serena, Katelyn, Luis, and Bryndis had each exhibited a talent for mastering air, fire, earth, and water. Which also explained the colors of their coats—gray for air, maroon for fire, brown for earth, and blue for water.

Across the field, Coralis easily caught a pass from Brianna, but just before he tossed it back, he made brief eye contact with Henry . . . and winked.

Talent-wise, the teams matched up fairly evenly. Katelyn versus Serena for finesse. Luis versus Bryndis for power and speed. Henry's clumsiness versus Brianna's recklessness. And while some of the players were more competitive than others, they all relished the opportunity to break free from the rigors of their training, if only for a few hours.

Henry laughed. For the first time, he had kicked the ball in the direction he was aiming, which surprised Luis so much that he nearly tripped over it. Bryndis easily swiped the ball away from him and used some dazzling footwork to sneak a shot past Molly for a goal.

Brianna and Serena locked arms with her, yelling "GOOOOOOAL!" with all the exuberance of a television announcer.

But their celebration was cut short by a terrifying screech from beyond the walls. A lone bird streaked skyward as if shot from a cannon. Henry quickly identified it as a falcon, but the three large birds that raced after it were much, much different. At first they appeared to be owls—until he saw that each bird had four deadly clawed legs.

"Strix," hissed Coralis. "Quickly, everyone take shelter within the shadow of the wall! It will be harder for them to see you."

Molly herded them toward the perimeter of the compound; they sprinted like lambs with a wolf hot on their tails.

But Henry felt rooted in place, watching the scene unfold beyond the walls, wishing there were something he could do to help.

The Strix and the falcon were too evenly matched. Predator hunting predator: It would never be able to shake off their pursuit. Henry stared intently at their bold red wings. When they dipped low enough he could see their bright yellow eyes—the eyes of something demonic.

The falcon raced furiously into a vertical climb, then looped over in a fantastic roller coaster move, plummeting toward the ground faster than physics should have allowed. Henry glanced at Coralis, who seemed momentarily stunned.

The avian quartet passed directly between Henry and Coralis in a blur of speed, pulling up at the last second. And in that split second, one of the Strix made eye contact with Henry. It broke off from the pack and turned like a fighter jet in a wide arc. And then it sped straight for him with an ear-shattering screech, extending its four legs forward, its long, sharp beak zeroing in for the kill.

Henry was frozen in place, eerily calm. He heard Coralis say something as if from far away. Something about their eyes and sunlight.

"Henry!" Brianna screamed, breaking him out of his hypnotic trance. In one fluid motion, he whipped his wand from his pocket and willed the power of the sun into it. Blinding light burst forth, slamming into the bird that was now mere centimeters away, reducing it instantly to ash.

"Henry, are you all right?" Serena rushed to his side. As she reached out for him, another of the Strix peeled off from its chase, taking aim at human prey.

Henry saw it coming, but Serena stood between him and the bird. "Serena, get down!"

Instead of following his order, she frowned—dark and angry. Serena reached for her wand and spun around. Feet spread slightly apart for balance, she pointed directly at the oncoming bird. "Be gone!" she screamed. There was no burst of light. Instead, a small, tight spiral of air thrust forward from the tip of her wand, growing into a cylinder of wind that surrounded the bird like an impenetrable cage.

Henry's wide eyes volleyed back and forth between Serena and the bird. He had never seen that look on her before. She was in total possession of her power as she held the bird trapped a mere meter away from her arm. The Strix fought viciously to free itself, snapping and clawing wildly at its invisible cell. Then its eyes began to change. Something was happening, and Coralis saw it, too.

"Serena, now!" Coralis shouted into her mind with such force that Henry felt it as well.

She pushed another burst of power through the wand. The spiral of wind spun faster in an ever-tightening tornado, squeezing the Strix until it, too, exploded in a haze of black ash. Then with a quick flick of her wrist, she sent the mini-tornado zooming skyward, where it gradually disappeared.

The third Strix must have realized it was outmatched and

quickly retreated beyond the compound walls. "Are you okay?" Henry caught Serena as she collapsed and helped her sit.

"What did I do? Where did *that* come from?" She rubbed her temples, exhausted and bewildered.

"That was awesome!" Luis jogged toward them. The others quickly followed, peppering Henry and Serena with questions they could not answer.

"I just suddenly knew what to do" was the best Serena could offer.

Coralis watched his apprentices with pride. He decided to let them have the moment to themselves and turned to leave, but the falcon blocked his path. He frowned. He was skeptical. But some part of him remained open to the slightest bit of hope.

He reached out with his mind. *"Randall."*

The falcon blinked and hopped forward but did not answer. Instead it squirted a sizable load of urine onto the lawn, then leapt to the side and took flight. It looped behind the castle and disappeared from sight.

Coralis cupped his chin in his hand. It was dangerous to allow wild hopes to preoccupy his thoughts. The falcon had to be nothing but a coincidence.

He grinned at the mess the falcon had left behind. Just maybe . . .

"The Strix should no longer exist." Coralis had gathered everyone, including Gretchen, in the Cryptoporticus. He activated the Sugi again with another ancient scroll. A beautiful landscape materialized in holographic-type imagery. Lush green hills ended abruptly at a cliff, pockmarked with caves. Tumultuous waves crashed at the foot of the rocky cliffside, pummeling away like a relentless battering ram that knew it would eventually win.

Small flocks of Strix engaged in battle, viciously tearing at one another yet never doing enough damage to emerge victorious. "These are creatures of ancient lore," Coralis continued. "There is not much that will harm them. In fact, in their time, their only natural predator was the Giant Roc. They were mindless creatures, and as far as we know, their sole purpose was to kill anything that crossed their paths."

Bryndis scowled. "How did these two know what to do?" She waved a hand in the direction of Henry and Serena, obviously irritated that she hadn't thought fast enough to join the battle.

Henry shuffled his feet nervously, glancing at Serena before replying. "For me, it was something Coralis said about their eyes. All I was trying to do was blind it. But then something inside me took over and I suddenly knew that blinding it wouldn't be enough. So I unleashed the power of the sun."

Katelyn smiled. "You're going to have to teach me that."

Coralis tapped the table and the image disappeared. "One cannot teach instinct. This is not the first time Henry has used it. What about you, Serena?"

"I, um . . . I'm not quite sure," she said tentatively. "It was like when someone throws something at you and you react to keep it from hitting you. I didn't have time to think. I let the wand take over."

"And how did you feel afterward?" Coralis asked.

She paused in thought. "Exhilarated. But that's wrong, isn't it? I mean . . . I destroyed something with my power—a living creature. I should feel bad." Her hands began to shake and she quickly rubbed them together.

"What about you, Henry?"

Coralis could see Serena was upset, yet he ignored her emotional turmoil. Henry saw tears welling in her eyes and was suddenly enraged at the old man's callousness. "You know I felt the same," he snapped indignantly.

"Uh-oh." Luis stepped away from Henry.

A dark cloud descended over Coralis's features as if an explosion was imminent. "As I said, the Strix are creatures of the ancient past." His voice was low and ominous. "I did not expect this to happen so soon, but it has. It can only mean one thing. A warning shot has been fired over our bow. Our war has begun."

Gretchen looked at the terrified faces of six frightened children. "Coralis." She poured the full force of her Voice into that single word.

Everyone in the chamber felt its impact—except Coralis, who turned on her with unsuppressed anger. "You cannot stop this, Gretchen, so please don't try."

Gretchen reeled, blinking rapidly. Her reaction led Henry to believe that this might be the first time her use of Voice did not work as she'd intended. She seemed confused, and even more than that, hurt.

Coralis saw it, too. He didn't apologize, but his tone softened. "While Molly has been saturating your minds with studies, I have been gathering information. Shortly before most of you arrived, Serena was presented with a valuable vision. She entered a pool of life in which the Earth Mother gave her a strong clue to Malachai's nefarious plan. To the best of my knowledge, the Earth Mother has only appeared to our kind one other time. That time, she appeared to Malachai."

Molly gasped but Coralis ignored it, forging ahead with urgency. "He was not always evil. He was one of my first apprentices. Even the Earth Mother could not have predicted how his soul would turn to blackness. It was a time of deep despair, and she took him into her confidence, revealing things that helped us avert a crisis of disastrous proportions. But tucked into those revelations was information that no one was ever supposed to know. I have spent weeks analyzing the scrolls Malachai left behind, considering their contents in relation to Serena's vision. I believe Malachai has found his way into the Temple of Time."

Molly whistled softly. "Talk about your myths."

"Unfortunately, not a myth," said Coralis. The dragon sat on the table, patiently awaiting instructions. A silent command from the Wand Master sent it scurrying to the center, where it transformed into a cloud of mist that began to swirl. Gradually, a solid sphere formed: a globe that looked much like Earth, but unlike any depiction Henry had ever seen. "Millions of years ago, our planet looked like this." Coralis spoke in a mesmerizing tone. "It consisted of a super-continent."

"Pangaea," said Bryndis.

"Yes, Pangaea." He nodded his approval. "If you have studied Earth's history the way our Greenlander has, you will know that the supercontinent gradually separated as tectonic plates shifted. It took millions of years to form the individual continents we have today." He waved a hand at the globe. The landmasses moved apart, but before they could finish, he froze the map. "As you can see, the land moved in such a way as to trap an enormous body of water, which is known as the Tethys Ocean."

"You said is, not was," Katelyn interrupted.

Coralis smiled. "I love an attentive apprentice." He started the globe in motion and the land continued to shift. "The Tethys Ocean became smaller individual bodies of water as the land divided it up. Some parts of the original ocean are still with us, in the form of the Mediterranean, Black, and Caspian Seas. But there is another part that became trapped below the surface. That should have been the end of the story.

"However, as mankind entered the picture, he began to wander and explore. In her infinite wisdom, the Earth Mother realized there was still a singular access point to the Tethys, and so she worked to create a defense with the ancient ones. I believe you know them as druids," he said to Katelyn.

"Then they're real?" Katelyn could not mask her surprise, which made Coralis chuckle.

"Not in the way you were taught. They were men and women like me and you. They were tasked with protecting the planet with undying loyalty and dedication. Several of them were members of the original High Council of Aratta. Under the Earth Mother's guidance, they traveled to the mountains of what is now known as Tibet, where they were charged with hiding and protecting an artifact. No one knows exactly what this artifact looks like, but we do know that it prevents all access to the Tethys Ocean."

"Why is it so important to keep this underground ocean from being discovered?" asked Henry.

"Think of all the animals that have become extinct throughout time." Coralis paused as he surveyed his charges.

Brianna spoke first. "Dinosaurs."

"The dodo," Katelyn chimed in.

"The giant sloth from the Ice Age," Luis added.

"Megalodon," said Bryndis.

"The Strix?" Serena shrugged, not entirely certain of what Coralis was after.

"Dragons?" Henry guessed.

"All correct," Coralis affirmed. "All of these and many, many more. All of them began as microbes and developed over millions of years. Now imagine a life source that contains billions of microbes that never had the chance to develop—prehistoric DNA, like lost blueprints to a thousand forgotten beasts. How much havoc could they wreak on the face of the planet?"

"But those blueprints might be for nothing more than kittens," said Henry. "How do you know they'd make more dinosaurs or dragons?"

"*We,*" Coralis said emphatically, "don't know. But the Earth Mother saw the need to protect us from the Tethys and what it contains. And I for one am not going to argue with her." He waved his hand once more, and the globe spun faster and faster until it was nothing but a blur. As it slowed down, it revealed a magnificent temple.

"I've been there." Serena's eyes were wide as saucers, filled with awe.

Coralis nodded. "This was your vision. The Temple of Time. The monks you saw are part of an elite force that has protected the artifact from ever being discovered. Not far from the temple is a cave that houses the artifact."

Serena frowned as she recalled a name implanted deep in her memory. "The Pangaea Particle."

"Hmmm," Coralis mumbled, rubbing his chin. "If the Earth Mother gave you that bit of knowledge, this is very serious indeed. The name of the artifact is as closely guarded as the location."

"But what does it do?" Luis asked at the same time as Bryndis, who then growled at him. He raised his hands defensively. "At least we're on the same page."

Coralis circled the table, never taking his eye off the temple. "One theory is that it is a device that, if exposed to the right conditions, could level an entire mountain range."

"That's one powerful device," Molly remarked.

"Yes, it is. But another more logical theory is that it is a source of power that keeps the creatures of the Tethys from emerging into our world. Less of a weapon, more of a shield." Coralis pursed his lips in a thin line of consternation. "The first theory was that of the High Council. The second was from . . ."

"Malachai." Henry knew beyond a shadow of a doubt that this was the case. "And now he has it."

"I think not." Coralis clapped his hands, startling them. "Malachai thinks he cannot be defeated. That is the hubris that almost led to his demise many years ago. I am certain he sent the Strix, but that was simply a test of our mettle. He wants to see what tricks I have up my sleeve. The Strix did not come from Tethys. They are a dormant species, and any Wand Master of his talent could resurrect them." He smiled broadly. "What he doesn't know is that Serena has given us the insight into what he is after. And we have *many* tricks up our sleeves."

Coralis motioned for them to follow him to a wall filled with ancient leather-bound volumes. He selected four of them, handing one each to Katelyn, Serena, Bryndis, and Luis. "Henry, why don't you explain," he said with a sly grin.

If this was a test, Henry did not want to fail. He took the book from Serena, whose smile gave him some measure of confidence. A pinwheel of symbols radiated out from the center. If he tried to focus on them, they shifted as if they did not want to be read. "These are the books from my father's study." His voice was a combination of wonder and joy. "The ones Mom took with her to Arizona."

"To prevent Malachai from getting them," Brianna added.

Henry stared at the cover again. Only one symbol remained stationary. "This is the symbol for air," he nearly shouted, then looked at the others. "Luis has earth, Bryndis has water, and Katelyn has fire. The four elements!"

"Our secret weapon." Coralis clapped Henry firmly on the back. "These books contain all the essential knowledge of the elements. They are the most difficult books you will ever read, but once you comprehend the concepts, they will be yours to command at will. Malachai knows that in the right hands, these books can offer immeasurable power. And yours, my young apprentices, are the right hands."

"But it's nothing but gibberish," Bryndis complained as she opened her book and flipped through page after page of a long-lost language.

"Not when you use this." Henry took his ulexite from his

pocket and ran it over a word. Bryndis gasped when she saw the translation appear on the upper face of the stone.

"Now comes the hard part," Coralis said grimly. "You must each study these books as if your lives depended on it."

Coralis dismissed most of the group. All that remained were Henry and Brianna. Their postures were a dead giveaway for how they felt—dejected, isolated, forgotten. Henry was so lost in his despair that he failed to notice Coralis standing over him. He finally looked up into the face of the Wand Master. "Does this mean I'm not needed?" His voice was barely audible.

"We," Brianna corrected.

"Oh, sorry." Henry mumbled an apology to his sister and held her hand.

"I am disappointed," said Coralis. "But only because you have drawn the wrong conclusion."

Henry was puzzled. "But the others . . . are different. They know how to use weapons. And now you're telling us they have a special bond with the elements. Where does that leave us?"

"Wait!" Brianna snapped. "Are there other elements we don't know about?"

Coralis suddenly burst out with laughter.

"I don't see what's so funny," Henry said angrily.

"You would if you were in my shoes," the old man commented. "You don't need the books, Henry. The power is within you. It always has been. Some are meant to master only one element. But others, on rare occasions, can master all of them."

Henry thought back to the intense light he could summon, the moonbeams he had inadvertently trapped, the surge of power to release the uranium atoms. He'd never understood why he could do the things he did. They just seemed to come naturally.

"Yes." Coralis spoke silently into his mind. *"You have them all. Now you must use them wisely."*

Henry's smile spread wider than he'd thought possible.

"Wait . . . what?" Brianna looked from one to the other. "Are you guys doing that telepathy thing again?" She squinted in concentration. "Oh great, something is blocking me from getting inside Henry's head. What did I miss?"

Henry laughed along with Coralis, but suddenly stopped. "What about Brianna?"

"As we've already determined, she has her own talent as an Enabler, which will be very valuable to us." Coralis took their hands in his. "We have a lot of work to do in the next week. When we are done, we will go after your father. He is as important to our success as the two of you. For he was the one temporarily bonded to Malachai—which means he had access to Malachai's memories. If we are to know the full extent of Malachai's plan, we must find him and go to him. And I can promise you this." Coralis burned with intensity.

"It will not be easy."

PART TWO

An old man sat on one of the balconies of his palatial home, eyes closed, his breathing shallow and slumberlike. Below him, a white-haired woman stumbled, struggling to push her small, wooden-wheeled cart of groceries along the cobblestone street. She had taken this same route for many years . . . but that was before the old man had taken her eyes.

She paused, her hollow eye sockets gazing in the direction of the balcony. "You can continue to torture me," she said, "but I will never submit to your will." She straightened to her full height and thrust her chin forward in defiance.

The man stood, his long black cloak fanning out to give his slender frame a deceptively large appearance. He bent over the elaborate millwork of the wooden railing. "You underestimate me. I will eventually break you." His voice possessed the clear, crisp quality of a much younger man. "But in the meantime, I want you to see the horrors that are to come. And so . . . your eyes will be temporarily returned."

Her confidence faltered. "Temporarily? But you said you only needed to borrow them."

"Indeed, I did. And I will need to borrow them again. And again. But you should know, it is for a very good cause."

"And what of the others?" she asked weakly, concerned about her friends whose eyes had also been taken.

"Alas, they are not so fortunate." He smiled at the thought of delivering the bad news to them.

Far in the distance, a shriek echoed off the mountains surrounding the village. It was a village that was lost to the civilized world, trapped in a medieval time warp by a powerful spell, created by and for the old man—Malachai.

He was absolute master of this realm, but he wasn't cruel. Over time he had given his people running water and an adequate heating system to get them through the cold winters. He had even given them a sewer system, and toilets—all located in one small building in the center of the village.

After all, he saw no need to spoil them.

The people numbered one hundred. No children. When the population dropped by a few, he opened a small door in the dome that kept the village hidden from prying eyes and enticed wayward hikers. Once the dome was resealed, they could never return to the outside world. Naturally, they would put up a fight. But he had ways to break them. And he usually had decades to come up with interesting, new ways to do so. The old woman was a prime example. For forty years she had been resisting him. Taking her sight might have been the final straw. Secretly, he hoped not. The others had given in much too easily.

Malachai had grown quite content with his life. He could leave the village for short periods of time—just long enough to stir up trouble and check on his Scorax brethren. It was during one of his more recent sojourns that he'd run across Henry Leach Sr. It had been several centuries since Malachai had encountered someone with a thirst for power that matched Malachai's own youthful ambitions. It took little effort to befriend the elder Henry Leach and gain his trust.

But Leach hadn't any idea he was dealing with the great Wand Master Malachai. The world thought he was long dead, and that was just the way he liked it. Conducting business from the shadows was so much more rewarding. And getting valuable information from Leach was easy. Each time they met, Malachai would present him with some rare item from his own well-stocked Kunstkammer. In this way, Malachai kept Leach on the hook . . . and through him discovered what his own son, Dai She, was up to.

He hadn't heard anything about the little toad in such a long time that he had begun to think he'd crawled into a hole and died. That outcome would have made him perfectly happy. Dai She was an unfortunate stain on his reputation, one that he'd just as soon be rid of.

Little by little, Dai She's plan came into focus, until Malachai felt he could no longer ignore it. Bringing the world to its knees by disrupting massive tectonic plates was actually genius—but for a fatal flaw. The resulting earthquakes would have released enormous pockets of methane gas trapped below the surface, killing every life-form on the planet.

That was unacceptable.

The only way to stop his son without revealing himself had been to take possession of Leach's life-force—his aura. Once he'd accomplished that, it was a simple matter to replace Leach entirely. The Wand Master wannabe had been locked away in a wand-proof prison in this very village while Malachai went out into the real world to have some fun. And when he discovered Coralis had also been drawn out of hiding by Dai She, well, then Malachai knew it was time to stir things up.

Unfortunately, Leach—now known as Markhor—had seen too much and had to be disposed of. Also unfortunately, Malachai couldn't kill him. They had been linked for too long and now shared an unbreakable metaphysical bond. Eventually, the passage of time would erode the link. Until then, Markhor must remain under lock and key.

Malachai smiled, thinking about his clever solution to the problem of Markhor.

Another shriek, this one much closer. Malachai gave a sharp whistle. Seconds later, a flash of red streaked toward the balcony. The Strix perched lightly on the railing. Its owl-like head swiveled to look at the desperate woman in the street. She could sense her own eyes looking down upon her. A dizziness washed over her. She staggered sideways before falling heavily onto the rough-edged cobblestones.

"Please," she begged. "My eyes."

"Oh, stop your groveling, you old fool." Malachai swiped a hand over the head of the Strix as if catching a fly, then flung his hand toward the woman.

Her head snapped back as if she had been struck. Her empty eye sockets bulged once more. Her sight returned. But something was wrong. "He-help me!" She tried standing but kept losing her balance. When she looked up, Malachai could see that her eyes were deeply crossed, pupils pointing straight down at her nose.

"Oops." He laughed. "Oh well. I'll get it right next time." He extended an arm for the Strix and carried it inside, where he placed it in a dome-shaped iron cage. He released a bag of mice, marveling at the efficiency of four claws and an exceptionally sharp beak. "You have done well," he murmured. "Now I know what that old man is up to. Not that it makes a difference."

He returned to the balcony. The woman had moved on. The sun was setting over the western peaks, casting a reddish glow. He took a deep breath, enjoying the serenity of the moment and looking forward to the excitement that was to come . . . until an all-too-familiar smell assaulted his nostrils.

"May I get you anything, master?" A man of medium build with a rodentlike snout entered the room. Once he'd been a formidable athlete; now he was just another experiment gone awry.

"Puteo, what have I told you about interrupting me?" Malachai scowled as he wrinkled his nose in disgust. "And when was the last time you bathed?"

"I am only to speak when spoken to, and three hours ago." Puteo tried slinking back into the shadows.

Any other time, Malachai would have enjoyed a good round of torture with his favorite slave. But the old woman had satisfied his sadistic craving for the time being. He would save Puteo for another day. "You may go now."

"Oh, thank you, master." Puteo groveled to make it seem as if he was happy to be spared the wrath of the Wand Master. In truth, he actually looked forward to the valuable lessons he learned through his punishment.

Malachai waited until Puteo had one hand on the doorknob. "On second thought, why don't you stay for a while."

Puteo gasped in horror—but inwardly, he cheered.

"Bahtzen bizzle!"

"Wow. We haven't heard that line in, oh, almost ten minutes." Henry nudged Katelyn in the ribs as he chuckled. They had paired off to practice some rudimentary wand skills and were taking a break in the kitchen when they heard the outburst.

"I wish Luis would at least pretend he's paying attention." Katelyn hummed happily as she smeared a hunk of Gretchen-made peanut butter on a slice of fresh-from-the-oven bread.

"I think he has WDD—wand deficit disorder. Ouch!" Henry's hand had slipped while he was slicing more bread. Blood quickly pooled on the tip of his thumb, spreading as the full extent of the gash opened up. "Whoa." He thumped into a chair before the sight of his own blood made him faint.

"Let me try something," Katelyn said eagerly. She held her wand at arm's length, whispered in an unfamiliar language, and watched proudly as the wand's tip began to glow.

Henry gulped. "What . . . what are you doing?"

"Just a wee bit of healing I picked up from my lessons. Oops! I almost forgot." She raced to the pantry and emerged with camphor leaves. "Now wipe off the blood and wrap your thumb with these."

"Why don't we just get a Band-Aid? It's not deep."

"Don't be such a scaredy-cat, Henry. I'm just going to cauterize the wound."

He knew that word. "You mean burn. You're going to burn me over a little scratch?" Panic began to seep in.

"It's not so little. You nearly fainted. And besides, it won't hurt a bit. That's what the leaves are for. They cool the skin as I apply the heat."

"Have you tried this before?" Henry nervously rubbed his other hand through his hair. His former buzz cut had long since grown out. His hair now stood on end, a rumpled mess.

"Just hold still and do as I say," Katelyn said sternly.

Henry did his best to keep from fidgeting as her wand glowed from red to white.

"Hmmm . . . too much." She turned the intensity back to red and touched the wand to the leaves above the wound.

First Henry's thumb, then his entire hand tingled with tiny pinpricks of pain.

Katelyn pulled back. "How does it feel?"

"Like my hand fell asleep. It's in the pins-and-needles stage of waking up." He shook his hand and the leaves, now brittle, fell away. "It's gone! The cut's gone!"

As Henry laughed and Katelyn clapped, reveling in their small victory, a shadowed figure retreated from the doorway. Serena hadn't meant to spy. She had been looking for Gretchen when she heard Henry's voice. She was about to join him, but when she heard Katelyn she stopped short. It wasn't the first time she'd caught the two of them together.

Jealousy was new to Serena. She tried to convince herself that Henry was simply interacting with another apprentice, but she'd seen the way he looked at the Irish girl. Much different from the way he acted toward Bryndis.

"Have you no ability to concentrate?" Coralis erupted again.

Poor Luis, Serena mused. She wanted him to succeed. He could be difficult around the others, but he was always friendly with her—sometimes almost flirty. At first it had been cute watching Henry's jealous reactions to that. But she also found that she rather enjoyed the attention from Luis. She wondered if there was more to it than simply trying to get on Henry's nerves.

She rounded a corner and nearly tripped on a vine that thrashed vigorously on the floor.

"I swear, I'm not doing anything!" Luis yelled back.

Serena sidestepped the vine, backtracking to approach them from the door on the opposite side of the room, when the slightest movement caught her eye. She pressed her lips tightly and frowned. There was only one person capable of controlling vines like that. Gliding down the hall without making a sound, she peeked around a corner and confirmed her suspicions.

Bryndis had her eyes closed in concentration. She never saw Serena coming, and when she finally opened her eyes, her mischievous smile evaporated under the steaming gaze of the angry apprentice. "Uh-oh."

"What are you doing?" Serena said loud enough for Coralis to hear. Tattling wasn't in her nature, but Luis didn't deserve this.

"Who's there?" Coralis shouted. "This is not the time for an interruption."

Bryndis slunk into the room, shoulders slumped. She could feel the heat of anger rolling off Serena behind her.

"What's this?" Coralis's eyebrows arched quizzically.

"Aha! Look there! I did it!" Luis announced in triumph as the vines retreated at his wand command.

Coralis nodded knowingly. "Yes, you did. Didn't he, young lady?"

"He is getting better." Bryndis spoke so softly she could barely be heard.

"Perhaps he is getting so much better that others might be jealous," Coralis prodded.

"What?" Her head snapped up. "No! Never!"

"Then there must be another explanation," Serena said.

"Wait a minute." Luis was finally catching on. "You were doing that? What is it with you and vines and tree roots?"

"I believe, Bryndis, you owe someone an apology." Coralis rose to his full height, hands locked behind his back.

Bryndis bowed her head for a few seconds and was about to do as Coralis asked when she looked up at the smirk on Luis's face. "No," she said defiantly. "I will not apologize to *him*." She spat the final word with hateful venom.

"I don't get you," Luis said. "What did I ever do to you? You've been after me since the day you arrived."

Bryndis's stare shifted toward a wall. The blaze in her eyes slowly diminished, her hardened features softening. "It's not you." She shook her head, clearing her thoughts. "It was someone like you. Someone from my village."

"Like a boyfriend?" Luis asked clumsily. "Did he break up with you?"

"Don't be an idiot!" she yelled. "I would never date a boy like you. But he hurt me in another way." She stopped, struggling for the right words. She looked to Coralis and Serena for some kind of support, but they had silently exited the room. For some reason, this relaxed her.

Finally she made a decision. "I will tell you, but if you laugh, I will strangle you with these vines. And if you ever tell the others, I will create many ways to torture and humiliate you."

"Jeez." Luis gulped. "Don't worry. I can keep a secret."

"Fine." Her face twitched with conflicting emotions. "There is a competition in my country. A singing competition."

Luis started to ask a question. She held up a hand. "Please, just let me talk. It is not singing as you know it. It is something the Inuit people—my people—have done as far back as anyone can remember. It is called throat singing."

She stopped abruptly and closed her eyes. Luis moved uncomfortably, until he heard a sound. It began as a hum, then deepened into a cross between a hum and a growl. Bryndis kept her eyes closed in concentration. The hum increased in intensity and rapidly evolved into a series of animal-like grunts and growls. At first, it sounded like noises animals would make to call one another—a secret language only they would understand. But there was something much more precise to it.

Her controlled breathing allowed her to make sounds Luis knew he could never hope to imitate, and soon he was mesmerized by the beauty of it—and in awe of the amount of practice it must have taken to master it.

The sounds rose to a feverish pitch. Small beads of sweat broke out on her forehead. The song reached a peak and she began to unwind it, bringing it back to the hum she had started with.

"That was amazing."

Bryndis gave Luis a long, hard look, ready to strike in anger, but she saw the sincerity in his eyes. "Thank you."

"I'm guessing the other boy didn't share my opinion."

"No. He did not." Her forehead pinched tightly at the memory. "Throat singing is not easy to master, especially for someone like me who does not have the natural talent. I practiced many long hours, always in private. I was determined to win the competition. Then one day I was careless, and he caught me. And mocked me," she said bitterly.

"I had thought this boy was cute, but he was suddenly very ugly. He would tease me at every opportunity, making disgusting animal noises behind my back, yet always within range of my ears. He urged his friends to join him. It was a terrible time. I stopped singing and gave up my dream."

"But that's horrible!"

"Yes," she said gravely. "But it gets worse. You see, my talent went beyond singing. I can mimic animal sounds. I can call to them as if I were one of their own. Sometimes, when meat was scarce, I would sing to the polar bears, even an occasional walrus. Lure them in for the kill."

"You cheated?"

She smiled mischievously. "Only when I had to."

He smiled back. "That doesn't sound so bad."

"That's because I did it for the right reasons. But then one day, I saw him alone on a kayak in the bay. The water was calm. I was not." She grimaced. "I called to the whales."

"You don't have to do this." Luis reached for her arm but she pulled away.

"I know, but if I don't finish now . . . never mind. I thank you for your concern. I had the whales do my dirty work for me. It was a time of broken ice. As the Earth warms more rapidly, the broken ice appears more often. Small icebergs are a daily hazard. I had the whales push the ice into the bay toward that horrible boy. Soon, the kayak was surrounded by ice. I saw the panic in his movements, nearly capsizing him, and yet I wasn't satisfied.

"I wanted to crush him like he crushed my dreams. The whales understood. They moved the ice closer and closer." Bryndis stopped as tears welled in her eyes.

"Did you . . ." Luis could not bring himself to finish.

"Kill him? No. Fortunately, or unfortunately, my father was nearby and heard the boy screaming for help. He saw what I was doing and pushed me roughly to the ground. The call was broken, the whales stopped, and the ice retreated. Suddenly, I was a danger to my village—and to myself. They sent me here."

Luis stepped back. Slowly a grin appeared. "So what you're saying is, we have something in common."

A path opened to their left. "Amazing!" Luis exclaimed in awe.

Henry and Serena smiled at each other knowingly. Rather than resume their studies in the Kunstkammer, Molly had decided to take them on a field trip into the forest. It was the first time Katelyn, Luis, and Bryndis had ventured out from the security of the castle walls. They walked in single file—Molly in the lead, Henry and Serena in the rear—as the forest directed them.

"How do we know we are not being led into a trap?" Bryndis asked warily.

In response, a long branch from a shrub whipped out, snakelike, and snapped her across the bottom.

"I'd say that's your answer," Brianna laughed.

Katelyn giggled and Bryndis glared at her. Luis gave Bryndis a pat on the back, which had an immediate calming effect on her.

Henry felt Serena stiffen and watched her eyes narrow as if she didn't like what she was seeing. He hadn't felt her usual warmth toward him recently and now wondered if he might be losing her affection because of Luis.

He reached for her hand just as Brianna pointed to a nearby tree and yelled, "Beech!"

"Spruce!" Katelyn countered.

"Honeysuckle!" Serena shouted, and plucked a small white flower from its shrub as she joined in.

They continued along the path for several kilometers, playing their impromptu game of botanical I Spy until, abruptly, the path ended. "Now what?" Luis asked.

The forest answered again, this time in dramatic fashion. The undergrowth of rhododendron and thorny raspberry slowly pulled back to reveal an open field that was filled with a dazzling display of wildflowers, much more concentrated than the one Henry and Serena had encountered weeks before. Majestic mountain peaks loomed far in the distance.

"Incredible," Molly exclaimed. "Every time I think I've seen it all, I realize I haven't even come close."

The path behind them closed, urging them forward. Luis grabbed Bryndis by the hand. "Come on!" he shouted as he sprinted into the field, pulling her in tow. The others looked at one another for only a second before sprinting after them. They laughed and whooped, jumping with infectious happiness. Henry caught up to Luis and slapped him on the arm—hard. "Tag, you're it!"

Luis brushed off Henry's slap with a condescending sneer, then raced after Serena.

Molly watched them play from a distance, smiling with delight, knowing this was just the release they needed.

But then the breeze shifted. The twinkle of mirth in her eyes gave way to concern. The breeze brought with it a scent. The scent of trouble. The scent of death.

"Stop!" The force of her voice carried across the field and echoed off the mountains.

The apprentices stopped in their tracks. One by one they noticed the smell and rapidly returned to Molly's side. "I know that smell." Bryndis lifted her head, sniffing the breeze. "This way."

They all looked to Molly, who nodded for them to follow. The breeze shifted several times but could not fool Bryndis. She had too much experience with tracking. A lone cloud passed in front of the sun as the breeze stopped. The scent of death drew closer with each step until it overpowered everything else. Bryndis stopped and pointed toward a large red mound a short distance away.

"Wait here," said Molly. She crept uncertainly toward the mound, dread in every footstep. She held her arm across her face, the sleeve of her shirt providing a filter that was mostly useless against the stench.

The mangled carcass was that of a bear—and not just any bear. A brown bear with an unusual patch of white fur between the ears. A bear that was often seen raiding Gretchen's garden—Sophia.

"Is that a bear?" Luis asked, then gagged. The others surrounded him with equally mortified faces.

Molly nodded solemnly. "A friend of the family, so to speak. A gentle old bear with an insatiable appetite for Gretchen's crops."

"Not Sophia!" Serena cried.

Then something caught Molly's eye and she gasped aloud. The others followed her line of sight.

"Is that a Strix?" asked Henry.

"Or what's left of one," Luis said, clamping his nose shut.

Henry's curiosity got the best of him. He cautiously side-stepped the bear to examine the Strix. Large claws had ripped open the underside of the bird, revealing something other than blood and guts. He poked at several good-sized stones— black with a sheen like wet tar—with the toe of his shoe. He looked closer and reached for one.

"No!" Molly hissed. "Don't touch them. We'll need to get Coralis to properly dispose of them."

"It's not coal or obsidian," Henry remarked. "It's almost like . . . oh!" Suddenly he recalled a passage from his earliest translations of the books from his attic. "Phenakite crystals, completely drained of their life-force."

"Yes, and deadly to the touch. Did you see the scorch marks on Sophia's claw? The poor beast was probably winning the battle when she unknowingly ripped the Strix open. She probably died on contact," Molly explained before bowing her head.

"I don't understand," said Katelyn. "If the bear and Strix died at the same time, what did the rest of this? They look . . . mangled."

"True," Bryndis grunted. "This is not the work of simple scavengers. This killing has another purpose."

"A warning." Molly squinted as her eyes settled on a single black feather. She quickly withdrew a sharp switchblade from her pocket and sliced it in half. The two halves flopped and squealed like a mouse with its tail caught in a trap. "Valraven!" Panicked, she scanned the skies. "Quickly, back to the castle."

No one needed a second warning as they ran from the field.

"The time has come." Coralis had gathered them in the Cryptoporticus. Hours had passed since the apprentices had arrived back at the castle, out of breath and visibly shaken. They had never seen Coralis move so fast once Molly briefed him. When he finally returned to the castle, he appeared distraught, and in his eyes was a look of fierce determination. "Molly is correct. Malachai has unleashed another horror. Bryndis, you are probably the only one with knowledge of this bird."

"Nay," said Katelyn. "I've heard the legend as well."

Bryndis was not about to lose the spotlight. "The Valraven is a myth. Or at least it was. It is a raven with supernatural power that eats the dead on a battlefield. It consumes the power and knowledge of those it has eaten and can change its shape, though if I'm not mistaken, not completely. According to the legend, it's usually seen as half wolf, half raven." She frowned. "Does this mean there's a half bear roaming the woods?"

Brianna had been trying her best to keep herself in check. In her time at the castle, she had grown fond of the bear. The vision of that playful creature now turned into some kind of monster was too much. She covered her mouth with her hands and could no longer prevent the tears from coming. Henry wrapped an arm around his sister. She turned into his shoulder and wept openly, as much for Gretchen as for the bear.

Coralis was visibly uncomfortable with Brianna's reaction. He did not elaborate on what he had to do to destroy the Valraven beast the bear had become. A most unpleasant task.

"As apprentices, your duty to protect the Earth is as strong as mine. However . . ." He nodded gravely. "You are young and inexperienced. What we must do is extremely danger-ous, and I am not certain you are up to the task." Henry started to object, but Coralis stopped him. "I believe Malachai is testing your mettle. He is trying to frighten you—and in doing so, to weaken *me*. To be honest, I am not certain I would win a head-to-head battle with him. As much as I need you, I cannot force you to risk your lives."

"Sir," Serena interrupted, "with all due respect—"

Coralis raised a hand. "You cannot speak for the group," he said sternly. "And I cannot protect all of you in the heat of battle. There is no pleasant way to put this—if you join me, I cannot guarantee your safe return." Frustration etched his features. He had seen this scenario unfold in the past. It never ended happily ever after.

Bryndis stepped forward, looking as forceful as she had on the day of her arrival. "Count me in." Then she smiled wryly.

"I am scared, but excited. And I am honored to serve the Guild."

"Aye," said Katelyn. "Count me in as well."

One by one they voiced their consent, locking their hands in unity. Coralis stared into the eyes of each of them, searching for a thread of doubt, but seeing nothing except unwavering commitment.

"Very well," he said solemnly. "May the spirits of the High Council be with us."

"A gathering of Wandbearers who have a specific mission is called a conclave." Coralis opened a cabinet drawer next to the wall. "Please, each of you take one of these wands."

Serena was closest. "Does it matter which one?" At first glance they seemed identical, but upon closer inspection she noticed slight differences in the details. Each wand had the grain of wood, yet the consistency of stone. The pattern in the grain varied, as did the pattern of colors, but they were all the orange-red sandstone color she was familiar with from her home valley. "This is petrified wood." She lifted one, feeling the weight in her palm.

"Correct," said Coralis. "Taken from your homeland in a place called the Petrified Forest."

"But that's illegal." Serena's tone scolded the Wand Master. "And there is a curse on those who take it."

"It's illegal now, but not when these were taken," Coralis countered. "Once the forest was discovered by tourists, the site was pilfered by those with no more respect than tomb robbers. But long ago, your ancestors took only what was needed. These fine specimens were selected for their value as Argus Wands. In Greek mythology, Argus was a giant with a hundred eyes. The Argus Wand has a specific purpose—to search for something. But its power is not to be taken lightly." He smiled. "As for the curse, there is no such thing. But superstition is more effective than fines to keep poachers at bay."

Each apprentice selected a piece of the prized wood. "It is wood, but not wood." Bryndis examined hers closely. "Interesting."

"And powerful," Coralis reminded her. "Its power to search can corrupt the user if he or she chooses to go after personal gain."

"Like buried treasure?" Luis asked. "Perhaps some gems to offer a loved one?" He smirked in Henry's direction.

"That is one example," Coralis agreed. "On the surface, a harmless pursuit. Yet one that can easily lead to an uncontrollable addiction to greed and power."

He directed them to equidistant points around the Sugi. "You are not fully trained. Therefore I am breaking the rules." With a twinkle in his eye, he added, "But since I made the rules, I am granting myself an exception. Place your wand on the slab like this." He placed his own wand with the tapered end pointing toward the center of the Sugi.

Coralis spoke to them as a hypnotist would—focusing their concentration, regulating their breathing, and slowing their heart rates until they beat in sync, as one. "Now press down on the end closest to you using your thumb and forefinger and concentrate on this." An image of the elder Henry Leach appeared above the table.

"Oh!" The sight of her father startled Brianna into releasing her wand, and the image abruptly disappeared.

"What happened?" Luis asked.

"That was our father," Henry said crossly.

"My fault," Coralis apologized. "I should have warned you. Let's try again, shall we? Concentrate and focus." When they were back in perfect synchronization, he gave one additional instruction. "Focus on this single word in your mind and transfer that thought into your wand . . . WHERE."

Henry stared into the eyes of his father. The image was of him as a younger man, not of the man he'd last seen over a year ago. It immediately raised so many questions. At the forefront: How did he ever get mixed up with the likes of Malachai?

"Focus, Henry." Coralis spoke to his mind. *"WHERE."*

Henry quickly pushed all other thoughts aside. More than anything, he wanted to find him. Questions needed to be answered. He bore the word forcefully into the wand. A spark of light jumped from its tip and raced to the center of the table, where it joined sparks from the others.

Gradually, the image of his father faded, replaced by that of a man painting a wall. He used short brushstrokes with his left hand, rendering his subject's beard in incredible detail. The painting took up an entire wall, almost twice as long as it was high. It was not finished, but Henry still recognized it. He had seen it numerous times in churches and knew what it was without hesitation. "*The Last Supper,*" he whispered.

In a wispy puff of smoke, the scene vanished. "No!" Brianna yelled. "Where is he? Who was that guy?" She wheeled angrily on Coralis. "How does that tell us anything? WHERE'S DAD?" The last words came out with a powerful burst of Voice that sent them all reeling from the table.

Coralis composed himself, adjusting his shirt and overcoat as he advanced on Brianna, who stood her ground defiantly. His furrowed brow relaxed. He began to chuckle, then laugh.

"It's not funny," Brianna said through clenched teeth.

"No, it's not," he said merrily. "It's perfect! You might be novices, but you are stellar novices. We not only know where . . . we know when!"

SEVENTEEN

Markhor rolled over on the damp earthen floor of his cage. A large sewer rat nibbled on his bootlace, yet he made no effort to stop it. Despair born of hopelessness had seeped so deep into his bones that his marrow began to fester with rot. He opened his eyes, staring into the darkness, wondering for the thousandth time how he could have let it happen. How he could have been so wrong. How he did not see the signs or detect the evil beneath the facade of the man he now knew was Malachai.

But he did know.

Yet he ignored it in his insatiable quest for power and knowledge. The double-edged sword of villainy.

Markhor. His name—no longer Henry Leach the Seventh. He detested it but was stuck with it, for once a Wand Master chose a name it was bound to the person like an eighth layer of skin. The fact that he did not choose the name was immaterial. It was chosen for him while Malachai was bound to him through his aura, and that was enough.

Markhor—named after a goat that was known as a snake killer. It was Malachai's idea of a joke. His son was Dai She, the "evil snake." Markhor, the snake killer. Malachai, vile and ruthless enough to cause his own son's destruction.

Markhor groaned as an image of his own son, Henry, flashed in his mind. He angrily kicked at the rat, which sailed across the room and hit the ragged stone wall with a sickening crunch. It twitched two, three times before succumbing to the throes of death, joining the pile of others that had met a similar fate. *At least you are out of your misery,* he thought.

He rolled again, trying to find a semi-comfortable position before giving up. He pushed himself into a sitting position and leaned against the wall. Just this simple exertion left him winded. He attempted to take a deep breath. Too much at once. The cough could not be suppressed as it bubbled to the surface. A hacking, wet cough—a sign of something seriously wrong in his lungs—that he was powerless to do anything about.

Gradually he managed to calm his breathing. Dirt-encrusted nails that were chipped and broken raked through the dull red hair that had grown like a wild shrub and covered his face. He removed his cracked glasses and pressed his eyes closed. The image of himself as a gaunt old man bound with manacles to a dungeon wall appeared on the inside of his eyelids.

He nearly laughed, catching himself before another coughing fit could take his breath away once more. He was wasting away and he knew it. He also knew he could never die—another unfortunate side effect of the binding. As long as Malachai lived, Markhor would live.

But it didn't mean he would live in peace or comfort. Malachai would let him decay into nothing but a breathing husk of skin and bones—something he found out from the prisoners in his neighboring cells.

In the pitch blackness, he had heard the faint, rasping breaths of cellmates who could not answer his call, unable to move from the floor. Eventually, the one in the cell closest to his own had gathered enough strength to tell his own story. How Malachai had used him the way he had used Markhor. It was a story Markhor knew all too well. The man in the cell, Paulo, also heard a similar tale from the cell next to him, who heard it from the cell next to him, and so on down the line of endless cells. Each cell held one prisoner. Each prisoner wasting away.

With the last of his strength, Paulo revealed what Markhor already suspected. They had been there many, many years. "How long?" he asked.

Paulo wheezed, hoarse and dry, which could have been an attempt at laughter. "Time is irrelevant here. But the Wand Master revels in our misery. He sends us cake on the anniversary of our jailing—every hundred years."

That marked the beginning of Markhor's despair. He could never escape, and even if he did, he was certain he could never find freedom—would never get his life back. His shoulders slumped, head knocking hard against the wall behind him.

Keys rattled in the distance. It was the old woman delivering their daily portion of water and gruel. For some reason he decided to try to get her to talk. He had given up months ago, as she appeared to be deaf and mute—something Malachai probably found amusing. But there was something different this day.

He sensed a surge of power as she made her way down the row and knew instinctively this was not the same servant. Markhor grasped the bars of his cell as the shadow approached in the dark.

"Move." A woman's voice, not too old.

He took a step back, waiting as she slid the water bucket through an opening near the floor. A metal ladle clanged as she scooped the slop he was supposed to eat onto a filthy plate. He fidgeted with anxious anticipation.

"He is an animal," she sighed as she lit a lamp. The wick was so low there was barely enough light to see, yet it provided welcome warmth in the darkness.

"Who are you?" His voice cracked from not speaking for weeks.

"Wrong question," she responded, and he could tell it was taking every ounce of effort to do so.

"Do you know who I am?"

"Yes."

Energy born of hope coursed through his veins. "Is there a way out of here?"

"Yes." He waited for more, but it became clear that her ability to answer was extremely limited. Malachai had probably cast a spell of silence over the dungeon. Markhor leaned forward to see into the shadows of her hooded cloak. Her face glistened with sweat, straining against the spell.

"Hurry," she whispered.

Markhor thought quickly. "Is there a way out for me?"

"No."

He cursed softly. "Did someone send you?"

"Yes."

He racked his brain. Who would know he was here? He had seen someone through his merge with Malachai. An old man with a powerful aura in a desert. He surged forward, gripping the bars. "Was it Coralis?"

"No."

No? Who else could possibly know? Suddenly the woman jerked her head up, meeting his eyes with hers. She reached for his hand, grasping it tightly with intense urgency. Markhor nearly stumbled as images rushed from her mind to his. A sprawling city with streets paved with stone; horse-drawn chariots; Roman-era soldiers; a large fort; an impressive cathedral; a canal filled with ships laden with supplies.

He knew this city. He had been there once to meet Malachai. But the image was an ancient version of the one he knew.

Milan. Italy.

The woman groaned as sweat streamed down her face. She looked as if she was about to faint as she pushed one more image—that of a man. Painter, inventor, genius. Markhor gasped in recognition as she quickly released her hold on him. She leaned against the bars, breathing heavily. He could only imagine the strength it had to take to do what she had done. He reached toward her and lightly touched her face. "Thank you."

Without a word or another glance, she doused the lamp, gathered her pails, and left. Markhor stared at her retreating figure, remaining there long after she had gone. He now knew where he was being held and who had sent the message, though he could hardly believe either one. "Thank you," he said once more to the darkness.

Midway across his cell he jolted to a sudden stop. His back arched as pain erupted in his head and a brief but powerful vision filled his sight. He gasped . . .

"Henry!"

"Ahhh!" Henry doubled over, squeezing his head between his hands to stop the pain.

Coralis rushed to his side. "What is it? What happened?"

"I don't know." He continued to massage his temples. The blast of pain lasted only a second, but took much longer to subside and even longer to decipher. It wasn't merely a headache. The blast was accompanied by a vision—grainy, blurry, and dark. A face smeared with dirt and grime, and overgrown with hair. Beyond that, he couldn't discern any further details. The vision faded along with the pain until it was gone, leaving Henry to wonder whether he had imagined it. "I'm okay now."

He could sense Coralis probing his mind, but he knew there would be nothing to see. The vision, if that's what it was, had disappeared. Coralis stood back, as if waiting for Henry to elaborate, but as far as Henry was concerned, there was nothing to share.

"Humph." Coralis obviously wasn't completely satisfied, but there was nothing he could do if Henry wasn't going to cooperate. He turned his attention back to the table. On command the dragon raised it and retrieved a scroll for Coralis. "*Castello Sforzesco*." A holographic image of a fortresslike castle materialized above the table. Coralis murmured words from an extinct language and the image began to turn, offering them a video-quality projection of the castle's perimeter.

"This magnificent structure, called 'Sforza Castle' in English, still stands in Milan, Italy. But what remains today is a tourist destination that houses several museums. What you see here is what the castle looked like in the year 1497."

As the image turned, Henry leaned forward. He had always had a fascination with medieval times. Not so much the knights in armor, but the castles and dungeons. This was exactly how he envisioned one should look like.

One side was anchored in either corner by large round towers—*anchored* being the appropriate term, since the entire structure was surrounded by a wide moat. The castle was built from orange-red brick, and the moat's murky green palette concealed any number of secrets, from sea life to the bones of fallen invaders. The rectangular shape of the main structure was connected to the main interior by a series of drawbridges.

He leaned in even closer to get a better view of the massive chain links used to raise the bridges and wondered at what it took to build such engineering marvels using only the ancient technology and tools they had at their disposal. One draw-bridge was connected to a fortification like a mini-castle that was erected in the middle of the moat—which, in turn, was connected to the main body of the castle by a more permanent bridge.

The image turned, revealing a long wall. Halfway down was another small round tower, and at the end of the wall was another tower, the smallest of the three but still impressive. When the image flipped on its side, Henry saw that the overall design was nearly symmetrical and was amazed to discover that there was an inner moat. This was certainly a structure built to withstand an enemy attack, and, in fact, looked to be impenetrable.

Suddenly a cannon fired directly at Henry. He jumped backward and fell flat on his rump, eliciting a chorus of laughter from the other apprentices. He had been so engrossed that he hadn't even realized he had climbed onto the edge of the table. The dragon stood at the edge, sternly waggling a clawed digit at him as a warning. "Mind your distance, Henry," Coralis said through a vainly disguised smile of his own.

"Sorry." He scrambled to his feet, apologizing to the dragon. "It's just that it's so . . . cool!"

"I doubt that Francesco Sforza would have used the word *cool* . . . but I happen to agree. What's the saying? They don't make them like they used to?" Coralis began a tutorial of the castle using words like *barbican*—the structure connected to, and used to defend, the outer drawbridges; *battlements*, from which men would shoot arrows; *turrets*, the towers used as lookouts; and *inner ward*, which was more or less a courtyard similar to the one at Castle Coralis.

Each term sparked a memory from books Henry had checked out from the library, and he found he was able to retain most of it fairly easily. Across the table from him, Bryndis yawned. He checked the others, similarly bored, eyes glazed over.

Brianna had edged up beside him. "Um . . . this is all fascinating stuff." She nudged Henry. "But what does it have to do with our father?"

Coralis frowned at their lack of interest but sent a thought to Henry that they would continue later in private. He placed a piece of faceted amber on the Sugi and touched it with his wand. The image zoomed in quickly. It raced past many people performing their daily tasks, unaware they were being observed. Down it went, swooping through the inner ward and pausing at a group of men hard at work building a . . .

"Is that a catapult?" Henry asked much louder than he'd intended. A tall man in a dark robe who was supervising the construction turned slowly to face them, as if he knew they were watching.

"Meet Leonardo da Vinci," Coralis announced. "This is how he looked in the year 1497."

Henry was the first to recognize him. "That's the man who was painting *The Last Supper*."

"The Argus Wand will seldom give direct answers, but it does provide clues. It is up to the user to decipher them," Coralis said giddily. "A student of history would be able to identify exactly where and when Leonardo painted that timeless piece of art. To be precise, the painting itself is on a wall

. in the Convent of Santa Maria delle Grazie, which is a short distance from Sforza Castle. But the castle is the place where prisoners were held."

"And you figured all this out just from seeing some guy in a goofy hat with a paintbrush?" Luis asked. "Seems like a pretty big leap to me."

The rest of the apprentices leaned forward, mouths agape. Leonardo was taller than most of the men working for him. But it wasn't just his height. There was an air of superiority about him that was unmistakable. A middle-aged man, he wore a simple cap, and his face was framed by a short beard. By far his most remarkable feature was his eyes. They sparkled with light, giving a glimpse of the wisdom and knowledge that was unparalleled in his time.

As if on cue, he dipped his head in a bow toward the apprentices, then looked directly at Coralis, indicating with a nod of his head a doorway to his right. Just before the scene shifted, Leonardo's eyes centered on Henry and Brianna and his mouth twitched with a thin-lipped smile.

"It's as if he sees us," Brianna whispered.

"That's because he can." It was moments like these that Coralis found most rewarding . . . and amusing. There was so much his apprentices had yet to learn and understand. He only wished he had more time to teach them.

"Wait . . . what?" Luis asked skeptically. "It's 1497 and he can see us? I mean, no offense, but that's impossible."

"As much as scholars know about the genius of Leonardo, there is so much more they will never know about his mystical connections to the unseen world." Coralis tapped the amber once more and the vision zoomed through the doorway. At first it was so dark Henry thought the camera (or whatever was giving them the image) had stopped moving. But slowly, a dim light emerged. A torch mounted to a wall, the flame so dim that it appeared to be in a constant struggle with the darkness it was trying to penetrate.

The vision advanced forward at a more measured pace, allowing for the lack of proper lighting. Along one wall, a row of bars separated jail cells from a narrow gravel walkway. Each cell was the size of a small bedroom and contained a solitary, rickety wooden bed frame. As the view progressed down the row, lumps became more pronounced on the beds. The walkway as well as the number of cells appeared to be endless.

The vision finally stopped at a cell that housed the only moving occupant. The figure, a man, sat on the edge of a filthy straw mattress, hunched over with his head in his hands—his posture indicating he had succumbed to the hopelessness his life had become. His head moved, cautiously, as if he could sense he was being watched.

This time Henry recognized him from the mind-image that had caused him so much pain. "Dad," he whispered, and reached for him. Immediately, the vision vanished.

"Wait!" Brianna shouted. "That was Dad? Henry, what did you do?"

"Nothing! I swear!" He turned pleadingly to Coralis for help.

"You did nothing wrong," he said. "The vision had run its course. It was designed to show us only what we needed to know."

"We need to know how to rescue him!" Brianna cried.

"Be still." Coralis reached out to her with mild Voice to calm her. "We will go to him."

"A time slip?" Henry asked for the fourth time.

Coralis had dismissed the other apprentices, instructing Molly to intensify their training. Only Brianna and Henry remained behind.

"I thought you told me time travel was impossible, Henry." Brianna sat heavily and rubbed her eyes. "And besides, I'm hungry." Her stomach growled in agreement. "Gretchen told me that using Voice would trigger my appetite. I should have believed her." Her stomach rumbled what sounded like *Yesssss.*

"You need to forget what you know—or what you think you know." Coralis paced the room, trying to think of an easy way to explain. "We are operating in a realm outside the rules of physics. There are forces in the universe that cannot be explained . . . partly because the human brain is wired to accept only the things it can comprehend."

"What's the other part?" asked Henry.

"Lack of imagination." Coralis smirked. "You are correct. Time travel is impossible—bound by the laws of the known universe. Which is why our world operates outside of it."

Brianna's stomach growled louder. "For goodness' sake, girl." Coralis pulled a bright red apple from his pocket and handed it to her.

She chomped into it like it was the first meal she'd had in a week. "Tanks."

"Don't talk with your mouth full," Henry scolded.

Coralis got right back to the point. "Some of your most brilliant scientists have theorized, and correctly, I might add, that all points in time exist simultaneously. Imagine stepping into a fourth dimension and being able to see every moment of your life like still frames of a motion picture, then reentering in real time at any one of those points."

Henry smiled. "You're kidding, right?"

"I do not kid, young man." Coralis glowered. "And if you do not open your imagination, you will never be able to go with me to see your father."

Brianna stopped in midchomp and swallowed hard. "Sounds good to me. When do we start slipping?"

Coralis walked them to a large globe of the Earth. "There is a mineral that is very rare on Earth. It is called tranquillityite. A very small sample was recently discovered in Australia, but until then, the only other place it was found was on the moon."

"No more moon stuff," Brianna groaned.

"Tranquillityite was named after the Sea of Tranquility, where it was found on the moon's surface. But long before that, it was known among Wand Masters as Umquam Crustallos— the time crystal." Coralis placed both hands on the globe and gave it a sharp, firm twist. A section of the top half came off. Etched into the flat surface of its interior was the figure of a man with four arms and four legs.

"I've seen that image somewhere . . . ," Henry started, then slapped his forehead. "In the *Guidebook!*"

"Correct." Coralis nodded. "It is a famous drawing by Leonardo da Vinci called *The Vitruvian Man*. Most people believe it is an illustration of the relation of the human body to the architecture of a Roman named Vitruvius—when in fact, it is a treasure map!" he exclaimed.

Brianna squinted. "Um . . . you kinda lost me at Leonardo."

Henry stared thoughtfully at the etching. "I think I get it. Each arm and leg is pointing to a location on the globe." He ran a finger along the surface, hovering over Romania. "Is this where we are?"

"Good lad!" Coralis congratulated him with a rousing clap of his hands.

"You're such a dork." Brianna elbowed him in the ribs.

Coralis ignored her, his excitement building. "And not only the arms and legs, but the head as well." He ran a finger from the center of the head along an imaginary line to the surface of the globe. "Leonardo had extraordinary talent that spawned many disciplines, and while he was not a member of our Guild, he worked with us to help our cause. This illustration is as remarkable for its face value as it is for its hidden meaning. Each of these points marks the location of a significant tranquillityite deposit."

"But what makes that so special?" Henry asked. He had read his share of books about minerals and studied them at the castle, but this was the first he had heard of tranquil-lityite.

"Fortunately, only the Guild is aware of its finest property," Coralis explained. "Geologists do not have enough material to experiment with. They suspect it can be used to estimate the age of very old rocks. Which is true. But in the case of a sizable deposit, that property expands exponentially, and essentially forms gates that allow passage into the fourth dimension. This is what we call the time slip. Leonardo was the first to discover it . . . completely by accident, I might add. At one point he even got lost in time for several years, but eventually he worked his way back to his original time period."

"I, uh . . ." Henry fidgeted with his hands, trying to comprehend the impossibility that Coralis laid out for them. He remembered some time travel rules from watching movies and now wondered if any of them were true. "Can we go to the future?" he finally asked.

"Yes and no," Coralis said. "We can go to *a* future, but it might not be the one that actually comes to pass because of all the decisions people will have to make between now and then. The slightest deviation can trigger a snowball effect that can radically change the future."

Henry was catching on. "Is the same true for the past? If we do something one hundred years ago, will it change the present?"

"For the most part, no," Coralis answered. "The past is the past, and interaction with people there will be long forgotten over time. You could hand someone a cell phone, but what good would it do? You could tell someone a significant fact about the future, but once you have left, it too will be forgotten. We use the term 'out of sight, out of mind.' You simply cannot leave a lasting imprint on the past.

"That said, there is a limit—if we managed to detonate a nuclear bomb, for example. But this is why the secret of the time slip is so tightly guarded by the Guild."

As Henry digested this information, a thought occurred to him. "Malachai must know about time slips, too, if he sent Dad back in time. What's to stop him from messing up the past in a big way?"

"In order to understand our enemy, we must identify his motivation." Coralis picked up his Argus Wand from the table and twirled it between his fingers. "Malachai desires power and control. He would have no control over the past and therefore has little reason to meddle with it. However, he can influence events in the present that will give him control in the future. And this is the reason we must see your father—to find out what Malachai intends to do with the Temple of Time and stop him from succeeding."

Brianna placed her arm around Henry's shoulder. "Enough blah, blah, blah," she said brightly. "Let's do this!" Her stomach let loose a thunderous growl. "After we grab some chow."

CHAPTER
NINETEEN

"Enough already!" Coralis yelled in frustration at the castle wall, which immediately created an opening for them to leave the castle's confines. It had given them fits, almost as if it knew what they were up to and wanted to prevent it.

Forest wasn't much more cooperative than the castle until a similar outburst set them on a clear path in a direction they had never taken before. Henry and Brianna followed Coralis in silence. Henry thought about what Coralis had told them, and he assumed his sister was doing the same. Using the time slip was not as easy as either of them had originally imagined. It was an "unnatural science," as Coralis had phrased it, that had inherent risks—the biggest of which was getting caught in a time loop.

The way Coralis explained it, he would assume the lead, tuning his voice to a specific pitch that would set the tranquillityite crystals vibrating. That would typically be enough to allow the Wand Master to pass through. But with three of them, Brianna was going to have to match his pitch while using her Nailinator Wand. Even that was going to be tricky, as too much power could scramble the crystals at the molecular level and ruin the gate.

There were nine gates, three of which were under oceans and not reachable with current technology. One of them was near Castle Coralis, and another close to Milan. "Slipping" was tricky. The location from which they exited the time slip would remain open for approximately ninety minutes. Within the ninety-minute pulse window (a term Coralis used to describe the opening), the travelers could still enter the time slip and return to their original place and time. Once it got beyond ninety minutes, "things could get a bit dicey," as Coralis put it.

Henry was very nervous about the short time window, but Coralis assured them they could get what they needed with time to spare. Yet Henry thought he detected a small twitch in the Wand Master's left eye as he said it. And there was something bothering him . . . something he couldn't put a finger on. Coralis had admitted he was taking an enormous risk by using two apprentices with very little training. If things got "dicey," they might lose their opportunity to stop Malachai. So why chance it? Henry's gut was telling him he was missing something.

They arrived at a rocky outcropping that was partially concealed in a copse of pine trees. A shadow moved and a Hutsul woman emerged. Coralis greeted her. "Good morning, Lesya."

"Good morning, old man," she replied with a wink in the children's direction. Her accent was thick but understandable—like Dracula might sound as a woman. She was as tall as Coralis, and slender. Henry thought under different circumstances she could easily be a volleyball player. But two things stuck out—she had only one arm, and that arm held an imposing rifle.

Coralis grumbled. "You know why we are here?"

"There can only be one reason. And yet . . ." Her eyes drifted toward Henry and Brianna and back to Coralis, though she didn't move her head in the slightest. "I question your wisdom."

"They are aware of the risks."

"And they accept them—all of them—willingly?"

It's as if she knows something is off, too, thought Henry.

"The stakes are high and their power is strong," he said sternly. "Do not concern yourself."

Lesya remained locked in place as if unsure she should allow Coralis to pass.

Henry wondered what power she might have that could stop him. He decided to speak on their behalf. "We are going to see our father, who is being held prisoner." And something washed over him like a twenty-meter wave—the thing Coralis had been keeping from them. He wobbled on his feet. Coralis always chose his words carefully. He was truthful enough about *seeing* their father, but he never said anything about *rescuing* him.

Suddenly Brianna was at his side. "Are you okay?"

He shook his head to clear it, and swallowed hard though his mouth was dry. He couldn't tell her—not yet. "Yeah. Yeah, I'm fine. Just a little dizzy."

Lesya bowed to him, short and tight. "Are you well enough to continue?" she asked.

Henry glanced at Coralis, whose lips were pursed in a grim scowl. His head dipped, almost imperceptibly, in response to Henry's unspoken question. Coralis had not deliberately lied, and yet Henry felt deceived. There was no choice but to move forward and accept the consequences as they unfolded. "Yes, I am well enough. We should go now."

Without another word, Lesya slipped back into the shadows and they advanced toward the rock . . . one of them with the weight of the world on his shoulders.

"Ah! Before I forget, please place these stones in your pockets." Coralis handed a small, clear rectangular rock to Henry and another to Brianna.

"It looks like ulexite, but it seems to be humming." Henry held the rock to his ear. "Are those voices I'm hearing?"

Coralis nodded. "This is a special kind of ulexite. If treated one way, it can translate the written word. But if treated another . . ."

"It translates the spoken word," Brianna finished. "Brilliant!"

"Because they don't speak English in Renaissance Italy," Henry said, marveling at the incredible rock that surpassed any piece of technology. "I'd have never thought of that." But something else occurred to him. "What about our clothes? How are we going to pass for natives in these?"

Coralis had been carrying a satchel slung over his shoulder. He removed three cloaks that glistened like sharkskin. "Never underestimate quality outerwear." Coralis winked as he held out one for each of them. The garment fit more like a poncho than a coat. He illuminated a wand and led them into the dark recesses of a cave set within the rocky outcropping.

Sketches on the interior cave walls drew Henry's attention. He paused to run his hand lightly over them. "These aren't the work of cavemen."

"Our friend Leonardo. His mind never stops," Coralis explained.

"But this looks like a flying machine," said Brianna. "How could he draw something like this if he never traveled to the future? I thought you said—"

Coralis stopped her with a raised hand. "I assure you, these illustrations are hundreds of years old. To say that Leonardo was a genius is an understatement. His ideas were centuries ahead of their time. When something popped into his head, he immediately went to work, getting his thoughts down on paper—or, as you can see, whatever surface was available to write upon."

A short while later they arrived at a side tunnel that ended abruptly after only a few meters. The walls were rounded into the shape of a chamber, but the dimensions were deceiving, as the walls wavered—not with light, but with a hazy blur, as if they were in constant motion.

"It feels . . . electric," Henry said loud enough that his voice echoed.

"A very astute analogy," Coralis replied. "A tranquillity-ite deposit as large as this emits an energy field. It's how Leonardo discovered them in the first place. So . . ." He looked at them with severity and withdrew another wand from his cloak, holding it aloft like a sacred object. Bloodred, the wand pulsed with a life-force all its own. "I need you to follow instructions to the letter."

"Do you understand?" Coralis spoke directly into their minds. *"We cannot speak normally while traveling through dimensions, but I encourage you to try."* He smiled mischievously. "Brianna, please hum at this pitch along with me."

Brianna nodded nervously. She cleared her throat, closed her eyes, and repeated the low, resonating pitch that Coralis hummed. When she opened her eyes, the cavern swirled around them at a dizzying pace.

"Excellent!" Coralis said with pride. He instructed them to hold hands. "Now take a deep breath and listen as you hum. Concentrate through your Nailinator Wand. We will need a very precise volume."

Henry could tell she was frightened by how tightly she gripped his hand. *"You can do this . . . for Dad."*

Brianna relaxed. It was all the encouragement she needed.

"Louder! Until I tell you to hold," Coralis silently commanded.

Henry's face shone with amazement and pride at his little sister. For the first time since the accident, he did not feel guilty about what he had done. It was as if some unseen destiny had led them to this point.

Coralis leaned toward the wall and pressed his wand against it.

Time sucked them in and collapsed around them. A loud shriek ripped the air and an abrupt burst of wind whipped past Henry's ear. He could not tell if his eyes were open or closed. The darkness was absolute, with only tiny pinpricks of light bouncing randomly in the distance. He had the sensation of moving forward but knew he wasn't walking. He squeezed Brianna's hand to make sure she was still there.

Slowly, scenes emerged. If Henry had to guess at what having your life pass before your eyes meant, this would be it. However, it wasn't his life. It was many others. They slipped past battlefields of horrendous wars, past great monuments under construction, past fields of grain with horse-drawn plows, and past artists and sculptors painting and chiseling.

"Are you seeing this?" Henry asked Brianna aloud. But his words became twisted into garbled grunts. He sensed Coralis chuckling at his expense.

Gradually the scenes slowed down until they were once again enveloped in darkness. Their walk through time had stopped. Coralis illuminated the cavern, similar to the one they had left, yet somehow different. Henry was about to ask if they had succeeded when he noticed the falcon perched on Coralis's shoulder. The old man's face conveyed surprise and confusion. But before any of them could speak, the bird launched from its perch and soared out of the tunnel.

Henry ran through a half dozen thoughts in his mind, yet couldn't form a coherent question.

Coralis anticipated what Henry and Brianna really wanted to ask. "I honestly don't know," he said, shaking his head. "The more I learn about the powers of the universe, the more I realize I've only scratched the surface. I know that Randall died, yet I cannot explain the presence of this bird—or what connection it might have to our mission. But I can tell you this: If you've never believed in good omens before, now would be a good time to start."

He was hustling them out of the cave and into the tunnel when Brianna began to laugh. "Henry, you're wearing stockings!"

"What?" He looked down at his clothes and grimaced. "Ahhh! What happened to my clothes? I look like a . . . I don't know what!"

Coralis grinned. "You've never looked more dashing."

Henry rubbed the fabric of his pants to make sure he wasn't imagining it. The cloak was gone—not a trace remained. It had transformed into a costume. His pants were now some sort of tight-fitting hosiery with broad yellow and brown vertical stripes. His shirt was more like a woman's blouse—dark green with long puffy sleeves—with a crimson shawl draped over his shoulders. "Ugh . . . if I wore this to school . . ." He shuddered at what others would do to him.

"Oh, come now, my boy." Coralis urged them forward. "I daresay the ladies of Milan will find you most attractive."

"At least I get to wear a dress." Brianna stopped to perform an exaggerated twirl. Her long gown had the same voluminous sleeves as Henry's shirt but were tapered at the wrist. As they stepped from the tunnel, sunlight caught the vibrant reds and golds of the floral design. "Can I take it home with me?" She laughed.

As did Henry, but his was directed at his sister's feet. "Sasquatch feet!"

Brianna gathered her dress out of the way for a better view. "Ew! They're hideous!" She stared down at flat-bottomed shoes made of scuffed brown leather with a broad front and an unflattering strap.

"Enough with the fashion show," said Coralis. "Let's get moving."

He strode forward at a brisk pace while the two apprentices snickered behind him. Coralis's clothes were very similar to Henry's except for his shirt, which sported an elaborately ruffled collar, and his pants, which fit like a second layer of skin. "And that's why grown men shouldn't wear skinny pants," Brianna whispered as Henry giggled.

The gaily attired threesome hurried down a grassy hillside to a dirt road lined with tall, conical trees.

"It's snowing!" Brianna opened her mouth to allow a floating white morsel to land on her tongue and immediately spat it out. "Blech! What are those things?"

"Seeds of the poplar trees." Coralis laughed as he hurried them forward.

"They look like puffballs from a dandelion." Henry scooped a handful that had accumulated on the ground and shoved them in his pocket.

"You'd think he could have warned me," Brianna pouted.

"And deny myself the pleasure of seeing that look upon your face?" Coralis chuckled.

They could see the Sforza Castle from atop the hill, and they half jogged toward it. Less than two minutes later, a team of horses pulling a large flatbed wagon drew alongside them and came to a stop.

"Buongiorno!" the robust driver shouted happily. Immediately, the ulexite translator kicked in so that Henry and Brianna heard it as "good day." "Leonardo has sent me. Please climb aboard." He had a full head of curly dark hair and a bushy beard with bits of food stuck in it. Unlike Henry and Coralis, his clothes had a much more rugged appearance, like those of a farmer. "I am Giovanni," he shouted over his shoulder as he urged the horses forward. "I am to deliver you to Sforza Castle as quickly as possible." He smiled at Brianna and his eyes widened. He reached below his bench seat and tossed a hat to her. "Even in fashionable Milan, women do not have blue hair. You will make others jealous," he added with a wink.

"How do I look?" she asked, modeling the hat.

"It's not quite as ugly as your shoes." Henry chuckled. As they neared the castle, he craned his neck for a better view.

"Come up here before you strain your neck." Giovanni patted the seat next to him.

Henry eagerly climbed out of the wagon to marvel at the immense structure looming before them. The hologram in the Cryptoporticus did not do it justice. They approached an outer gate, posted with a sentry.

"I will speak for us," Giovanni said sternly, his jovial nature now very serious. "You speak our language well," he said, and Henry realized the ulexite worked both ways. "But you do not know our ways, so do not talk. They will know you are not from here and take you for questioning. The duke has his share of enemies."

The sentry asked several no-nonsense questions, but it was clear that Giovanni was a regular visitor. He glanced briefly at Coralis and Brianna but stared long and hard at Henry.

"My new farmhand," Giovanni offered as an explanation, which seemed to satisfy the sentry. He allowed them to pass. Giovanni visibly relaxed.

"Why was he staring at me?" Henry asked as they crossed the bridge over the outer moat.

"Your skin," Giovanni answered. "It is not Milanese. Too dark."

Henry examined the light brown skin of his hand, courtesy of his Navajo ancestry, which had tanned rapidly as he spent more time in the sun.

"Is that going to be a problem?" Coralis asked.

"Just stay close to me." Giovanni clapped Henry on the back. "We will move quickly. But to be safe, perhaps you should return to the wagon."

Henry scrambled back but couldn't help but stare upward at the castle walls and towering turrets. They crossed the inner moat and entered an immense courtyard teeming with activity. Giovanni waved and greeted many people. It was obvious he was well liked. Henry could not imagine how they would have gotten inside without his assistance and silently thanked Leonardo for sending him.

Momentarily, they approached a hive of activity, at the center of which was the catapult they had seen in the Crypto-porticus.

The wagon continued past it and rolled behind several tents in the far corner of the courtyard, disappearing from sight. Giovanni quickly led them into one of the tents, securing the flap tightly. Henry gulped. Until now, he could almost chalk up the time slip to some kind of surreal dream, but suddenly it became very real. He was face-to-face with one of the most legendary figures in history—Leonardo da Vinci. As impressive as he was in holographic form, in person, he was ten times that.

"Good morning, my friends." His eyes were alive with activity, yet his face remained impassive, as if he was incapable of smiling. "Coralis, it has been too long. Or was it only yesterday? Time is so elusive when it's within one's grasp. And these are . . . ?" He motioned Henry and Brianna forward.

"My apprentices," Coralis said as he placed his hands on their shoulders.

"So young," Leonardo commented.

"Yet already seasoned." Coralis squeezed their shoulders gently.

Henry felt the Wand Master's pride in him, giving him a measure of confidence. "Pleased to meet you, sir." He offered his hand, which Leonardo clasped firmly. The inventor's hand was rough and calloused, no stranger to hard work. An uncomfortable silence followed, one that Henry attempted to fill. "I saw your painting of the Last Supper."

"Did you?" Leonardo's face finally twitched with an element of humor. "And was it finished to your liking?"

"Oh yes . . . I mean, it's magnificent!" Henry blurted.

Leonardo frowned. "It's good enough, I suppose. But you are not here to fan the flames of my ego. That is the duke's job. A more urgent purpose awaits."

He thanked Giovanni for his help, tossed him a coin, and asked him to leave. "We have little time and much to do." Leonardo led them to a large wooden table and pointed to a meticulous drawing of the castle's courtyard. "We are here." He slid his finger to an entrance not far from their current position. "This will lead you to the dungeon."

Brianna whimpered before she could catch herself.

"It is not a nice place for children." Leonardo scowled at Coralis before unrolling a second sketch. "This is my original design of the dungeon, though it has been modified slightly."

Henry detected anger in the man's voice. He noticed lines and arrows that had obviously been added at a later date and wondered who would have the nerve to tamper with the work of a genius.

"Your pupil, Malachai," Leonardo said to Coralis with disdain, "added this passage. Most cannot enter. Most cannot detect its existence. There are unnatural powers at work here, of which I strongly disapprove but am powerless to change."

Henry drew upon his lessons and tuned in to Leonardo's aura. It sparked with red energy, which indicated a controlled but deep-seated anger. When Henry let the aura fade, he found Leonardo staring intently into his eyes. "I'm s-sorry," Henry stammered.

"Do not be," Leonardo replied. He raised an eyebrow at Coralis. "Seasoned indeed." Then he quickly explained how to get into the hidden dungeon without being detected. "There are no sentries—there's no need for them. The man you seek is in the next-to-last cell."

He turned to Brianna. "I am told he is still healthy of body and sound of mind, though his appearance would indicate otherwise. Do you still wish to go?"

"Yes," she replied emphatically. "He is our father and we have come to rescue him."

"Rescue?" Leonardo stepped back and glared at Coralis. A horrible cloud of foreboding permeated the tent. "You should go. Now!" He hurried to the entrance and held the flap open for them to pass.

Brianna looked frantically to Henry for some kind of explanation. Henry could not bear to look at her and rushed out after Coralis.

Brianna caught up to him and grabbed him forcefully by the arm. "What's going on? What did he mean by that? Tell me!" her voice commanded too loudly.

Several of the men working on the catapult turned to stare at them, and Leonardo shouted at them to get back to work before wheeling his anger at Coralis. "You cannot keep secrets, old man. Have you learned nothing?" He dismissed them with a wave of his hand and marched back into the tent.

Henry glared at Coralis. The Wand Master had been soundly rebuked and appeared flustered and embarrassed.

"I will explain," he said to Brianna. "After we are out of sight."

A few workers huddled in hushed conversation, peeking nervously in their direction. "Come on." Henry pulled his sister's arm. "We're running out of time." Fortunately, she did not resist. Unfortunately, she connected with his mind and screamed at him with some very unladylike obscenities.

CHAPTER

TWENTY-ONE

Leonardo was correct. There were no sentries because—much to Henry's surprise—there were no prisoners. They walked quickly down a corridor of empty cells. Following Leonardo's instructions, they turned left into a shadow and ran into a shimmering wall—like heat waves rising off the pavement on a summer day. "Is that a protective spell?" His whisper reverberated around them like an echo that had no place else to go.

"Do not attempt to use your wands," Coralis said grimly. "I can get us through, but you must stay close." He took a tentative step forward with the apprentices close on his heels. Passing through the invisible wall was like going through a dense curtain of fog—one that was laced with power that pushed back at them. Once inside, the air remained heavy and every step took effort. But it did nothing to suppress the stench of rot. Rats scurried out of their way, unaffected by the spell.

Brianna began to cry.

"Dad's okay," Henry said gently.

She hiccuped a short laugh. "It's not that. It's the rats. They're trapped here too."

He'd forgotten she could communicate with them. He draped an arm over her shoulder.

The row of cells was long and dismal. Having seen this in the hologram, they were still unprepared for the squalid conditions and the hopelessness that emanated from whatever life remained in the prisoners. A few lumps stirred on their cots as the trio passed, expending energy they did not have for a glimpse at the people who had penetrated the spell.

"Here." A familiar voice came from a cell at the end of the corridor.

Brianna attempted to rush forward but Coralis held her back. "Stay with me," he said, his voice strained.

They arrived at the cell. Something moved deep in the shadows. "Dad?" Brianna asked softly.

Markhor hobbled forward into the light. "Henry." His voice cracked like dry leaves as he addressed his son for the first time in well over a year. He tried to focus on the young girl through his broken glasses. "You called me Dad, yet . . ." It suddenly registered. "Brianna?"

She smiled weakly. "Surprise." A tear rolled down her cheek.

"But how?" Markhor removed his glasses to rub his eyes.

"It's a long story." Henry shuffled his feet, embarrassed. "But a really good one."

Markhor stood in silence. He smiled, then laughed briefly, but his laughter erupted into a terrible cough.

"Oh, Dad!" Brianna reached for him and was immediately thrown backward against the wall.

"Brianna, no!" Markhor lunged at the bars of his cell. "Are you all right?"

She propped herself against the wall and worked herself into a standing position, still stinging with residual power. Henry reached to steady her but she slapped his hand away. "We can't help him, can we?" The full force of her anger slammed into Coralis, yet she held her Voice in check.

"We cannot." Coralis was drenched in sweat, his voice quivering as he strained against the spell.

"I brought this upon myself," Markhor said sadly. "There is nothing anyone can do for me now."

"Then why are we here?" she cried.

"Do not lose sight of our goal," Coralis said meekly. "We need information about Malachai."

"Malachai," Markhor spat. "I was such a fool. He baited me like a fish and not once did I think to look for the hook. But you have to believe . . . I never intended to cause any harm."

Henry stepped back. Pity for his father's situation easily dissolved into anger. "Harm? Everything you did was wrong! You told me nothing about who I am or what I could do. Do you have any idea what I've been through? I changed your daughter into a hedgehog!"

Markhor withered under his son's attack, burying his face in his hands. "I'm so sorry . . . Wait, did you say *hedgehog*? How is that even possible?"

"It doesn't matter." Henry remained on the offensive. "You put our family in danger. And for what? Power? Glory? What made you ever think that what you were doing would turn out well? And yes, for your information, not only was it possible, but it aged her by three years, which makes us virtually twins, which is another thing I will never forgive you for."

Henry had never had so many words come out at one time. Having spent his wrath, he slumped forward, dejected and overwhelmed. "We defeated you . . . or him, or whomever. But now he's up to no good again. Coralis thinks you might still have a connection and can give us some information. Maybe you can help set things right. I've got friends now, and I don't want them to get hurt."

"We have reason to suspect he will attempt something at the Temple of Time." Coralis's voice was barely audible. The strain of warding off the protection spell was rapidly depleting his energy. Henry knew it took much more power to work undetected within a spell. And the weaker he got, the greater the chance that Malachai would know they were there. He could already feel minute cracks forming in the Wand Master's protective dome.

Markhor seemed to recognize that Coralis's strength was rapidly failing. He spoke quickly. "He knows I still have the mind-link and has taken pains to hide from me what he can." A smile tugged at his lips. "But he underestimates me." Another burst of coughing doubled him over. As he stood, there was renewed fire in his eyes.

"He is going after the Pangaea Particle," Markhor continued. "He knows that by taking it he will disrupt the Earth's ecological balance, but he has something else in mind. He has gone to great lengths to shield his true purpose, yet occasionally he has let his guard down. Essentially, he believes the Particle will give him the powers of a god. I don't know how he plans to steal it. I am fairly certain he doesn't know how it works, but he is willing to take the chance that he can figure it out and control its power. If even a smidgen of what he is thinking is true, then we have to stop him."

Coralis nodded. "It's enough to get us started. And now we must hurry. We have little time to return to the portal."

"Henry, Brianna," Markhor called to them. "I've made enough mistakes for several lifetimes, but I swear to you that when the time comes, I will be right there with you as we defeat this monster. And who knows? Maybe someday I'll be able to return home."

Henry turned away with a jerk. His father had sent the briefest of images into his mind—one that confirmed what Henry had suspected all along. This might possibly be the last time they would ever see him alive. He couldn't let Brianna know. He quickly wiped the image clear and regained his composure. "Thanks, Dad." Henry held Brianna's hand. "Good-bye for now."

"Bye, Daddy," Brianna sobbed. "I miss you."

"I miss you, too. Tell your mother I love her." Markhor watched them leave, his heart so heavy with guilt and remorse that it literally pulled him to the floor. He lay and wept for all the people he had hurt until another coughing fit left him drained and exhausted.

A rat crept up and sniffed his ear—and there wasn't a thing he could do about it.

TWENTY-TWO

"Come on! We have to hurry!" Henry urged.

Brianna had hesitated just before leaving the dungeon. "I spoke to the rats," she whispered. "I asked them to leave Dad alone."

"So will they?"

"They will try." She winced in pain. "But they are so very hungry."

"You did all you could." Henry smiled tersely.

They emerged into the courtyard to a most unusual sight. Leonardo stood a short distance from the catapult. Perched upon his outstretched arm was the falcon. At Leonardo's command the bird soared skyward, performing a series of loops and dives to the delight of the growing crowd.

From behind the tent, Giovanni waved them over. "Leonardo has given us a distraction. I almost wish I could stay and watch." He winked.

Coralis lifted Brianna into the wagon as Henry scrambled in beside her. "Do we have enough time to get back?" Henry asked.

"Yes, but it will be close," Coralis answered. He accepted

a jug from Giovanni and took a long drink of water. "Let's hope we don't run into any roadblocks."

Giovanni kept close to the walls to remain as inconspicuous as possible. Thirty meters from the gate, a shout arose from a lookout in a tower, followed immediately by a chorus of cheers from soldiers on the battlements.

"Oh no." Giovanni reined in the horses as the first of a very long line of soldiers dressed in varying degrees of armor marched three by three across the inner bridge and into the courtyard.

"What is this?" Coralis asked urgently.

"There is much war—Germans, French, Swiss, Milan, Naples. Ludovico Sforza makes much trouble for us." Giovanni ushered them out of the wagon to stand at attention as an elaborately decorated carriage came into view. "The Duke of Milan, our fearless leader, arrives."

The drawbridge slowly rose until it came to rest firmly against the castle wall, sealing everyone inside.

Brianna kicked a pebble. "I'd say that's a roadblock."

Leonardo stepped forward as the carriage rolled to a stop. Henry craned his neck to see what was happening, but Leonardo was blocked from view on the far side of the carriage.

"Leonardo and the duke are close. He is the best at making the war machines the duke needs. He will find out what kind of trouble Ludovico has brought with him." Giovanni adjusted the hat on Brianna's head as the blue hair tried to peek out.

Coralis frowned as he checked the time on his pocket watch.

"What happens if we don't get back to the portal within ninety minutes?" Henry asked. All along, he had assumed they would get in and out without any complications. In the face of this huge problem, he wondered why he hadn't thought it through. *I'm going to have to work on anticipating this kind of thing.* He hoped Coralis had planned for such an obstacle, but the look on his face said otherwise.

"Let's worry about that when the time comes." Coralis tapped a finger on the edge of the wagon, anxiously awaiting Leonardo's word.

Precious minutes slipped away. Finally, the carriage pulled forward. Leonardo called to the falcon, which landed lightly on his forearm. "An unusual bird," he said, arching an eyebrow with curiosity. "I sense it wishes to remain here with me."

"That bird has always had a mind of its own," Coralis said. "If it wishes to stay, there is a good reason."

Leonardo pursed his lips and nodded. "Follow me. You don't have much time." He led them brusquely to a corner opposite the catapult. Using a skeleton key, he unlocked the heavy wooden door and hurried them inside, locking the door behind them. At the end of a short hall he unlocked another door and entered a voluminous workspace occupied wall to wall and floor to ceiling with wooden frames of random contraptions in various stages of completion.

"Remember this," Coralis said to his apprentices' minds. *"You are witnessing living history."*

Henry wanted desperately to stop and soak up every detail, but Leonardo rushed them through.

"Remind me to bring a camera next time," Brianna whispered.

"Let's hope there is a next time," Henry replied.

"Give me a hand with this, Henry." Leonardo took one side of a large chest and, with Henry's help, slid it forward. They moved several rolls of canvas, revealing a small door. Just before they entered, the falcon flew into the rafters and shrieked.

"I think he's saying good-bye," Brianna said sadly.

"Maybe we'll see him again someday." Brother and sister waved one final time and turned back to Coralis. "Let's get out of here," Henry urged.

Brianna had to duck through the small doorway into the secret tunnel, which meant Coralis and Leonardo needed to fold in half. Leonardo lit a candle and pushed it through the bottom of a brass canister. The light reflecting from the canister created what was essentially a spotlight.

"Neat trick," Brianna commented.

"Out of necessity is born invention." Leonardo led them down a long flight of stairs. Anticipating their questions, he explained how he'd helped design the castle—along with a few modifications. "One never knows when an escape route will be useful."

Henry tried to hide his enthusiasm. Ancient castles with secret passages! Things he'd read about but never thought he'd see. *Wait till I tell Serena!* Granted, it fell far short of meeting the Earth Mother, but it was still pretty cool.

The stairs were endless. The air grew thick with humidity when they reached the bottom. As they hurried through a tunnel encased in stone, droplets of water fell from the ceiling, which barely cleared the top of Leonardo's head.

"I think we're under the moat," Henry whispered to Brianna.

"Duh."

It was good to hear her sarcastic reply, though he could tell she was still angry over Coralis's deception. *"When this is over, we'll come back for Dad."*

"I really want to believe that," she said silently.

Gradually the ground sloped upward. They emerged into a storage shed well beyond the castle walls. Clouds had moved in and a light mist fell.

"Good," Leonardo stated. "Rain and impending battle. Two things that will keep travelers out of your path." He gave Coralis brief directions back to the cave before addressing Henry and Brianna. "I will do what I can to give your father comfort."

Henry glanced at his sister, who was on the verge of tears. "Thank you." He offered Leonardo his hand.

"Accept what life has to offer you." Then he winked. "But always bend the rules."

They set forth in a steady jog over rolling hills. Mist turned to rain, slowing their progress. "We're not going to make it, are we?" Brianna panted.

As an answer, Coralis picked up the pace. At the top of a rise he paused to get his bearings. Henry reached out with his senses and detected the unmistakable hum of the portal's energy field. "That way!" he exclaimed, and ran down the hillside.

He heard their footsteps thumping behind him as they followed his lead into the mouth of the cave. "Are we in time?" he asked, breathing hard.

"Yes and no," Coralis said, deep in thought.

"That's not an answer." Brianna threw her hat against the cave wall.

"Sometimes that guy really gets on my nerves," Brianna said silently to Henry.

He smiled and held her hand as she began to hum.

"We have arrived with seconds to spare." Coralis checked his watch again and shrugged. "However, seconds are not necessarily as good as minutes."

"You mean we're stuck here?" Brianna panicked.

"Nonsense," Coralis scoffed. "It just makes our return trip more interesting."

They emerged from the cave, and Henry knew immediately something was wrong. "Where's Lesya?"

A path in the forest opened to their right. Coralis led them with the same urgency Henry felt. Even the castle wall cooperated, creating a door as soon as they broke free from the forest.

Gretchen was waiting for them on the other side. Her wild eyes confirmed Henry's fear.

TWENTY-THREE

"You have been gone for six days," Gretchen informed them. She had to move quickly to keep up with Coralis, who growled angrily.

"Six days?" Brianna jogged with Henry, desperate to keep pace with the long strides of the Wand Master. "I guess that's what he meant by more interesting."

From the second they emerged from the cave, Henry could sense something was terribly wrong. Everything in nature contains a power unto itself, and a Wandmaker's abilities stem from a connection to this life-force. It was like having a direct line to nature. Henry and his fellow apprentices were still in the early stages of developing their abilities and the sensitivities that came with them. But despite his limitations, Henry could tell that something had gone sour. He could hardly imagine the damaging effect it must be having on Coralis.

They swiftly covered the grounds and entered the castle. Gretchen led them directly to the front foyer. Gathered around the tree-trunk columns, Lesya and many of her Hutsul companions shuffled anxiously. Henry read the look on their faces as worry, but quickly found out differently.

A small man stepped forward to confront Coralis. "What have you done?"

"Please remain calm, Pesha." Coralis tried a small measure of Voice to soothe their anger.

"No! No Voice tricks!" Pesha spat. "Three of our people are dead—one guarding the cave, two guarding the springs. Attacked from the skies. Torn apart by a flock of large black birds." He winced. "I will never wipe that sight from my eyes."

"That is not all," said Lesya. "We heard the screams but arrived too late. Once the birds killed our people, they gathered in an arrow formation and dove into the springs, where they exploded. The springs have turned. The water has gone bad. Sour—like vinegar."

"That's impossible," Coralis said warily. "Nothing can affect the Earth Mother's domain. She would protect it at all cost."

"She is gone!" Pesha's voice thundered within the small confines of the lobby. "She is weakened. You can feel it!"

Immediately, Henry knew Pesha was telling the truth, and a brief glance at Coralis confirmed he knew it as well.

"What have I done?" Coralis said weakly as his shoulders slumped.

Henry's mind raced to search for what they might have done to bring harm to the Earth Mother. It could not have been the act of slipping through time or she would have been weakened before this and Coralis would never have risked it. Furthermore, Leonardo could not have done anything. And

Henry's father was trapped and incapable of . . . "Oh no." The color drained from Henry's face as he recalled the aura link between his father and Malachai. "He knew. Malachai knew we were there."

"And he took advantage of Coralis's absence to poison the springs," Brianna added somberly.

"And thus to keep the Earth Mother from interfering with his plans." Coralis stared helplessly at the floor. All motion in the room stopped as if time were frozen. The silence became overwhelming as they awaited the Wand Master's instructions.

They waited a long time.

Six days earlier, Malachai casually walked down the main street of his hidden village. He smiled at several people he passed and they smiled back, thankful their master was in a good mood. And indeed he was! He found immense pleasure in picking at Coralis's defenses, toying with him to find out what weapons he had left in his pitiful arsenal.

Children. His former mentor had fallen to pieces, allowing his Guild to flounder into obscurity, and now he was scrambling to make up for lost time by recruiting children.

They'd be no more trouble than the bear.

Malachai waved happily to the woman with crossed eyes and laughed as she stumbled . . . when a sudden dizziness washed over him and sent him to his knees. The woman ran into a nearby alley, fearful at what she might have done. The streets cleared in an instant. Whatever was happening, they did not want to be a part of it.

Slowly Malachai rose to his feet, his eyes blazing red with anger. "That fool!" he shouted.

Quickly, he retraced his steps to his home. The caged Strix shrieked as he slammed the door behind him. "Shut up!" He pointed his wand at the bird to silence it, but his anger was such that it immediately turned to ash. He squinted at the smoldering remains, relaxing his breathing to regain control of his emotions.

The spell at Sforza Castle was one of his most powerful. Only someone as masterful as Coralis could have penetrated it. Fortunately, he had installed a safety spell that he wove into the main spell, which acted like a silent, undetectable alarm.

Malachai reached into the cage and grabbed a handful of ash. He squeezed it tightly, immune to the heat and poisonous vapors, until it formed a solid egg. The bird might be gone, but the essence of its evil contained in the egg would be useful.

His composure returned. He wasn't sure if his anger was more from Coralis's intrusion or because he had underestimated the old man. He suspected it had to be the latter. Coralis might be a fool, but he still had some fight left in him. And to Malachai, this was an act of war.

A war he would win.

Malachai's village was not the only one hidden from time. Deep within the Himalayan mountain range, surrounded by impenetrable gorges hundreds of meters deep, sat one of the oldest man-made structures ever built. It began on top of a three-thousand-meter peak and draped over the mountainside, facing the morning sun. A castle of immense proportions, it spanned twelve hundred meters across the peak, sprawling outward as it ran down the cliff face, seemingly molded from the earth as a child might construct a sand castle at the beach.

One could only imagine the years of manual labor and the lives that were lost using the most primitive tools to erect it in all its magnificence. Yet even with modern technology, the structure could not be duplicated. It was indeed a wonder of the ancient world—one that was unknown to most of mankind.

For like Malachai's village, this sacred place was shielded from prying eyes. Even the most ardent explorer, given its exact location, would never find it. And that was just the way the Wandmakers' Guild liked it.

This was the Temple of Time. A source of life shrouded in myth. This particular mountain was riddled with caves that ran for thousands of kilometers, splintering off in so many directions that only a mole could navigate them. A human would die of terminal confusion long before ever seeing the light of day. But should one succeed, he would find himself at the entrance to the long-buried Tethys Ocean.

While the oceans of the planet's surface contain creatures and anomalies that mankind is only beginning to explore, the Tethys Ocean contains creatures that were never meant to rise from the depths. Life-forms that are capable of decimating the habitats of every living thing and throwing the ecological balance into a tailspin from which it would never recover.

In order to keep those creatures in check, the Earth Mother created an artifact. She gathered great quantities of some of the rarest elements in existence, some of which have never been seen by anyone since the dawn of man. Elements that were essentially poison to the Tethys' life-forms. She condensed these elements into a powerful artifact—much the way extreme pressure would turn ordinary carbon into a diamond—and she gave it a name. The Pangaea Particle.

The location of this artifact remained known only to her for millions of years. But when man emerged and multiplied and explored every mountain, forest, valley, and crevice on the planet, she sought the aid of those who could help shield it from being accidentally discovered. The High Council of Aratta was entrusted with knowledge of its existence and challenged to keep it safe.

But even the High Council came under the influence of political differences, and from this division in fundamental beliefs, the Wandmakers' Guild was formed. As sworn protectors of the Earth, the Guild worked tirelessly to build the Temple of Time, and thus, the sanctity of the Pangaea Particle was preserved.

Only once did the Earth Mother err in judgment. She did not foresee the change in Coralis's most dedicated apprentice,

Malachai. The day she took him into her confidence was a day she would always regret. Yet as much as she could protect life, she could not take it away, and she relied on the Guild to keep Malachai at bay until such time when he would finally pass away.

The Guild had failed.

Malachai knew he had to act in haste. He no longer had the luxury of amassing an army of Scorax followers to storm the temple. He had willingly taken part in his son's plan over a year ago, if for no better reason than to make sure it failed. He had his own plans for the Earth, and nothing, not even his own son, would get in his way.

But now Coralis was up to his meddling ways. Given time, the old Wand Master—his mentor—could be a formidable foe. And while Malachai was confident he could eventually squash Coralis's meager forces, there was no point in getting into a prolonged fight. Instead, he turned to plan B.

He smiled. Deep down, he had probably been looking for a reason to use plan B all along. When he devised the plan, even he was impressed at how ruthlessly efficient it could be. His experiments with the Strix and Valraven had proven effective. But those were creatures that were already at his disposal. Now was the time for some manipulation. Time to turn to his private menagerie.

Malachai was nearly giddy as he descended several floors to a subbasement where he kept his collection of pets. The old woman responsible for their upkeep eagerly fled when he demanded she leave. He wrinkled his nose in disgust at her appearance, but smiled nonetheless at the fresh bite marks on her forearms.

The upper tier of cages held various species of monkeys. He examined each one thoughtfully until he came to the white-thighed surili. The gorgeous young male with long, grayish fur leapt at him, baring its teeth and screaming in defiance.

"Now, now, my pet," he murmured. "You will soon be free."

Malachai paused. He stared thoughtfully at the monkey, admiring its unique appendages. He had gotten the idea from a movie he had seen years earlier. At the time, he admired the author for his ingenuity. He even went so far as to label the creation an act of genius, surprised that nature had never seen fit to evolve that way on its own. The film was *The Wizard of Oz*, and the creatures were winged monkeys.

Malachai extended a hand toward the cage and quickly retracted it as the monkey snapped viciously. "Still not happy with me, are you?" He chuckled. "I guess I can't blame you. But once I let you out, I daresay you will be thanking me."

He selected a vial from a nearby cabinet and attached a mister to it. Covering his mouth and nose with a handkerchief, he sprayed a single shot of vapor at the monkey, which stared at him in wide-eyed shock before collapsing unconscious. "That's better," he said as he gently examined the body.

While the Strix and Valraven were mindless creatures that were easily controlled, the intelligence of the monkey presented a problem. There was only one way around it—he would have to see through its eyes, and there was only one way to do that. He smiled. That woman's eyes weren't doing her any good anyway.

Logistics also presented a challenge. Malachai had several winged monkeys at his disposal. The white-thighed surili had been combined with a bar-tailed godwit—a bird that could fly incredibly long distances without stopping. But the Temple of Time was over six thousand kilometers away, and at an average nonstop speed of forty-eight kilometers an hour, it would still take over five days to make the trip.

Malachai shrugged. He would just have to find some favorable wind currents. The monkey was his best option, and he swore to himself that he would not fail. And it would be as taxing for him as it was for the monkey. In order to guide it, he would have to remain awake the entire time.

Four nights later, under the cloak of darkness, the exhausted monkey landed on the roof of the temple. Malachai directed it to a fountain for a long drink of water and spotted a basket of apples nearby. Once nourished, he allowed it (and himself) to sleep for two hours before directing it to the cave entrance. Despite his own exhaustion, Malachai projected his senses outward, easily locating the presence of the Pangaea Particle.

Several hours of scampering later, the monkey turned the corner and came face-to-face with two guards, heavily armed with an arsenal of wands. But the monkey had the element of surprise. It took the guards several seconds to acknowledge there was a monkey in their midst, and several more to realize it had wings. Before they could unsling their weapons, the monkey threw a vial at the guards. It exploded into steam that temporarily paralyzed the guards.

Malachai waited for the vapor to dissipate before sending the monkey past the immobilized guards toward the Particle. There was only one more obstacle, which would have been impossible to overcome had the Earth Mother not shared her secret with him.

The Particle was encased in a transparent sphere composed of Earth's earliest and now extinct elements.

The only thing that could penetrate the Earth Mother's defenses was the Diffluonium Wand. Malachai hated entrusting it to the monkey but had no choice. The tiny primate grasped the wand firmly and pressed it against the transparent sphere. At first nothing happened, causing Malachai to have a momentary anxiety attack. Then smoke began to fill the sphere. The monkey panicked and tried to pull away, but Malachai's control was too strong. Smoke thickened, and as the solid elements turned into their gaseous form, they began to react with one another on a molecular level.

Sparking arcs of light danced like heat lightning within a cloud. The monkey screeched wildly but Malachai held it in a viselike grip. Its eyes bulged, straining with effort. Then, as suddenly as the smoke appeared, it vanished—along with the wand, which dissolved into the sphere just before it disappeared.

The Pangaea Particle had been released.

TWENTY-FOUR

"You're telling us that you went to Italy for six days while Malachai was stealing an artifact that could throw the world into total chaos?" Bryndis was not only the first to speak, but the first to challenge Coralis. And while the other apprentices might not have been so direct, Bryndis had nailed what they were thinking as well.

"We didn't go anywhere for six days," Henry said. He wanted to reason with her. He would have had more success in stopping a charging rhino.

Luis snorted, making his allegiance clear.

"You were absolutely gone for six days," Bryndis scoffed. "The fact that you got lost on your way home doesn't lessen the amount of time you spent away from here—where it really matters. Did you at least find out anything useful?"

Henry looked to Molly for support but could tell even she was dubious about whether their trip had been worthwhile. And Coralis seemed to have wrapped himself in a cocoon of isolation, smoldering in some kind of self-pity.

Finally Henry took a deep breath. "Look. You're right. We didn't know it at the time, but it was a huge risk. At least now we know what Malachai is up to." Henry scanned their faces. He still had some convincing to do, which was difficult because he, too, had his doubts. Granted, they learned a few important details. But was it worth the cost? Unless . . . had Coralis actually taken the risk so they could say good-bye to their father?

Brianna came to his side and grasped his hand, squeezing it and giving him confidence. "When Malachai took over our dad, he created a mind-link that will last for as long as either of them are alive. Their auras are connected. That's why Malachai has him in prison in another time period—because it's too dangerous for him. If Dad were to escape, or if someone could get to him, Malachai could be exposed."

Henry had their attention, yet he couldn't help but notice how Luis leaned toward Serena—and how she didn't seem to mind the shoulder-to-shoulder contact. He forced himself to continue. "We've seen what he can do with Strix and Valraven."

"And we fought them and won," Bryndis said emphatically.

"We did. But those creatures could be kittens compared to the ones in the Tethys Ocean."

"Or they could be the lions," Bryndis countered. "You don't know—"

"Enough!" Coralis cut through the bickering. "We *do* know. The Earth Mother would not have put that safeguard in place if it was not needed. Whatever is down there is not meant to see the light of day. This is one instance in which we do not have to see in order to believe. Because once we actually *see*, it might be too late."

But Bryndis was not to be deterred. "Then why did you leave when you should be training us to fight?"

"Because no battle can be won without knowledge. We needed something more concrete than an educated guess!" Coralis pounded a fist into his hand.

"Those six days gave Malachai a pretty good head start," Molly said warily.

"Which is why we must act quickly," Coralis urged. "And for the sake of humanity, I hope we are ready."

Malachai cradled the monkey in his arms and silently mourned its passing. The creature was almost unrecognizable. It was as if something had attacked its face and head, which was now heavily scarred and clumped with small bits of remaining hair. Its hands were bloody, and all but three nails were missing.

But the monkey hadn't been attacked—not in the traditional sense. Proximity to the Particle had done this gruesome work. Despite wearing specially designed gloves to carry the artifact, the animal had suffered the toxic and corrosive effects of the elements contained within it.

Malachai had prepared a thick box made from solid lead, thinking radiation would be his primary concern. However, from the looks of the monkey, it appeared as though he had more serious side effects to contend with. This went beyond radiation poisoning. He wondered whether the lead would be at all useful.

He called the animal's keeper to give the monkey a proper burial. She gave him a strange look, as if puzzled by his pity for the creature. But it was the least he could do. He wasn't a complete monster.

Malachai stared long and hard at the Particle. Was there something he was missing? Some small detail the Earth Mother might have shared that he could have forgotten? No, impossible. Besides, if he dwelled on it for too long he would get sidetracked from his mission. He needed to concentrate.

He carried the lead box with the Particle inside into his workroom.

Something tickled his palm.

He laughed.

Consensus among the apprentices was split. Henry, Brianna, and Katelyn chose the Kunstkammer as their favorite place in the castle. Bryndis, Luis, and Serena favored the Cryptoporticus, which was where Coralis had gathered them.

"The Particle could never be found through ordinary means—as long as it was protected within the Temple of Time. Even now that it has been removed, it will take the six of you to narrow down its location." Coralis positioned them around the large wooden table and activated a holographic image of the Earth. "Now use your Argus Wands to locate the Pangaea Particle."

One by one, they placed their wands on the table, pointing them directly at the image. There was no hesitation among any of them. In the weeks they had studied under Molly and Coralis, they had grown in confidence and ability. They no longer had the nervousness of rookie apprentices. And while far from being Wand Masters themselves, they approached their assigned task with the firm resolve that they could succeed.

Henry stood between Serena and Luis. He glanced at Serena for one brief second, hoping to catch her eye, confident that his wand would be the first to react. However, that one-second delay cost him his edge.

Luis's wand pulsed. He poured his newfound knowledge of the earth element into it and a ray of light connected with a large area of the globe. A small grin tugged at the corners of his mouth. His eyes shifted toward Henry.

And that was all the time Henry needed to catch up. A burst of light from his wand joined that of Luis and narrowed the area. The other apprentices concentrated harder, until they had all joined beams and narrowed the area to a specific pinpoint on the globe.

Coralis marked the position and told them to relax. He adjusted the hologram to a flat surface and zoomed in on the area. "You have done well."

"All right!" said Luis.

"But don't get cocky about it," Coralis huffed. "Now that it is no longer contained, the Pangaea Particle emits a strong life-force, which made it easier to locate."

"So when do we leave?" Bryndis asked, her face set in fierce determination.

"Not until we have a plan," Coralis warned. "This is a rugged mountainous region and, no doubt, Malachai has his defenses in place. Molly, please take them through the exercises we planned. Henry and Luis, stay here."

"But—" Bryndis began.

Coralis cut her off. "Go. Now. And follow Molly's instructions to the letter. You will need these final lessons if we are to succeed. The boys will follow shortly."

Henry blanched. He had gotten used to Coralis referring to them as young men. Calling him a boy was not a good sign.

As the others filed out, Coralis wheeled on Henry and Luis. "This is not a competition." Luis started to speak, and Coralis shot him a look that could cut through steel. "This is not some game to see who can do better than the other. You are a team. After that juvenile display of arrogance between the two of you, I am tempted to leave you behind. You must act in concert with each other. The slightest hesitation in concentration can cost you your lives—and not just yours, but the entire team's. I am not blind. I can do nothing to stop your growing affection toward other apprentices, but you must put your emotions aside for the greater good. Am. I. Clear?"

Sufficiently scolded, they mumbled, "Yes, sir." Luis held out his hand and Henry shook it.

"Good. Now go join the others. We have no time to waste."

But as they left the Cryptoporticus, Henry was annoyed with himself that he had not offered his hand first.

TWENTY-FIVE

"Malachai has tested us and seen firsthand that we are not defenseless." Coralis had gathered everyone into the classroom. On the front wall he had tacked a large map of Romania. "What he does not know is how strong we've become—something of which even I am not certain. Your training has gone well. You are all to be commended on the level to which you have honed your skills."

The apprentices glanced sideways at one another, wary of the Wand Master's praise, waiting for a "but." It came not from Coralis but from Bryndis. "But are we a match for him? Assuming Molly goes with us, we are eight against one. Unless he has an army of Scorax hiding in the wings. Or a flock of Strix. Or abominations from the Tethys."

"All good concerns." Coralis nodded. "Let's address them one by one. Malachai has recruited thousands of followers."

Luis shot out of his chair. "Wait, what? How can we—"

"Please." Coralis held up a hand and Luis sat back down, nervously, on the edge of his seat. "The Scorax are not a unified force," he continued. "They are individuals positioned around the globe whose purpose is to keep the world in a continuous state of upheaval—causing chaos at every opportunity, keeping people in a constant state of fear. They range from arms dealers to owners of major news syndicates. But Malachai's network is not designed to amass and function as an army."

"But you can't be certain of that, can you?" Henry asked.

"You have met a small band of Hutsuls." Coralis pointed to positions on the map. "There are hundreds more scattered throughout these mountains, giving us access to information and communication." He jabbed a finger at an area labeled *Transylvanian Alps*. "Your Argus Wands have located the Pangaea Particle in this region. Dozens of Hutsul scouts have scoured these mountains. They are familiar with every movement and have assured me there has been nothing to indicate Malachai is gathering ground support."

"You're making this sound like a military maneuver," Serena said.

"That's because, in a manner of speaking, we are at war," Coralis said grimly. "To answer the second of your concerns, Bryndis, we know Malachai has created more Strix and Valraven. However, because of the vicious nature of these creatures, he would not be able to contain a large number of them."

"And that number would be?" Katelyn asked.

"My guess is no more than a hundred . . . give or take." Coralis paused, waiting for the group to explode. Instead, he was surprised as they seemed to relax. "Would any of you care to explain why you don't find this worrisome?"

"Tell him, Bryndis," Molly urged.

Bryndis hesitated, her eyes darting from Molly to Coralis and back again. Molly nodded encouragingly. "While you were off time-traveling, I was doing some research."

"Indeed?" Coralis sat on the edge of a desk, curious as to where this was leading.

Bryndis squirmed uncomfortably and continued. "I was able to locate some ancient scrolls . . . with the help of the dragon."

"Bahtzen bizzle! You entered the Cryptoporticus without permission?" Coralis yelled as he advanced toward her.

Serena stood to block his path. "Let her explain."

Coralis's steely gaze burned through Serena but she held her ground. When he finally stepped back, Bryndis spoke again.

"It wasn't my idea . . . at first. I was jogging laps around the castle when suddenly the wall opened. I hesitated for a moment and it closed up so quickly that I thought I had imagined it. But on my next lap it opened again, so I went through. I've watched you open the Cryptoporticus door and repeated what you did."

"And it let you in?" Coralis saw her confusion and explained. "It will not allow you to enter if you are not a Wand Master . . . or unless it can sense your aura is pure. Congratulations, young lady."

The apprentices turned to Bryndis, pride and respect reflecting on their faces. She blushed a deep shade of crimson and continued. "I entered the Cryptoporticus and . . . the dragon was waiting."

"You have made some valuable allies," Coralis said approvingly.

"Perhaps, but the dragon was not very cooperative." She frowned. "No matter how many questions I asked, it wouldn't answer them . . ."

"Until you asked the right ones," Coralis finished.

"Fortunately, the Strix had been on my mind," Bryndis said quickly. "If my elemental strength is water, I didn't see how that would help fight them. It turned out I was right. They are right at home around water. But . . ." She grinned cagily. "I remembered something you said about them."

"Indeed?" Coralis pressed.

"You said the Roc was their only natural predator," Luis piped in. "And thanks to Bryndis, we know where to find one."

"Finding a Roc is one thing. Controlling it is quite another," Coralis warned.

"The dragon seemed to think that *he* could." Bryndis pointed at Henry.

"Um . . . I'm not following." Henry swallowed hard. "What exactly is a Giant Roc?"

Luis smirked. "Picture an eagle that's big enough to lift an elephant."

"Whoa! That's one big eagle!" Brianna exclaimed.

"And what am I supposed to do with it?" Henry felt a bead of sweat trickle down his back.

"Beats me." Bryndis shrugged. "You'll have to ask the dragon yourself."

"He will do nothing of the sort." Coralis bristled. "I will explain it to you later, after I've had a talk with that confounded dragon."

"But if Bryndis could—"

"Now is not the time," the Wand Master growled in warning. He turned to Bryndis. "Was that all?"

"No. I also asked for some history, especially in regard to my ancestor, Laars Thornkill." She stared boldly at Coralis, her face unreadable.

"I see," Coralis said respectfully. "Then you know his lifeblood is still with us. We will speak of this in private."

Henry wondered what kind of secrets were being kept between the two of them. He was also jealous that Bryndis had been allowed into the Cryptoporticus. What did it mean to have a pure aura? Was Bryndis the only apprentice with that attribute? Did that mean the rest of them had some kind of character flaw? He felt a competitive urge rise within him but quickly repressed it as Coralis's earlier warning rang in his ears. He could not allow his drive to be better than everyone else to cloud his thoughts. He looked up to see Coralis appraising him, eyebrows raised.

"As for the creatures of the Tethys . . ." Coralis paused. "It will take some time for them to reach the surface."

"How much time?" asked Molly.

"I don't know," Coralis admitted. "But I know it's not like pulling a drain plug and watching the water drain. The

Tethys is deep below the surface, and even if the creatures could sense that their prison door has opened, they might be wary of leaving the confines of their domain. This might allow us enough time to regain possession of the Particle and return it to its proper place."

"Sounds like an awful lot of guesswork," Katelyn said.

"Perhaps, but there is more to Malachai's plan. And this was the importance of going to Milan." Coralis returned to the front of the room. "While the Hutsuls have not detected any movement by the Scorax, they have encountered suspicious activity in this sector." He pointed to the map. "Over the years, people have gone in but never come out."

"Wolf attacks?" Serena asked.

Instead of answering, Coralis withdrew a wand. Henry recognized the shape from when he'd first met Serena's grandfather, Joseph. "Is that a Revealer?"

"Yes, but with a unique quality." Coralis held it close enough for Henry to examine.

It had the familiar shape of a human finger bone but was capped on both ends with a bulging node. He decided to take a guess. "The Revealer Wand you used in Arizona could only be used once. Those nodes must be trapping something inside this one to let you use it more, or in different ways."

Coralis winked. "Excellent deduction. This Revealer has the additional property of detecting concealment spells." He turned to Serena. "Wolf attacks would have left remains of the victims. In this case, the victims did not die. They were trapped behind an invisible wall. One created by Malachai."

It would appear our nemesis has been operating under my very nose—the last place I would think to look. Shame on me."

"Is he spying on us?" Henry asked.

"Spying would be beneath him. No, this is his way of taunting me. He believes he can sleep in my backyard and I'd never know it."

"And he was right," Henry projected, to which Coralis nodded glumly.

"But he knew we were in Milan," said Brianna.

"A result of us breaching his spell, I fear. But that's the beauty of this Revealer. It can detect the concealment spell without penetrating it."

"So we know where he is, and that he has the Pangaea Particle, and he doesn't know what we know," Luis said. "What's the catch? What did Markhor tell you?"

"Smoke and mirrors," Coralis said. "Malachai could not care less about the creatures that might come crawling out of the earth. Although if they did, it would be a bonus prize that would aid in diverting us away from his real goal."

He moved to a side wall, where a large chart of the periodic table of elements hung. "You are all familiar with this?"

"Please don't tell me we have to memorize it," Luis groaned.

"It wouldn't hurt for you to do so. But there will be time for that later." Coralis pressed an indentation on the rock wall. The chart was attached to a hidden panel, which rotated 180 degrees to reveal another chart. It had the same configuration as the periodic table, but many of the squares were blank. And the ones that were filled in contained symbols, not letters.

"Are those hieroglyphics?" Henry asked.

"Many languages have been lost throughout the millennia. This one is Sumerian, one of the oldest written languages," Coralis said.

"It looks alien," said Katelyn.

"Rest assured, it is not alien, but the elements these symbols represent could very well be." Coralis stared at the chart, his brow creased with worry. "This chart is the only known copy in existence. The original was lost in the fire that took the Royal Library of Alexandria in Egypt several thousand years ago. But it would have been easy enough for Malachai to use a time slip to secure a copy for himself. Each of the symbols represents an element that no longer exists in the known universe."

"How much of the universe is unknown?" Brianna asked.

"Most of it," Coralis replied glumly. "Scientists have only begun to scratch the surface. They have tools that enable them to see into the far reaches of space and allow them to formulate hypotheses based on assumptions."

"More guesswork," Bryndis scoffed.

"Yes. Which is why this chart is so remarkable. Each symbol is not just a name of an element but a descriptor as well."

Henry squinted at the symbols, hoping for a glimmer of recognition from all the books he had read, but they were as foreign to him as if he were trying to read Klingon. He felt overwhelmed by the mysteries of the universe and wondered . . . "Wait. If no one knows about these elements, how could anyone possibly know what they can do?"

Coralis smiled. "What do *you* think?"

"Alien visitation?" Katelyn barely whispered.

"Ha!" Bryndis laughed.

"Perhaps," Coralis admitted. "Or perhaps something closer to home. You see, these are the elements from which the Pangaea Particle is made."

"Gaia," Serena said.

Coralis nodded. "The Earth Mother has had very limited direct contact with humans, yet tends to reveal information on a need-to-know basis. Our best guess is that she gave this information to an ancient Sumerian who felt the need to record it."

"So what can Malachai do with the Particle?" Bryndis asked impatiently.

"That depends on the level to which he can deconstruct it—take it apart—isolate the elements. This one"—Coralis pointed to a square in the center of the chart—"is of most concern. The name and descriptor are one and the same. It is called the dominator. It is speculated to be the key element that holds the Tethys at bay and keeps the creatures contained. Malachai believes that if he can access it, he will have control over every living thing on the planet. He will rule the world . . . no, he will control the world."

"But unlike his son, he won't have to destroy anything in the process." Henry only meant to think it, but the words came out. Everyone turned to look at him, but something about the chart got his attention. "Why is that symbol separated from the rest?" He indicated a square in the far-right corner.

"Roughly translated, it means the great unknown," Coralis answered. "It could be an inhibitor or an enhancer to any of the other elements. It is something the Earth Mother would not reveal. And since she protects the planet, we must assume there is a very good reason."

"Do you think Malachai knows?" Henry asked. "If the Earth Mother told him about the Pangaea Particle, maybe she told him about the unknown."

"It is possible, but unlikely," Coralis said warily. "Call it a hunch, but I believe this element has much more to do with preservation than domination."

TWENTY-SIX

Malachai removed the Pangaea Particle from the lead box, hoping this time it would reveal one or more of its secrets. *Third time's the charm,* he thought, and giggled. "I really must stop that," he mumbled. "I'm beginning to sound like my son." He shivered at the thought and looked deep within the Particle, marveling at the intricate design. It was the most complex puzzle he had ever seen and he was determined to unlock its components.

The spherical artifact was about the size of a baseball, the surface covered in a silvery, opalescent sheen that shifted and shimmered with a fluid motion, giving it the appearance of a liquid. Visible beneath this outer layer, veins appeared like dry riverbeds, widening and contracting along the stormy surface. Malachai suspected that if not for the outer shell, the innards would explode. It was as if the elements were being held captive against their will.

He longed to touch it with his bare hand but was reluctant to remove his protective gloves. He saw what it had done to the monkey, though he still did not understand *how* it had done so much damage.

A tingling sensation tickled his palm. He almost removed a glove to scratch it but caught himself in time. He giggled again. "Tricky little thing, aren't you?" The sphere responded with another tingle. "Can you understand me?" Malachai whispered to the sphere.

The opalescence swirled faster.

"You can!" He gasped in awe. He brought the sphere closer and closer to his eyes, staring with intense concentration. *Is it trying to tell me something?*

While the swirling pattern mesmerized him, an invisible, odorless gas seeped out and found its way to Malachai's nose. His face froze, paralyzed, as a thin tendril poked through the surface of the Particle, attaching itself to his face, just below his left eye. Like a mosquito, it penetrated his numbed skin, injecting something never intended for any human.

Seconds later, the sphere was back to its normal state. Malachai blinked twice before deciding he must have imagined it. After all, it was silly to think the Particle could actually communicate. He carefully returned the sphere to its box, sealing it until he could figure out a better way to approach the puzzle.

He removed his gloves and, using the heels of his palms, rubbed his eyes, vigorously applying more and more pressure. Suddenly he jerked his head up. What was that? Was someone laughing at him? Whoever it was, he would find them and make them pay. He tracked the laughter to room after room . . .

But the house was empty. Eventually, he stumbled back into the room where he kept the Particle.

"Puteo!" he screamed.

Malachai's lackey emerged from the shadows behind his master. His head bobbed from side to side as if he were ducking from imaginary jabs to his face. He had seen something he should not have seen and it scared him. His master had always had a volatile temper, but the look in his eyes told Puteo he was on the verge of doing something extreme. "I am here, master."

Malachai spun and lunged at his slave. He grabbed him by the throat, lifted him off the floor, and pinned him against the wall. "What took you so long?"

Puteo struggled to breathe. He tried to contain his self-defense mechanism—to no avail. A putrid odor arose from his pores, overpowering Malachai, who dropped him in disgust.

"Why, you foul . . ." Malachai covered his nose and retreated from the room. Once outside, his eyes widened with a brilliant idea. He clapped his hands and applauded the genius of his own villainy. He ducked his head back into the room. "Sound the gong and round up the village. Then bring me a puppy—the cutest one you can find—and meet me in the square in ten minutes. I'll gather my . . . tools. It's time to show you pitiful human beings the true meaning of evil."

In a prison cell over five hundred years in the past, Markhor huddled in a dark corner, his eyes wide with fright. Something had happened. Ever since he had been locked in his cell, his connection with Malachai had been through their respective auras—which gave Markhor a link to Malachai's sick mind.

But this was different. He had actually *seen* through Malachai's eyes. And what he saw terrified him.

Malachai had been numbed by the Particle and felt nothing. But Markhor was stabbed with pain so great he screamed for mercy. Along with the pain came the visions. The world in ruins. Hideous beasts adding to the carnage. And in the center of it all, Malachai, his skin shredded by his own hands.

Whatever was inside the Particle was now inside Malachai. It would slowly drive him mad . . . and it was going to take Markhor along for the ride.

Part of what a scientist does is to draw conclusions based on evidence and facts. Geologists explored the Himalaya Mountains and found fossils of sea creatures, which meant that those rock formations were once underwater. That water was an ocean named after the Greek goddess of fresh water, Tethys. Fossils from the Tethys Ocean were also found in other areas, such as the Solnhofen Limestone Formation in Bavaria, which was where the archaeopteryx—the feathered dinosaur—was discovered.

The Tethys was rich with life. Some of it swam; some of it eventually walked. One hundred million years is a long time for an ocean to be buried. A lot can happen in that time.

A lot *DID* happen in that time.

One would think that evolving in a dark environment would lead to certain physical features, like nonfunctioning eyes or no skin pigment. But perhaps—just perhaps—luminescent microorganisms were also trapped below the surface. It might not be sunlight, but it is nonetheless light. Which enabled creatures to see and grow and change into some of the strangest life-forms imaginable.

And perhaps some of these creatures had highly developed senses. Senses that could tell they were no longer held in check by the dominator element.

And just for the sake of argument, perhaps a highly intelligent species emerged—a biped that walked upright with wicked spines protruding from its vertebrae, with raptorlike claws and multiple rows of sharp, serrated teeth. One with the predatory instincts of a great white shark and the intelligence of a great ape.

It might also be worth mentioning that this creature carried germs never before seen by man and for which there was no cure. This was the creature that began its ascent toward sunlight and freedom. Soon others would follow.

And they were worse . . . oh, so much worse.

TWENTY-SEVEN

B lack clouds hung so low in the morning sky that Henry thought he might be able to touch them if he was able to jump high enough. Which wasn't about to happen, given the weight he now carried. He tightened the left strap on his fully loaded backpack and shrugged it higher up on his shoulders.

Henry had struggled to keep up with the others in Molly's exercise regimen. There were mornings when his leg muscles screamed at him, but he had learned how to stretch properly to relieve some of the tightness. And now all of his hard work was paying off.

Suddenly the wind shifted and the first heavy drop of rain smacked Henry in the nose. He hunched his shoulders and tilted his head skyward as three more drops hit their mark.

They began walking in single-file formation. For the first kilometer the rain held off. But any hope Henry had of a semi-dry hike dissipated when the intermittent drops increased in volume to a steady, soaking rain. And even though their coats kept their bodies dry, their legs, feet, and heads were exposed.

They continued, Coralis in the lead, Molly in the rear, until they were joined by a tall Hutsul man. His clothes were sufficiently drab as to blend into the surroundings. He wore no rain gear but the water didn't seem to faze him. The group pulled into a tight circle. Henry could sense the tension in the air as, one by one, they noticed the rifle slung over one shoulder and a powerful crossbow fastened to his back.

"Something has happened." The Hutsul addressed Coralis in a strained voice that spoke to the weapons he carried. "There has been strange activity where we are going."

"Define strange," Bryndis said sharply.

The Hutsul man narrowed his eyes, warning her silently to watch her tone. "You will soon see." He turned and strode quickly along a narrow path in the woods.

"You have a real knack for making friends," Molly chided.

Bryndis scowled. "Talking in riddles isn't going to help us be prepared."

"Dumitru is on our side," Coralis insisted. "Let's follow him now."

They continued at a brisk pace for over an hour, most of it at a gradual incline. Henry was somewhat relieved that he wasn't the only one struggling.

As the densely packed trees began to thin out, a hissing sound that had been a dull background noise increased in volume. Henry thought it had something to do with the rain and was surprised when they crested a small ridge and came face-to-face with a train. Wispy white steam rose from the top, sides, and rear, partially obscuring the black engine, which looked to Henry as if it had been transported from the Old West. A separate compartment was stacked full of wood. Two dark green passenger cars completed the short train.

The rain increased in intensity but Henry hardly noticed as he walked around the front of the engine. A plaque bolted to the steam stack read RESITA, and he wondered if that was the name for this model of train, or just a cute name the engineer had come up with. A grizzly man with a grease-smeared face stared down at him, looking very much like he did not want to be there.

Henry lowered his head and was walking back toward the others when he tripped over the tracks. They were nothing like tracks from the Southwest Chief he had ridden on his way to Monument Valley. These rails were set closer together and appeared rickety in comparison, as if they had been hastily assembled and not well maintained. Panic over riding on them must have shown on his face. The engineer laughed and pulled a cord, which blasted a high-shrieking steam whistle. Henry heard the others scream, just as startled as he was.

Dumitru ushered them onto one of the passenger cars. Plain, worn wooden benches were arranged in staggered rows, fastened in place with black metal poles that ran from floor to ceiling.

Henry was relieved to see Luis sitting next to Bryndis, and quickly took the space next to Serena. "I have a feeling this is going to be a bumpy ri—" His head snapped back as the train lurched forward. "Ow!" The train picked up speed, but compared with the Southwest Chief, it moved at a crawl.

Henry soon realized how dangerous it would have been to travel any faster. The train wobbled from side to side and negotiated tight turns that threatened to derail them.

Coralis sat toward the front of the car in deep conversation with Dumitru. When he finally glanced over his shoulder, he saw seven frightened faces gripping their seats in white-knuckled horror. He quickly whispered something to Dumitru, who stood and addressed them.

"This train is many years old, but is very reliable." None of the apprentices relaxed. "The locomotive was made by the Resita Company and it is almost indestructible." He smiled awkwardly. No one smiled back.

Brianna leaned forward and whispered to Henry. "He shouldn't smile. It's scary."

Dumitru realized his attempt to put them at ease was not going well and turned to Coralis for help. The train jolted to one side, causing Coralis to stumble forward. Katelyn and Brianna giggled, relieving some of the tension.

Coralis grasped his seat back firmly. "This train belongs to a narrow-gauge railway system that is part of the logging industry of Romania. While it might appear to be somewhat unstable, I have traveled on it many times and can assure you it is completely safe." The passenger car tipped dangerously to one side in response, forcing Coralis to sit while he continued.

"Our journey will keep us to the western edge of the Carpathian Mountains, and to the northern edge of the Transylvanian Alps as we travel westward. At times, we will travel along main rail lines, but for the most part we will stay to the secondary lines that run through the backcountry to avoid large areas of population. There is no point in announcing our presence until we have to. As you can see, the train does not go fast, and we have about four hundred kilometers to go. So sit back, relax, and enjoy the scenery. In one hour we shall review our strategy."

Coralis and Dumitru turned away and resumed their discussion. Luis was first to speak. "I spy rain," he said sarcastically.

Bryndis laughed. "I spy more rain."

"I spy mud." Katelyn giggled.

"I spy nothing," Serena said in a spooky voice as they entered a tunnel.

One by one they added to the game until Brianna frowned. "I spy a wolf . . . with glowing red eyes. Seriously. Check it out."

They crowded onto the left side of the train where the wolf sat on the outskirts of the tree line. It never flinched as the train rumbled past, and its unblinking glare clearly revealed the eyes were not only red, but glowing like warning lights on the dashboard of a car.

"Looks like a robot," Luis remarked. Then the engineer blasted the steam whistle, and the wolf snarled viciously and bolted into the woods. "I take it back. Not a robot."

But as the train rolled onward, they "spied" more oddities. A large black bird with teeth slammed into a window. A wild boar with claws attempted to climb a tree. The waving branches of trees seemed to reach for them. Something that looked like a cross between an armadillo and a mountain cat sprinted alongside them before curling into an armored ball and rolling out of sight.

Coralis joined them at the window. "As Dumitru said, strange happenings."

"What does it mean?" asked Henry.

"I don't know," Coralis replied. "According to Dumitru, they first appeared yesterday. We can only assume they have something to do with Malachai, but what it means is anyone's guess."

"Reminds me of *The Island of Dr. Moreau*." Katelyn shivered at the thought.

"Is that in Ireland?" Brianna asked.

"No." Katelyn smiled. "It's an old book about a mad scientist who created creatures that were part human and part animal."

Luis made a gagging sound. "Gross! If I see anything like that, I'm outta here."

Coralis rubbed his forehead in thought. "Only a few more hours to go. Let's review the plan."

As it turned out, "a few more hours" was a bit of an understatement. They crossed the Olt River and continued southward until the train suddenly ground to a halt. Coralis and Dumitru disembarked and entered into a lively and heated conversation with the engineer.

"What's bugging him?" Serena murmured.

The argument continued until Dumitru reached into a pouch and handed over some coins. As the train resumed its journey, Coralis could not ignore the expectant faces of the group. "No point in beating around the bush," he sighed. "Rumors about this area have spread rapidly, and our engineer felt he should be compensated for the risk."

Another of the toothed birds slammed into a window. Brianna yelped as it cracked but didn't shatter. The rain became a steady downpour. They were going over the plan for the umpteenth time when Henry felt something beneath the train—as if the wheels had slipped on the tracks. "Did you feel that?" he whispered to Serena. She shook her head no, but seconds later it happened again.

Suddenly the train began to slide sideways. "Mudslide!" Dumitru shouted. "Everyone—"

The train wrenched violently as the engine screamed with an outburst of steam. Dumitru took his rifle and smashed several windows. "Out!" he yelled. "You must jump!"

Bryndis did not need to be told twice. She saw the wide eyes of Luis backing away from the window, grabbed him by the front of his coat, and nearly heaved him out before leaping after him. Molly followed, yelling something like a battle cry before disappearing from sight. Coralis and Dumitru grabbed Serena and Brianna and pushed them through, but as they reached for Henry and Katelyn, the train swung wildly in one direction, snapping loose from the passenger cars and throwing the two men out the windows.

Henry did the only thing he could think of. He threw himself on top of Katelyn and wedged them beneath a wooden bench as the passenger cars crashed over the edge of a ravine . . . and disappeared from sight.

TWENTY-EIGHT

Henry raced through the forest, his feet pounding the sodden earth as underbrush whipped past him. At one point he looked down to discover he had lost his shoes. The mud soothed his feet but soon it thickened, and he found it harder and harder to lift them. Several steps later he was knee-deep in muck. The harder he pulled his feet the lower he sank.

Quicksand!

He panicked, waving his arms wildly in hopes of grabbing a branch overhead to pull himself out. A large white bird with a red streak on its head appeared and hovered over him. "Henry!" it yelled over and over.

"I'm trying!" he yelled back. The bird flew away but appeared moments later with a bucket of water in its talons—which it dumped on Henry's head. "Gaah!" he screamed as he awoke from the nightmare.

"Are you all right?" Katelyn sat beside him, a bleeding gash on her forehead. She cradled his head with one arm and raised the water bottle to his lips.

"I . . . I think so." He sat up and winced as he felt the sizable lump on his forehead. "You're bleeding."

She gave a short laugh. "At least we're alive, thanks to your quick thinking." She kissed him on the cheek. "I don't know what possessed you to do that, but thank you."

"Where are the others?" Henry's vision was foggy. He thought perhaps night had fallen, then realized they were in the midst of a dense fog. A brief wind swirled and cleared it enough to show a momentary glimpse of what was left of the passenger cars several meters away.

"I only woke up a few minutes ago. Then this fog rolled in. I haven't seen or heard anyone yet."

"We should go find them." He stood, and a wave of dizziness washed over him, plunking him back down.

"Stay still!" Katelyn commanded. "If they landed clear, they'll come looking for us."

He nodded, glad that she was taking charge. "You were a beautiful white bird."

"What?" She laughed.

Henry blushed. "When I was unconscious, I dreamed there was a white bird trying to help me. I guess it was you."

"Hmmm . . . let's hope you don't have a concussion."

"If I do, at least I'm in good hands." He thought back to when she had healed the cut on his hand. "How did we get out here?"

She shrugged. "I dragged you clear."

He squeezed her upper arm. "You're stronger than you

look." The fog thickened to the point that he could barely see her. "Katelyn, there's something weird about this fog."

"Aye. I noticed. It's not damp like a mist should be after a rain."

Something suddenly thrashed about in the undergrowth. "Here!" he yelled. "We're over—"

Katelyn clamped a hand over his mouth, her eyes wide.

Dread and fear formed a knot in Henry's stomach as the mist slowly coalesced into his worst nightmare. They stared into the face of madness.

"Welcome to my playground, children," said Malachai.

Henry's head throbbed to the beat of his heart. He tentatively opened one eye, then, not quite believing what he saw, closed it in an attempt to gather his wits. *Why am I behind bars?* The last thing he remembered was . . . His eyes flew open and he sat up too quickly, only to bang his head against the top of his cage. "Ow," he grunted.

"Henry?" Katelyn whispered urgently. "Are you okay?"

"Maybe." Henry squirmed into a semi-comfortable sitting position. "Where are we?"

"I'm not sure, but from what I can tell it's somewhat of a cross between a prison and a zoo."

"Technically, they're the same thing." A single dim bulb at the end of a row of cages flickered, threatening to cut off their only source of light. But perhaps not. Henry reached into his coat for his wand and summoned light. Nothing happened. He examined it for any signs of damage. "What happened to my power?"

Katelyn had been squatting against the front of her cage, directly across a two-meter-wide walkway. She sat back, tiny lines creasing her forehead. "Malachai said we'd have no power here, which is why he didn't bother to take our wands. Something about a nullification spell. Henry," she said worriedly, "I think he's gone totally bonkers in the head."

"Probably a side effect of being evil," he joked in a feeble attempt to allay her fears.

"I'm not kidding!" She scooted forward. "He's gone daft."

"There's a reason people are called mad scientists." But the panicky look in her eyes was impossible to ignore. He channeled his inner practical Bryndis. "Define daft."

"This place, for starters." She motioned to the cages. "Aside from us, this room is empty. But on the way here he took us through several rooms that were full of creatures, the likes of which I've never seen. Creatures like the ones we saw before the crash . . . and worse. Malachai is quite proud of them. He pointed out some of the work he's done. A gorilla with the legs and tail of a kangaroo. A zebra with tusks like a wild boar. And monkeys with wings! 'Tis like we've landed in Oz, Henry. It's just not right! What's he doing here and why?"

Henry wished he had his sister's gift of Voice to calm her down. He decided to employ a logical approach instead. "What was that book you mentioned about a Dr. Moreau?

He's just crossbreeding animals in some twisted way. Lots of scientists dabble in genetics, but it doesn't make them insane. When you come right down to it, they're still just animals."

"And what do you suppose he's going to do with them? Open a safari park?" she spat angrily. "You were unconscious. You didn't hear the way he talked . . . and laughed. Like this is all a big joke! He showed me his prize—his greatest achievement." She shuddered and winced at the memory. "He combined a cheetah with a Komodo dragon. Do you have any idea what that thing could do if he let it out?"

Henry knew exactly what it could do. "Tell me about the laugh."

Katelyn sensed she had gotten her point across and relaxed . . . or at least turned down her intensity. "You've seen movies about people in insane asylums?" He nodded. "Like that, but it wasn't an act. Coralis talked about him being clever and cunning in a diabolical way. But I'm telling you, Henry, he's a certifiable loon! He thinks he's a god and that nothing on Earth can stop him—his words, not mine."

"Okay, but . . ."

"Then there's his skin," she whispered, and shook her head as if trying to remove an image from her head. "He keeps scratching his face and arms, picking away scabs and opening new wounds, laughing all the while. I'm telling you he's not the same person Coralis described to us. Something very bad is happening. Can you imagine what a madman with his power could do?"

"Yes," Henry said, but his thoughts had drifted as she spoke. All he could think about was the link Malachai had to his father. He leaned back and buried his face in his hands.

Coralis surveyed the wreckage and wondered how they had made it out alive. Most of them. The engineer hadn't been so lucky, but at least his death was quick. Coralis covered him with a tarp and whispered a protective spell over him that would keep animals away until his body could be retrieved and properly buried.

While the mudslide had been enough to derail the train, it did not cover a wide area. Only Luis and Bryndis, being the first to leap, had caught the edge of the slide. But their Wandmaker coats had kept them safe and relatively mud free—although from the knees on down they were encased in reddish-brown muck.

Considering the severity of the accident and what could have happened, the rest of the group was fortunate to come through with only minor scratches to their face and hands. It was Dumitru's quick thinking that had saved them from worse harm. And so it was somewhat ironic that his wound was the worst of the lot—an ugly gash that bisected an enormous purple bruise on his forehead, the result of making hard contact with the window frame.

The rain had slackened off to a drizzle by the time Coralis approached his anxious apprentices.

"Where are Henry and Katelyn?" Serena demanded. She had attempted to mind-link with Henry. Usually the link would either be clear or totally blank. This time she received a strange static, as if something was interfering with her signal.

"The passenger cars are at the bottom of that ravine." Coralis pointed to a path of destruction, where trees and shrubs had been savagely ripped away. "But I can tell you with certainty that Henry and Katelyn are not there."

"What do you mean not there?" Bryndis scowled. "We should be helping them."

"Trust me. I would know if they were there and they are not," Coralis said with finality. "But you are correct. We need to find them. Is everyone up to the task?"

Brianna, Serena, Bryndis, Luis, and Molly grabbed their packs. Dumitru tried to stand and slid back down against a tree trunk. "I am sorry, my friend," Coralis said as he examined Dumitru's head. "You may have a concussion. Unfortunately . . ."

Dumitru waved him off. "Go. I will be fine." He patted the rifle that lay across his lap.

Coralis led the apprentices farther down the tracks until he located a rocky path that allowed sure footing into the ravine. The two cars had separated during their downward plunge. Despite the destruction they caused as they pummeled through the trees, they remained relatively intact, lying on their sides about two hundred meters apart. As they approached the crash site, Serena and Brianna ran ahead. "Henry! Katelyn!" they shouted.

Using the undercarriage as a ladder, Serena climbed into the lead car, Brianna right behind her. "Be careful," Serena grunted as she balanced herself on the side of a wooden seat. Working their way down the length of the tipped-over car, using the seat poles for support, they eventually found a bloody smear on a windowsill.

"Looks like they might have climbed out here." Serena tried to keep the worry out of her voice as she examined the handprint. Brianna growled as she pulled herself up toward Serena. "They're not here, so they're obviously well enough to move." She wrapped an arm around Brianna in a comforting hug. "They probably just got disoriented after the crash."

She grabbed a window frame and hoisted herself up, looking down at the others, who were combing the area for clues. "There's only a small amount of blood in here. Any signs of where they might have gone?"

"Over here!" Molly shouted. Bryndis was closest. She jogged over and quickly examined the ground, going immediately into tracking mode. Molly pointed at a small sapling. "There's some blood on these leaves."

"And three distinct sets of footprints," Bryndis noted with concern. She asked everyone to stand back so she could get a clear picture of what happened. She walked in a wide arc, occasionally squatting to examine leaves and mud in closer detail. "These smaller footprints are Katelyn's. Here is where she lowered Henry from the train and dragged him to here." She returned to the location Molly had identified. "At some point they sat here." She pointed to two impressions in the soil. "But a third person approached from that direction— much larger footprints—probably over two meters tall. And strong. His tracks leading away from here leave deeper impressions. He was carrying something—or someone. Probably Henry. Katelyn's prints are clear. But . . ." Her brow furrowed. "There is no sign of a struggle, which means they knew the person."

"Or maybe they didn't think he was a threat," said Luis.

"Or they knew there was no point in fighting him," Molly said gravely.

Coralis had remained silent, his eyes tracing the footprint trail into the forest. He reached into his coat for a wand and blew a gentle breath over it as he extended it toward one of the large footprints. Immediately, a glow of black and deep crimson surrounded the print. "Malachai," he said with contempt. "His aura lingers and he took no measures to conceal it."

"So he knows we're here?" Serena asked.

"Worse. He knew we were coming." Coralis walked hastily back to the body of the dead engineer. He removed the protection spell and, employing a similar procedure, found traces of Malachai's aura. "Bahtzen bizzle," he grumbled softly.

He returned to the others to deliver the bad news, but did not reinstate the protection spell. The engineer was a large man. The animals would feed well.

Coralis instructed Bryndis and Serena, his best trackers, to lead the search. He could have easily traced Malachai's aura, but use of his wand could aid Malachai in tracing them as well. Instead, he covered them with a low-level concealment spell that he drew directly from the Earth.

They had traveled for almost an hour when they abruptly came upon a well-worn hiking path that led upward toward a mountain peak. Instead of using the path, Bryndis and Serena split the group in two and led them along either side, looking for footprints that might have split off into the forest. Minutes later, Bryndis slowed to a crawl. "Something isn't right."

Coralis told them to stop as he cautiously walked ahead of them. The gravel path continued up the slope and curved around the mountain, but he didn't follow it. Instead, he closed his eyes and concentrated on extending his senses outward. He had only begun to probe when a wave of powerful energy pushed back at him, knocking him to the ground.

"Coralis!" Molly rushed forward.

"Stop!" he yelled. The command forced her to skid to a clumsy halt. He brushed himself off angrily and turned around, walking briskly past the group and waving a hand for them to follow. He pushed through the undergrowth until he arrived at a clearing. "We need rocks. This size." He held one up that filled his palm. "Find as many as you can."

The apprentices quickly spread out to do as he instructed while Molly held back. "Coralis," she said nervously. "If you're doing what I think you're doing, you're going to give away our position."

Coralis's lips tightened into a thin line. "You saw what just happened. He already knows where we are," he said grimly.

One by one the apprentices returned, their arms loaded with rocks. Coralis arranged them in a circle and took out his Revealer Wand. He chanted a spell and a transparent dome appeared, enclosing the rocks. "Bah!" Coralis released the spell.

"What?" Luis asked. "Why did you stop?"

"Malachai's containment dome shows no sign of weakness," Molly explained.

"He's good. But let's see how good," Coralis said eagerly. He began to dig a trench around the exterior of the rocks and the rest dove in to help. Once they had finished digging, he tried the spell again. This time he placed a palm over the invisible dome and pressed downward. The dome pushed back at him but he fought back, exerting greater pressure until a puff of air escaped through a mouse-sized hole in the trench. Coralis released the spell and smiled. "We found our way in."

TWENTY-NINE

A high-pitched giggle interrupted Henry's nightmare. The mad cackles had come with increasing frequency, occasionally accompanied by the tormented screeching of an animal.

Katelyn sat up and rubbed her tired eyes. "You'd think he'd take a break."

Henry focused on making a mind-link with Coralis, but once again his head filled with static. "We can't just sit here," he grumped.

"No, we can't." Katelyn squirmed uncomfortably. "I have something to tell you, but you have to promise you won't be mad."

Henry squinted suspiciously. "What?"

"Promise."

Henry looked around at the bars of their prison, then back at Katelyn, who stared at him with grim determination. "Okay, I promise."

"I found something in a book at the castle. A spell."

"Will it help us escape?" he asked eagerly.

"Nay, but it might help the others find us." She leaned forward. "You know how you and Serena can do that thing where you talk to each other's minds? Well, I tried and tried to do that with Brianna, but we don't have that kind of power. So instead we tried . . . a spell."

"A what?" he exploded. "You experimented on my sister?"

"You promised," she said sternly. As he slumped back, pouting, she pulled out a small twig, stripped of its outer bark and finely polished. She held it out so he could see the tiny filaments tied around the base.

"Is that hair?" he asked.

"Aye. 'Tis Brianna's. And she has one similar with my hair. It's an Imprint Wand. It allows us to find each other. It started as a game, but as we became closer, it took on more meaning. And as our friendship grew, so did the wand's power. Over time it allowed us to sense each other's feelings." She paused for his reaction but was greeted with a puzzled expression. "Feelings. Like besties. Maybe even more than besties . . ." She paused and waited for a reaction.

Henry shrugged. Whatever she was hinting at rolled right on past him. "And?"

"For a bright lad, sometimes you can be thick as a brick." Katelyn frowned. "After Malachai found us, he carried you as I walked. Then he blindfolded me and took my hand to lead me." She shivered recalling his evil touch. "It was like holding an ice cube. Shortly after, I felt a change in the air pressure, and sound seemed to echo. I sensed we were in a tunnel of some kind and used this wand. Tapped it against the wall as discreetly as I could. It wasn't much, but maybe just enough to help them find us."

"Or lead them into a trap," Henry snapped.

"Aye, I hadn't considered that at the time, which is why I made you promise."

"That still doesn't help us . . ." Henry heard a door latch turning. He quickly motioned to Katelyn to sit back and be quiet. The door at the end of the hall opened. A small woman dressed in rags shuffled slowly forward and placed wooden bowls of mush through the bars of their cages. Her hands and arms were covered with cuts and scratches. Henry gasped as he recognized teeth marks.

"The master said it was time to feed the animals." Her voice cracked and her lower lip trembled. She turned to leave.

"Wait!" Henry lunged and knocked into the bowl, which clattered to the floor. But the woman left and closed the door behind her. "Come back!" he yelled. He slid back against the bars, aware that any help for escape had just walked away, when his eyes rested on the slop that had spilled from the bowl.

"Henry!" Katelyn pointed urgently at something in the mush. "Is that a key?"

"Yes." He grunted and strained before collapsing in despair. It was just out of reach.

Malachai placed the lead box on a shelf inside his workroom. The more he held it, the more he needed it. He craved the power the Particle provided. Physical separation caused a degree of discomfort that grew as his distance from it increased.

But direct contact with the Particle also amplified the side effects. One side of his face oozed thick white puss from open sores. Twice more, the Particle had injected Malachai with its foreign substance. Only his incredible Wand Master power kept him from collapsing.

Only one person stood in his way—Coralis.

Malachai giggled. Coralis was on his way, and thanks to a series of sensor spells—and a cleverly crafted weakness in the protective dome—Malachai knew exactly where the old man was. He reveled in delight at the invincibility the Particle had given him, peeling a crumbling piece of skin from his arm and flicking it to the side. He looked at it with a detached sense of curiosity. It occurred to him that if he were not encumbered by physical limitations, he could operate on a far more powerful spiritual plane. Losing his skin was bringing him that much closer.

He peeled off three more strips and formed an M with them on the table. Another giggle erupted, but this time he unleashed it into an uncontrollable, maniacal laugh.

He was still laughing as he turned to leave—to spring his trap on Coralis. He turned the lights off and closed the door. On the table, the M of skin emitted an eerie glow. The top of the lead box moved the tiniest sliver of a millimeter—just enough for a thin tendril to snake its way out and attach to the skin, absorbing it until there was nothing left but a greasy stain.

Leading the apprentices westward toward the break in the spell, Coralis was lost in thought. His main concern was developing a plan that would allow them to capture Malachai with no loss of life within his own ranks. The evil Wand Master had defeated so many of their own kind over the centuries that Coralis had almost allowed himself to think that perhaps they were acceptable losses—casualties of war. But a loss among his apprentices now would be unacceptable.

Malachai's greatest fault had always been his arrogance. He truly believed he could never be defeated. Yet his hubris made him careless. Finding the hole in his spell was just the bit of luck Coralis needed to give him the advantage of surprise.

He glanced back over his shoulder at the single-file line of apprentices . . . and Molly. He had called for her to help stabilize the individuals into a cohesive group, never expecting that she would also supply much-needed firepower in their battle. Another piece of luck.

He casually and purposely broke another branch of a low-hanging shrub, just as he had done several times since leaving the crash site. If he was correct, Dumitru would summon help and they would need a trail to follow. For all they knew, there could be Scorax soldiers within the protective dome, and he would need the Hutsul then.

He flexed his senses and located the breach in the dome two hundred meters ahead. Had it not been for his abilities, he would have walked right past the well-concealed cave entrance. He directed Luis and Bryndis to pull on two very large limbs, creating a hole big enough for him to enter and check for safe passage.

Brianna had edged alongside him. "Katelyn!" she gasped, and shot past Coralis into the tunnel.

"Wait!" Coralis yelled, and barreled after her. As soon as he stepped through, the dome slammed down behind him like an invisible wall. The force of the spell blew outward, sending Luis and Bryndis flying in opposite directions and tossing Serena and Molly to the ground.

Coralis and Brianna skidded to a halt and stared helplessly at the transparent wall . . . as an unearthly laugh echoed down the tunnel.

"Hello, old friend."

L eonardo da Vinci's legs kicked restlessly in his sleep, another night disturbed by the recurring nightmare. The thoughts of prisoners wasting away in their cells that haunted him in the daytime were compounded at night. But helping them was beyond his control. On nights like this he wished he had taken Coralis up on his offer to learn the craft of a Wandmaker.

Leonardo preferred the certainties of science over what he perceived to be the sorcery and wizardry of the Wand Masters. Using the time slip portal that the tranquillityite provided was as far as he would allow himself to step into their world. His destiny was to assist man through advancement in science.

But on this night, the nightmare was different. There was another presence—something guiding him. He could see it . . . no, not an it . . . a man. A very young man. He concentrated within his dream, trying to bring the young man into focus. There was an ethereal quality about him. Suddenly, Leonardo knew he was in the presence of a spirit. A soft, glowing mist that was more than a ghostly apparition. This was the essence—the life-force of the young man.

Within the dream, Leonardo followed him through the castle courtyard and into the dungeon. He had not stepped foot into this part of the castle since Malachai had transformed a section of it into a place of unspeakable horror.

The stench of rot assaulted his senses. He stood at the entrance of Malachai's personal dungeon. The young man waved a cloudlike hand and the entrance began to glow.

A spell!

The words appeared in his mind. He cursed. This was the sorcery he sought to avoid. It was an abomination of the natural order of the world. The young man waved his hand again and something else appeared—a network of crisscrossed lines as wide and tall as the tunnel. It reminded him of a fishing net.

Spread equidistant around the perimeter of the net were rocks. Leonardo looked closer. These were not the river rocks a fisherman would use to anchor his net. These were unique. He had seen them before—in a cave.

The young man sent a thought wave that confirmed Leonardo's suspicions. These were rocks of tranquillityite, and this net would break through the spell. But why would he do that? What purpose would it serve to bring the wrath of Malachai down upon himself?

The dream shifted violently. Leonardo was no longer himself but the spirit of someone looking down upon another Leonardo. He gasped, realizing he was wrapped within the life-force of the young man. Together they looked down upon the real Leonardo, who was seated at a table. Spread out before

him were tubular roots that had a distinctively human quality
to them.

The real Leonardo sliced precise sections of the root in
measured quantities while the ethereal Leonardo commit-
ted the science to memory. The process fascinated him, as
he had never thought to prepare the root in this manner. He
had witnessed the effects of the deadly mandrake root in
the past, and yet there was something about this new process
that would make it less lethal. In fact . . .

A terrifying shriek jolted him out of his dream. His arms
and legs flailed in alarm as he thought he was under attack.
His eyes searched wildly for signs of an assailant and came to
an abrupt stop on the falcon that was perched at the foot of
his bed.

He slowly sat up, never taking his eyes off the bird, which
stared back at him with the intensity of a predator eyeing its
next meal. "You are indeed a most curious creature."

Leonardo rubbed his eyes. After all . . . it must have been
the lingering effects of sleep that made it look as though the
falcon winked at him.

Coralis blinked away the remnants of the fog that penetrated
his mind. He tried to rub some life back into his face and
immediately discovered his hands were bound behind him.
He shook his head, much like a dog would shake the water
from its fur, and took stock of his predicament.

The chair to which his arms, legs, and torso were firmly

tied sat in the center of a room of indeterminate size. A dull
bulb swaying on the end of a cord in a far corner provided
the only illumination.

Swaying?

Coralis tensed and attempted to flex his senses. He grunted
in pain as an intense pressure pushed against his chest. As
he withdrew his probing, the pressure subsided. The bulb began
to swing in a greater arc, like a pendulum gathering momentum. Coralis peered into the gloomy darkness and caught
the briefest outline of a shadow.

"My old friend." The voice rasped as if the words were
being dragged over a rocky bed of sharp stones.

"Malachai." Coralis cautiously extended his senses and
was rewarded with another blast of compressed air. It was as
if the molecules in the room were reacting angrily to his
efforts. Coarse laughter mocked him from the shadows. "Old
friend, indeed." Coralis concentrated on the rope around his
hands. He silently mouthed the words to an unbinding spell
and gasped as the rope grew intensely hot.

"Tsk, tsk, tsk," Malachai admonished him. "First you walk
directly into a trap—one, if I may say so, that wasn't even
well concealed. Then you blunder about with your pathetic
attempt to escape as if I would have forgotten to set up
countermeasures. You taught me this spell. Don't you remember? The first time you tried to defeat me."

Coralis sat still as stone, willing the pain from his hands.
Malachai had employed a reversal spell—a powerful one.
Every use of his power would be exponentially reversed

against him. Coralis expelled a deep breath to relax, conceding defeat for the moment. "What have you done?"

More laughter grated from the shadows. "It's not what I've done. It's what you haven't done. You gave up, old man. You forsook your charge to protect the world and crawled into a shell of self-pity. And in doing so, you gave me an opening—an opportunity." He laughed again, so hard that it ended in a wet cough. "Now look what you've made me do. Coughing up blood is a bad sign, is it not?"

"You're sick, Malachai. End this nonsense and I will help you."

The bulb shattered. Bits of glass embedded into Coralis's face.

"*YOU* will help *ME*?" Malachai exploded. "Look around you! Do you seriously think I need your help? For years I have shielded this village right under your nose. I have collected knowledge far beyond anything you could ever hope to learn. I have amassed an army of followers who await my command. And now . . . I possess the ultimate weapon."

"You stole from the Earth Mother," Coralis spat.

"She gave me the knowledge to find it," Malachai said smugly. "She recognized in me what she could never find in you. A champion of the Earth."

"A destroyer!" Coralis shouted.

"Calm down before you have a heart attack." Malachai pinched his thumb and forefinger together. Coralis gasped from the pain that squeezed his chest. "You have nothing left, old man. I will keep you bound here forever, rotting away like those wretched souls in Milan."

"You will never win," Coralis grunted.

"Oh? And who will stop me? Those children you call apprentices? Three of them are locked away in my dungeon for safekeeping and the rest are . . . occupied." Another wet cough erupted.

"What has happened to you?" Coralis knew that reasoning with him was futile, but he had to try. "You know the limits to power and yet you seek to control that which cannot be controlled. All that makes us human forces upon us a natural boundary that cannot be exceeded. If you continue, you will collapse under the weight of—"Another blast of pressure slammed into Coralis, forcing the air from his lungs.

"Oh, shut up already." Malachai squeezed until Coralis felt himself slipping into unconsciousness. Then he stepped forward and slapped Coralis across the face. "Stay with me, old man. I need you to witness the end of your old world and the fresh beginning of my new one."

Coralis gasped as he saw the shredded mess of Malachai's face. It glowed softly, outlined in a green haze.

"Ah. You see it now." Malachai stepped back. "Soon I will leave the confines of this body and become an ethereal force that cannot be stopped. I will bring to an end the mess that humanity has created and reboot the world with new life. *That* is the reason the Earth Mother has given me her gift."

"No, you are wrong," Coralis growled angrily. "By removing the Pangaea Particle, you are unleashing unspeakable horror that no one can control. The Earth Mother trusted you with a secret that was never meant to be exploited. Stop now and I will help you restore balance." *And your face.*

Malachai read his last thought and leaned in close. "What about my face? Don't you like the inner me?" He peeled a strip of skin from his forehead, examined it quizzically, and flicked it onto the floor.

Coralis stared back, masking the revulsion he felt rising to his throat. "You are mad."

"Crazy? Insane?" Malachai's fetid breath washed over Coralis. "No. But I am angry—so, in a sense, I guess I am mad. In any case, I've had enough of your preaching. Soon I will have control of all your fledging apprentices and I will bend their power to obey my will." Malachai began walking away, then stopped. "But I guess I should thank you for bringing them to me."

The door latch clicked with finality, leaving Coralis alone with only his thoughts.

Of how he had failed.

THIRTY-ONE

Molly, Bryndis, Serena, and Luis were cornered. No sooner had Coralis and Brianna disappeared than the battle had begun. A nest of two-headed snakes erupted from beneath a mound of rocks. Dozens of them squirmed their way out and made a beeline for the group, hissing angrily.

Shock quickly morphed into action as Molly shouted at the others to run. They had not gotten far when the first of the scorpions dropped from the trees. Serena dodged left, barely avoiding being stung by its twin tails, which dripped with deadly venom. It was the size of a healthy crow. Its carapace glistened like polished ebony.

Luis grabbed a sturdy stick from the ground and wielded it like a baseball bat. He swung with uncanny accuracy, batting several more scorpions into the forest before the stick shattered in half. As more fell from the canopy, he was momentarily paralyzed by the same fear that had gripped him when the giant centipedes descended upon the bats near his village.

Bryndis locked a fist onto the collar of his coat and roughly pushed him forward. "Keep moving!"

Molly scanned the trees for an escape route and shouted for them to follow. Hacking furiously through the undergrowth, she failed to see the cliff before her. Only Serena's quick hands kept her from tumbling hundreds of meters down the sheer mountain wall.

They turned to face the advancing horde of reptiles and arachnids. Luis was the first to act. He rammed his wand into the rocky ground. Leafy, ropelike vines whipped free from their moorings on the trees and attacked the snakes. They wrapped tightly around the writhing bodies while the snakes snapped helplessly—their venom having no effect.

Sensing the danger, the scorpions stopped their advance, but instead of retreating, they clicked their tails together.

"Now what?" Molly attempted to shield the apprentices behind her.

"Listen." Serena tilted her head.

Luis also heard it. "What is that? It sounds like a bunch of people stepping on crackers."

"I don't like it." Bryndis edged closer to the cliff to search for a way out.

"Look!" Serena shouted as she pointed at a wall of humongous spiders rappelling out of the trees like an arachnid SWAT team. "What is it with this guy and his menagerie of mutants?"

Molly took a step forward and stopped as one of the spiders raced toward her and reared up on its hind legs, warning her to stop. "It can't be . . ."

"It can't be what?" Luis asked. He held steady, focusing on the vines that were becoming outnumbered by more and more snakes.

"I have several specimens of these back home, but they're usually only about five centimeters long. These are easily five times that. They're Australian funnel-web spiders—some say the most venomous spider in the world."

"Is there anything in Australia that isn't venomous?" Bryndis asked bitterly.

"Not much," Molly answered. "But if being five times the size means they are five times as deadly, we're in some serious trouble."

"Like we weren't in trouble already?" Luis's face glistened with sweat from the strain of maintaining his concentration.

"What in the world?" Molly stepped back in amazement as the spiders quickly scurried into the trees and back down, time and again, releasing thread after thread of coarse webbing. Their graceful movements looked like a choreographed dance and would have been awesome if they weren't so frightening.

An intricate web rapidly formed and hemmed them in. The apprentices looked apprehensively at one another as they realized there were only moments left before the web would be complete and they would be at the mercy of an army of snakes, spiders, and scorpions.

Serena concentrated as she raised her wand and commanded the air molecules into action. What began as a light wind grew in intensity. She held the wind back until it crackled with energy, then released it at the forest.

The first line of arachnids blew backward, a number of them caught in their own webbing. But the rest quickly flattened themselves against the ground. The cyclonic force blew harmlessly over them and through the webbing, doing very little to tear it apart.

Bryndis stood closest to the cliff. As the wind died down she heard another sound and looked over the edge. Another battalion of eight-legged freaks scrambled up the rocky cliff. She growled loudly.

"What now?" Luis yelped. "Flying sharks?"

Molly hurried over to Bryndis. "Oh, for the love of Pete. Does anyone know how to fly?"

Bryndis's head snapped up. A wicked grin crossed her face. "Get your wind ready," she said to Serena. She closed her eyes and lifted her arms up. A low rumble gathered in her throat like an advancing freight train. She opened her eyes and released an enormous squawk, which she followed up with several more in rapid succession—the war cry of an angry bird of prey.

Molly watched as the spiders stopped their advance. They reared back in a defensive posture, long fangs fully exposed and ready to take on the threat.

Bryndis grinned wider. "Luis, get over here!" she yelled, bringing the group together. The spiders lowered their front legs to the ground and resumed their ascent. Bryndis shrieked her war cry again, but the spiders kept coming.

Luis glanced back at the tree line, where spiders and scorpions moved toward them like a black army of death. Snakes began to wriggle free of their bindings. "Um, it's not working." His voice shook worriedly.

"Ha!" Bryndis laughed and pointed skyward as a flock of eagles zoomed in with incredible speed. "Follow my lead." She pulled her Wandmaker coat over her head and raised her arms parallel to the ground. "Get ready, Serena." The eagles descended, four to a person. They landed, one on each arm and one on either side of their necks. Bryndis felt the iron grip of their talons as they dug in but could not penetrate the unique material of the coat. As they spread their wings, she said, "Okay, give us a lift."

Serena smiled and focused on the air beneath them. They began to rise. Too slowly. The dark army sensed their prey was about to escape and rushed madly forward. "I need more open space beneath us to create a big enough updraft," she said as she lowered them to the ground.

"No problem." Bryndis laughed. "Run!"

"Wait . . . what?" Luis shouted. He hesitated for just a brief moment, realized he could die either way, and followed his friends as they leapt off the cliff.

Serena grunted with effort as they began to drop past the cliff spiders, which whirled about in confusion. Several leaned so far back they lost their grip and tumbled down the mountain.

With a final push, Serena regained control of the wind. The eagles flapped furiously, sliding into the wind current.

The group began to rise, cleared the cliff, and soared higher into the sky.

"We're flying!" Molly shouted triumphantly. "You did it!" She laughed out loud while Serena and Bryndis joined in. They looked at Luis, whose face was drained of color, which made them laugh even louder.

"N-n-n-ot fu-fu-funny," he stammered.

As they glided over the forest they glanced back at the cliff. The creatures had lost their prey but not their bloodlust. Angrily, they turned on one another and engaged in a vicious battle. The laughter faded as reality set in. They had escaped with their lives . . . barely.

But they were in full retreat.

"Let me get this straight." Henry fidgeted uncomfortably in his cramped cage. "Coralis led you into a trap?"

Brianna shrugged. "Not intentionally. He found the only way into this place and took us to it. But getting captured was my own fault. I sensed Katelyn's trail and ran past him before he could stop me."

"Aye, if anyone is to blame, 'tis me," Katelyn said, sulking.

"That's just crazy talk," Brianna said flatly. "We would have found you sooner or later, and now there's three of us to come up with an escape plan."

Henry pointed at the key that was out of reach. "There's our escape plan, for all the good it's doing us." He remembered the smelly man who had delivered Brianna and how he had smiled when he saw the key, nudging it farther out of reach with his foot.

"You said Malachai somehow blocked your wand power?" Brianna squirmed and pressed tightly against the cage, stretching her fingertips as far as she could to reach for the key, when she suddenly stopped. "Well, that's weird."

"That's not weird," Henry said sarcastically. "You can't just make your arm grow."

"No, not that . . . Listen." Brianna tilted her head. "I wonder . . ." She closed her eyes to concentrate on some faint sound only she could hear. A few seconds later, a tiny mouse squirmed its flattened body under the door and sat up, looking quizzically around the room.

"Did you just call that mouse?" Katelyn leaned forward, obviously impressed.

Brianna and the mouse stared at each other. "Maybe my link with animals is not a power. Maybe it's more of an ability. Gretchen told me something like that. She said I could speak Mouse the way others can speak German or French. That means Malachai can't stop it."

"Great news." Henry slumped back. "It should only take a year or so for that little guy to chew through these bars."

Katelyn rolled her eyes. "I don't think that's what she has in mind."

Brianna smiled as she connected with the mouse. It walked cautiously past the empty cages, stopping every meter or so to sniff the air, its tiny whiskers twitching nervously.

"What are you doing?" At the sound of Henry's voice, the mouse immediately scampered for cover.

Katelyn shushed him.

Brianna frowned at her brother and called to the mouse again. Gradually it approached the key and clamped its teeth down on the ring. It dragged the key toward Brianna, but she still couldn't reach to the floor. And the mouse could not climb the bars with the key in its mouth. Brianna growled in frustration as the mouse dropped the key and ran off. She looked toward Katelyn, who nodded encouragement at her.

Brianna squinted as she searched for another voice. Her eyes lit up when she found what she was looking for. Another nose poked out from under the door. Little by little the large body of a rat appeared, easily five times the size of the mouse.

"I knew rats could squeeze through tight openings, but that's impressive," Henry said with admiration. The rat was pure white with pink eyes. "Probably an escaped lab rat."

"Good guess," said Brianna. "And she's not happy to be around humans again." The rat chattered angrily in response. Brianna sent reassuring thoughts to the rodent. Several long minutes later the key was within reach, but the rat would not let it go. Locked in a staring contest, Brianna didn't realize what the rat was up to until it suddenly released the key and nipped her on the finger.

"Ouch! Why you little . . ." The rat ran halfway to the door, stopped to deposit a fair-sized puddle of pee, then squeezed its way back to freedom.

Henry and Katelyn burst out in laughter. "I'd call that an unwilling accomplice." Katelyn giggled.

Brianna wiped a tiny speck of blood against her coat and called to the rat again. A pink nose appeared under the door. "Thank you," she said aloud. And the nose popped back out of sight.

The three apprentices pressed their ears to the door. "Do you think your mouse friend can act as a scout for us?" Katelyn whispered.

"Already on it." Brianna smiled. "He says . . . He says the food is this way." She opened the door a crack and peeked out. "Which apparently means the coast is clear."

They exited into a dimly lit hallway and tiptoed past three more doors, each one secured with heavy padlocks. The hall ended and branched at a 90-degree angle to the left. Henry stopped and turned to look back down the hall. "Something's not right. Why wasn't our door locked like the others?"

"Maybe Malachai didn't think we could escape," Katelyn said. But something in her voice told Henry she wasn't convinced.

"Or maybe he's leading us into another trap," Brianna said warily.

Henry extended his senses and focused on the nearest door. Something flickered in his vision. He walked up to the door and grabbed the padlock, but his hand passed right through it.

"An illusion?" Katelyn asked.

"Which means he's not trying to keep something in. He's trying to keep someone out," Henry reasoned. "What's he hiding?" He turned the doorknob.

"Not a good idea," Brianna warned.

"Maybe not," said Katelyn. "But I'm with Henry. We need to know what's going on here."

Henry cautiously opened the door and immediately closed it as a foul stench poured outward like a wave. "Auggh!" He covered his nose quickly as the girls gagged.

"Smells like sewage." Katelyn spat on the floor as if that would remove the smell.

Not sewage, Henry thought. He opened the drawers in his mind. He recalled all the lessons with Coralis when he had to compartmentalize scents. There was something familiar about the stench, but it was too potent to identify. He recalled how Coralis had taught him to break a mixture of scents into separate components. He opened the door by a sliver for another sniff and he nailed it. "Bird droppings," he said confidently.

"*That* is coming from bird poo?" Brianna still covered her nose. "I don't believe it."

"Well, usually bird droppings don't have an odor, but they do if the birds are sick and . . ." Henry stopped when he noticed the stop-right-there-nerd-boy look on their faces. He shrugged, pinched his nose, held his breath, and went inside. It was like a battle scene from a war movie. He lasted only half a minute before his eyes began to burn, but that was all he needed. He closed the door firmly behind him and sucked in a lungful of clean air.

"What is it?" Brianna asked.

"From the description Bryndis gave us, I'd say they are Valravens. Hundreds of them—and half of them dead." Henry shuddered. "I think they've been abandoned in there for a long time. They're feeding off one another."

"That's just sick." Katelyn wrinkled her nose in disgust.

"And twisted," Brianna added. "Let's get out of here."

Henry had no desire to see what was behind the other doors and led them quickly down hall after hall. It was like a maze, except there were no choices—just one long path that had them turning one corner after another. Until they ended up right where they'd started.

Henry bit his lower lip, mad at himself for not paying better attention to his surroundings. It should have been obvious, but he hadn't stopped to think. There were several turns where he'd totally ignored something that had tugged at his senses. "More illusions," he grumbled. "Follow me."

Four turns later he "felt" the hidden hallway. *Learn from your mistakes,* Coralis's voice said from his subconscious. Henry cautiously passed a hand through the illusory wall and hissed in pain, immediately retracting it. In that brief second his fingertips had turned blue and burned as if they had been encased in ice. He rubbed them vigorously and continued to the next hidden intersection. "Anyone else care to try?" he asked hopefully.

But they didn't have to, as the rat strolled through the illusion, casually carrying a piece of cheese. Startled to see the humans, it chattered angrily and fled back through the false wall.

Katelyn's stomach grumbled. "Sorry, but that cheese looked good."

As they passed through the illusion, Brianna said, "Did you feel that?"

"Aye, like spiderwebs," Katelyn answered, wiping her face at something that wasn't there.

"Wait." Henry raised a hand to stop them. "Illusions have no physical properties."

"You sound like you're quoting a line from a textbook," Brianna chided.

"That's because I did." Henry ignored her as he attempted to decipher the purpose behind the illusion. He visualized the page of text from memory. There! A handwritten note in the margin. "Oh crap!" He quickly scanned the hall ahead of them. "C'mon, let's get out of here!"

"What's happening?" Katelyn asked as they broke into a jog.

"Trip wires," Henry answered. "The illusion was laced with a spell that acts as a trip wire. Which means Malachai will know we've escaped."

"But the rat . . . ," Brianna started.

"Was too small," Henry finished. Then he stopped jogging so suddenly the girls ran right into him. "Shhh!" he whispered as they began to argue. He ran his hand against a wall until it brushed against an invisible knob. As he grabbed it, a door materialized. "Brianna, can you send your mouse inside?"

She examined the frame. "No, this one's airtight." Henry began to turn the knob. "Are you sure we have time for this?"

A loud sound screeched in his mind. It startled him until he realized it wasn't a warning. It was a cry for help. "Something in there needs us." He twisted the knob and walked inside.

THIRTY-TWO

Bryndis picked up a rock and threw it at a nearby tree with enough force that it broke off a chunk of bark. "We can't just sit here doing nothing."

The eagles had deposited them on a hilltop overlooking the area where the dome should have been. The spell was so powerful that whatever was hidden beneath it looked like nothing but an expanse of forest.

Night had fallen. A spectacular sunset was lost on them—each trapped in their thoughts about what to do next. Molly understood Bryndis's frustration but knew better than the apprentices what they were up against. A chill in the air reminded her of their first priority—survival. She asked Serena and Luis to gather wood for a fire.

Serena expected him to make some kind of flirty remark or facial expression. Instead, he simply followed instructions and walked into the woods. She smiled. *So he does it to irritate Henry after all.* She caught a glimpse of Bryndis giving her the stink-eye as if to say *hands off.* Serena held her hands up in mock surrender and walked the opposite way as her smile broadened.

Alone with Bryndis, Molly asked, "How did you do that . . . call the eagles?"

Bryndis frowned. "It's just something I can do."

"Just with eagles?" Molly prodded. Bryndis answered with a scowl. Molly was still pondering how to get the girl to open up when she finally spoke.

"My father called me . . . a mimic." She spat the word like a curse. "I was very young when I first tried it. Our village was starving but the seals could not be caught. I listened to their sounds and imitated them. The seals came to me and the village was fed." A pained look crossed her face. "But my father forbade me from doing it again. He made me promise. If others found out they would brand me a . . . witch." She wrinkled her nose. "I am not a witch. I am guided by the spirits of many animals. Later, I broke my promise, but secretly. I called my animals and they answered me."

"Like Brianna does?" Molly asked.

"Perhaps." A sly grin tugged at her lips. "But mine takes talent."

Molly stood and walked to the edge of the hill. She clenched her fists as she watched the colors of the sky turning from crimson to deep purple. There had to be some way into the dome. Something they were missing.

Suddenly a hawk materialized out of thin air. One second there was nothing, and the next there was a hawk. She thought her eyes were playing tricks on her when a second one appeared trailing the first.

Bryndis joined her and together they watched as the birds soared overhead. The girls looked at each other and grinned. A plan was born.

The night passed uneventfully. Surprisingly, they all managed to sleep. Molly had set a watch schedule to guard the camp, but the closest any of them got to excitement was when Serena saw a large brown bear. They had no food at their campsite and the bear was merely curious when it wandered in a little too close for comfort. Serena sent a brief blast of wind that zapped it in the nose and it lumbered off.

Just before dawn, Molly woke them with news of their plan.

"You want us to what?" Luis tried to wrap his mind around what Bryndis and Molly had proposed.

"Stop being a wimp," Bryndis scolded, but her tone was playful.

"Your plan calls for the taking of a life. That's nothing to scoff at," Serena insisted. "And it's going to be pretty messy."

"You want us to cover ourselves in animal blood?" Luis blanched. "It's disgusting!"

"It's necessary," said Molly. "The dome only prevents humans from passing through." She explained what she and Bryndis had seen. "The spell must be set to recognize a specific DNA."

"He can do that?" Serena's eyes widened.

"I've not heard of it done before, but I told you this is not your run-of-the-mill Wand Master," said Molly. "He is in full command of everything nature has to offer. I only hope I'm right." Luis groaned, but she continued. "Look, not only does it make sense, but it's the only choice we have. And in the end, we'll never get anywhere without taking a few chances."

"So we're just going to kill some defenseless animals?" Luis argued.

Molly smiled. "No . . . *we're* not." She nodded to Bryndis.

The Greenlander walked to the edge of the campsite with her back to the others. A low rumble gathered shape in her throat. Seconds later she howled to the wolves with perfection. She spoke to them with a series of barks, yips, and howls that only they could understand. She repeated the pattern a second time and rejoined the others. "Now we wait."

"Okay . . . I've heard people imitate wolves before, but that was impressive." Serena leaned across to high-five Bryndis.

Luis's stomach rumbled loudly. "Do you think we might be able to roast some of the—"

"No!" the others yelled in unison.

"Jeez! Isn't anyone else hungry?"

Bryndis rammed her wand into the ground with force and large earthworms slithered out. "Roast those," she said with a cagey smirk.

To her surprise, he eagerly twisted two of the squirmers around a stick and placed it over the flame. "Too bad we don't have any hot sauce," he said, relishing the moment of catching Bryndis off guard for once.

"I hear something." Serena crouched behind the fire and gripped her wand.

A pair of wolves appeared where Bryndis had stood earlier, dragging a fresh deer carcass into the open. Another pair appeared with a second carcass. Bryndis growled a thank-you at them and they slunk back into the forest.

Luis tossed the roasting worms aside. "I suddenly lost my appetite."

"Okay, kids, let's hustle," Molly urged. "We have about an hour before the blood dries and I want to be inside the dome before it does."

Molly theorized that the spell wouldn't be able to detect the human DNA beneath the deer's blood. Before "going crazy" (as Luis put it) with the blood smearing, they had experimented with their coats to see just how much they would need to cover. By treating the coats more like blankets, they could wrap them around their bodies and over their heads. Then if they squatted slightly as they walked, only their shoes to their shins were exposed.

They made quick work of covering coats and legs with the deer's lifeblood. Once they had finished, they joined hands to ask forgiveness and to offer thanks for the deer's lives.

Bryndis summoned the wolves, which returned quickly to retrieve their bounty. The apprentices followed Molly as best they could through the difficult terrain. The shortest route took them through sections of scree, which made for treacherous footing. They averted one final crisis when they located a log that spanned a small creek and were able to teeter across without getting wet and rinsing the blood off.

The dome was unusual in that it was an invisible wall that projected a mirrorlike 3-D image of its surroundings. As they got close, their senses buzzed like the tail of a rattlesnake. "It's probably best if we all don't go through at the same time or place," Molly said. "I'll go first. Then Serena, Bryndis, and Luis, in that order. At least a minute between each of you." The apprentices spread out until they stood about thirty meters apart. She tried to bolster their confidence with a warm smile, but she knew she was only kidding herself. If this didn't work . . .

Molly pursed her lips, took a deep breath, cinched the coat around her as tight as she could, and stepped through the spell.

Molly didn't know what to expect, but nonetheless she was caught totally by surprise when the ground dropped away from her on a steep slope. She immediately fell forward into a headlong roll and tumbled out of control. The coat she had wrapped around her body protected her until she lost her grip. As it fell away, she tried desperately to cover her head and face as her arms and hands took a beating.

She flipped forward and for one brief second looked up to see a massive rock wall. She screamed with effort as she torqued her body so that she slid feetfirst down the hill. Seconds later, her legs slammed into the wall, sending a jolt of pain from her lower back to her neck and causing her teeth to clamp down hard on her tongue.

The taste of blood in her mouth helped her retain consciousness. Molly's eyes fluttered open. A chipmunk sat nearby. It leaned its head from side to side as if to say *you clumsy oaf*, then scampered through a tiny hole at the base of the wall.

She slowly stretched out muscles and ligaments, testing for breaks, bruises, and sprains. "Ouch!" Her legs buckled as she attempted to stand. She fell awkwardly and dragged herself to the wall. As soon as she removed her boot, she saw her ankle had swollen to twice its normal size. *This is bad.*

But one glance back up the steep hill had her counting her blessings that she wasn't more seriously injured. The forest grew thick here, partially obscuring a gravel road that ran down the hill to end abruptly at the rock wall. Above, the road did not extend past where Molly knew the dome to be, but she could see the trees beyond and the dull gray sky as well. This was a very complex spell, and she wondered what mineral deposits were beneath them that could help perpetuate it.

Watch out for booby traps. It was one of Henry's favorite sayings during training exercises. She had to hand it to Malachai. Placing the edge of the spell at the top of a steep hill was a clever idea. It added one more layer to his security.

"Serena!" she whispered. She looked in the direction she had last seen the girl, but the forest was blocking her view beyond the first few meters.

She gingerly placed a hand against the stone wall. From the dense patches of greenish-brown moss that covered the lower half, and the weather-beaten facade of the gray stone blocks, she estimated it was probably built in medieval times—which meant that what lay behind it could be a fortress.

She was going to have to take a chance. "Serena!" she yelled as loud as she dared. She thought she heard a response, but it was muffled.

"Serena!" she called again.

"Coming!" Serena emerged from the forest and carefully slid down the steep path. "What happened?"

"I'm in a wee bit of a pickle." Molly pointed to her ankle, then noticed a tear in Serena's pants that exposed a bloody welt on her calf. "Are you okay?"

"Considering what could have happened, I'm in pretty good shape," Serena said. "Some kind of wicked vine wrapped around my leg and tried pulling me up into the trees, but I managed to burn through it. Some rescue party we are. I heard Bryndis and Luis yell as they came through. I'm pretty sure they got snagged."

Molly examined the wound. "You were lucky. If he meant business, the vines would have had thorns laced with poison. The trap was probably set to capture animals for food." She quickly gave Serena instructions for reversing the vine spell. "I'm sorry, but it looks like you'll have to go on without me."

Serena's eyes widened. "Maybe we can splint it and carry—"

"It's okay," Molly insisted. "You can do this. Use your instincts. They won't betray you. Just be careful. With some luck, I'll be able to weave a few spells to get the swelling down and join you soon.

"We're all counting on you, Serena."

Serena eventually found Bryndis dangling upside down. She was struggling against a vine that had a tight grip on her ankles. Serena traced the vine to its source and murmured as she touched her wand to it. The vine slowly lowered Bryndis to the ground.

"This is embarrassing." Bryndis landed with a soft bump and angrily tore through her vine, uttering a series of Greenlandic curses. "How did you know what to do?"

Serena gave her the bad news about Molly.

"So we're down to three." Bryndis pursed her lips, then nodded. "Challenge accepted. Let's go find Luis."

Luis hung motionless by one foot—his concentration so intense that the sound of Serena's voice startled him. "Quick! Let me down. I can see something . . . odd. Over there." He pointed in the direction of the dome. As soon as he hit the ground, he charged through the undergrowth and led them to a rounded, oblong boulder about the size of an adult box-turtle shell. "Wait, where's Molly?"

"Injured," Bryndis answered. "She won't be coming." Luis started to protest, but she cut him off. "It's done. We keep going. Now what's so odd about a rock in the woods?"

He walked several paces and found another. Then another. They appeared to be laid down in a pattern.

Serena had an eerie feeling. "What did the rocks look like from up there?"

"From what I could tell, they go on forever. And to me, they looked like a giant snake."

Serena examined the nearest rock. But as she rubbed her hand over the smooth surface it tingled her palm.

"It takes incredible energy to maintain a dome like this." She carefully lifted one side of the boulder—just enough to reveal another rock beneath it. But this one was dull green with large splotches of red. "I learned about this. It's a mineral called bloodstone. In ancient times, magicians claimed it gave them the power of invisibility. Seems they might have been right. And see these darker red spots? My guess is it's human blood, which would explain the DNA part of the puzzle.

"The boulders serve to conceal the bloodstone and probably act as conductors to maximize their power. Absolute genius."

"So let's just move the stones and change the pattern," Luis suggested eagerly. "That should mess up the dome, right?"

"Don't touch them," Bryndis commanded. "Malachai is always a step ahead. My guess is he has a fail-safe or two built in. Best we leave them alone for now."

They worked their way down to the wall. Bryndis cupped her hands and Serena stepped into them, hoisting herself upward. She wedged a foot into a seam between the boulders and pulled herself up to stand on it. "I don't see any breaks in the wall," she said. "Looks like we'll have to climb over."

She reached for Luis's hand as Bryndis pushed from below. By lying on their bellies, they were able to pull Bryndis to the top. The three of them scanned the countryside. The opposite side of the wall opened up into a wide expanse of rolling hills. In the near distance, a hamlet consisting of half a dozen homes was surrounded by farms and fences where cattle and goats grazed peacefully. A woman emerged from a home and tossed a bucket of something liquid into a pasture before limping back inside.

The apprentices crouched down. When there were no other signs of activity, they lowered themselves to the ground. With nothing to offer them cover, they advanced in single file, hoping they wouldn't be spotted. Their luck almost held out . . . almost.

An old man in threadbare jeans stepped from the corner of the closest home and leveled a rifle at them. Bryndis halted the group and motioned for Serena and Luis to flank her. She wanted the old man to see they were just children.

"Who are you?" he asked in Romanian.

Bryndis turned to her friends, who shrugged. "We are looking for friends of ours," she said, hoping the man knew some English.

The man cocked his head. He used the gun to motion them to go inside.

"I don't trust him," Bryndis whispered.

"We don't have much choice," Serena answered.

As they stepped inside, they were met with the mouth-watering aroma of hot food. An even older woman stood next to a rough-hewn table that appeared to be more stable than the walls of their home. Five bowls of hot stew sat on the table.

"So much for sneaking up on them," Luis said as his stomach growled loudly.

The old woman laughed. *"Stai. Manca."* She used her hands to translate. *Sit. Eat.*

Bryndis pulled up a chair and the others followed. "How do we know it's not poisoned?" she asked as Luis scooped a spoonful of delicious meat into his mouth.

His eyes widened. He held his hands to his throat as if choking. The old woman chuckled as she ladled more stew into his bowl. "How do you say thank you in Romanian?" he asked.

"You are welcome." The old woman surprised them by switching to English. "We learn your language from other visitors."

The old man wiped a finger across Serena's coat and sniffed it. He squinted, then looked past them into the distance, putting two and two together. "Clever." He smiled warmly. "You are familiar with our wizard?"

"Shhh!" The old woman glanced worriedly at the door.

"Sorry . . . our *Wand Master.*" He rolled his eyes.

"He has killed for less," she said sternly.

"Our friends have been captured." Bryndis wiped her lips and set the spoon down. "We've come to rescue them."

The old man laughed. "You waste your time. No one escapes. We have been here over forty years." His voice trailed off, a man defeated. "But you are here, so you have, well, nothing to lose. Correct?"

Bryndis nodded.

"Perhaps we don't, either." He left the table and went into another room. He emerged holding a rolled parchment, which he spread out on the table. An elaborate sketch of a village had been drawn in exquisite detail. "I used to be an artist . . . before," he said proudly. "The village is a half-day walk, but you are young so maybe quicker. Here"—he stabbed a finger at the illustration—"is where he lives."

For the next hour, they pored over the sketch. The old man pointed out the safest route as well as the traps and pitfalls they would encounter. "But you must arrive before dark," he said ominously. "Many strange flying creatures keep us indoors."

As they made final preparations to leave, the old woman hobbled over to offer food for their journey. She had wrapped strips of dried beef and a loaf of brown bread into a tight bundle, which Luis offered too willingly to carry.

"If I catch you picking the caraway seeds out of that bread, I will break your fingers," Bryndis warned.

"It will be worth it." He laughed.

The old woman fidgeted with her hands as if she were troubled. "I have a favor to ask."

"Anything you want." Serena knew it would be difficult to repay the kindness they'd been shown.

"I have a sister. Natalia. She always loved to hike in the forest. We brought her to these mountains for her birthday and we never left. Bad present. Every year he makes her wear a tiara and eat a cake made from things no human should eat. And every year she spits it back at him." She smiled briefly, a twinkle of admiration in her eyes. "She is strong-willed and would not surrender to him. To this day, he still tries to break her.

"Not long ago, he took her beautiful eyes. She will never see me again." Her shoulders began to shudder with a sob but she shook it off. "If you see her, tell her we are well." She stepped forward and gripped Serena's wrists firmly. "And if you can, make him pay."

Serena stared into her eyes and saw the fire that burned within her soul. "You have my word."

THIRTY-THREE

Henry ran through the list in his head. Giant moa, elephant bird, diatryma, phoenix—all giant birds he had read about, both real and fictional. But nothing could have prepared him for what he faced when he entered that room. The resting creature was too big for a cage—or perhaps the room was cage enough, as there was hardly any space for it to move about.

Unlike the other rooms, this one had a sunken floor that doubled its height, and the bird needed every inch of it. The walls were constructed of enormous blocks of marble that had faded from white to beige over time, while the floor appeared to be the bedrock upon which the prison was built.

Henry felt Brianna and Katelyn move in behind him. "Don't say a word," he said softly. Not softly enough. The bird slowly opened one eye and gazed down upon them as the rest of its massive body also began to awaken. Long brownish-gray feathers unruffled as it drew up to its full height, nearly touching the ceiling, fifteen meters tall.

"Maybe we should leave now." Brianna's voice wavered.

Henry winced as a wave of thought collided with his mind. He clutched his chest as his original wand—the one he had used to summon a flock of blue jays over a year ago—began to emit short bursts of electricity. *Either my wand connects me to all birds, or this giant is an ancient ancestor of the blue jay,* he thought.

He glanced up and met the bird's cold, hard stare. "It . . . she won't hurt us," he said. His head bucked as another wave of thought slammed into him.

"Henry, what's wrong?" Katelyn reached for his arm but he pulled away.

"She's trying to tell me something. But it's so loud . . . she's in pain!" Henry's ankle began to throb and his arm got a sudden kink in it. He was feeling what she felt, and he didn't fight it. He allowed his senses to open up and found the sources of the bird's pain. An invisible chain large enough to secure a battleship held the bird's leg to the floor, and an invisible wire was binding her wings.

"Is this what I think it is?" Brianna asked.

Henry nodded. "She's the Roc that Bryndis had located with the help of the dragon. She's been locked up here for years. The dragon must have told Bryndis about her so we could help her escape."

Katelyn suddenly laughed, which startled the giant bird. "Sorry, but in your wildest imagination, did you ever think you'd see dragons and Giant Rocs?"

Henry smiled. *Your imagination knows no bounds,* Coralis had told him once. But he also knew his limitations. He could feel the power of the spell that held the Roc captive. He connected silently with the bird and told her they would be back.

In response, the bird tucked her razor-sharp beak beneath her wing and plucked off a downy feather. Brianna gasped as the Roc extended her neck toward Henry. Her head was easily the size of a full-grown elephant.

The bird gently nudged the feather into Henry's hand. He felt the life-force of the bird through the feather as he tucked it into his coat and led the others from the room. As he closed the door behind them, the feather was no longer bound by its spell. A surge of power flooded Henry's senses, and the world exploded in exceptional clarity. He grinned from ear to ear as he continued to absorb the power of the Roc. "Let's get out of here."

Henry, Katelyn, and Brianna crept through the alley behind Malachai's prison. Henry's newfound "sight" had saved them hours of fumbling about. Whatever he had absorbed from the Roc's feather enabled him to visualize a path with no obstructions. He literally had them walking through walls, as he was able to see right through all of Malachai's illusions.

But as they entered the alley, he became very cautious. The trip-wire illusion should have tipped off Malachai that they had escaped, but the evil Wand Master had not confronted them, nor had he sent any kind of minion—smelly human or otherwise. Which meant that Henry could be leading them right into a trap. "Do either of you sense anything?"

"Nay, but I get your meaning," said Katelyn. "That was too easy. But on the other hand, maybe he's gone completely mad. Lost touch with reality."

Henry poked his head around the corner of the building and examined the rear and side facades. There was nothing about the three-story house that would lead anyone to believe the horrors that were held inside. He led them down the alley. The fieldstone walls that lined it were a full meter over Henry's head. They had been built in long sections, separated by thick blocks of timber that reminded Henry of railroad ties. Every four sections were further divided by stone arches that provided entrance to other alleys. Henry rushed the girls across the alley, but smelled something familiar. He approached one of the timber columns. It glistened with a black sheen that smelled like tar. He quickly identified it as creosote, which he knew was used to weatherproof wood. It was still moist, which meant it had recently been applied.

He examined his surroundings and realized how meticulously everything had been maintained. Cobblestones had been swept clean. Paint evenly brushed, with no stains or chips. Window casements . . . He pulled Katelyn and Brianna out of sight into an arch as a shadow passed in front of a second-story window. His heart thumped like a rabbit's foot in his chest; he was afraid that they had been spotted.

Evil resonated through the glass. With his heightened acuity, it felt like needles poking through his skin. He knew without a doubt it was Malachai. The Wand Master stepped into clear view of the apprentices, his eyes trained on the distant skies.

Henry gasped. Either Katelyn had understated the horror or it had gotten much worse. Malachai's face was an absolute mess. He seemed to be oblivious to their presence. His lips moved as if he was talking to someone. Then he slowly raised his hands, which held a sphere of swirling energy.

He suddenly burst out in laughter that dissolved into a retching cough. Henry grimaced as Malachai wiped blood from his mouth against his sleeve. That's when he noticed that the Wand Master's shirt was covered in dark red splotches. He held the sphere close to his face.

"What on Earth?" Brianna whispered.

The sphere swirled faster. At least half a dozen snake-like cords grew from its surface and attached themselves to Malachai's face. His eyes began to glow with an unearthly green light. His mouth opened as if to scream but nothing came out.

Henry couldn't watch any longer. He grabbed Katelyn and Brianna by the arm and sprinted down a side alley. They turned left, then right, then left again, picking up speed with every turn. Only when they were safely enclosed in a stone tunnel did they stop to catch their breath.

"What was that thing?" Brianna clutched Henry by the front of his coat. Her white-knuckled fists shook with a mixture of anger and fear. "It was doing something to him. *Changing* him!"

"I think that was the Pangaea Particle." As he said the words, he knew instinctively he was right.

Brianna leaned heavily against a wall and buried her face in her hands. Katelyn placed an arm around her and tried to calm her.

Henry's thoughts drifted back to the chart of the Particle's elements. "The great unknown." Again, he knew it was right as he said it. "Coralis told us there was an element in the Particle that could not be identified. I think we just saw why. Maybe it's some kind of self-defense mechanism."

"I still think he's gone mad." Katelyn began to walk away.

"Insane is more like it." The voice came from the far end of the tunnel.

Henry ran to Katelyn's side and pulled his wand from his coat, though he wasn't sure what to do with it. "Who's there?" His voice cracked and he cringed. He could not show weakness. "Show yourself," he said with more authority.

The voice chuckled. "Or what? Do you think you can do worse to me than what that wizard has done?" A figure stepped into the mouth of the tunnel. With the light at its back, only an outline was discernable to the trio of apprentices. "Come. I won't bite."

As they approached, they could see it was an old woman hunched over with age and afflictions. A well-worn shawl was draped loosely over her shoulders and her hair was tucked into a floral-patterned babushka.

"And what might three children be doing running like rabbits fleeing a fox?" She lifted her head to reveal empty sockets where her eyes should be. Katelyn unsuccessfully attempted to stifle a cry. "Yes, he did this to me, which should answer some of your questions." Her body was feeble but her voice was firm, as if she took a measure of pride in her condition. "Now, what about you? Give me a reason I should not report you to him." She spat onto the cobblestones.

"Something is wrong with him," Henry said shakily.

She laughed again, then cocked her head. "Have you seen him?" They nodded. "You're going to have to speak up." She smiled grimly as she pointed to an eye socket.

"Sorry." Henry gave her a brief account of how they'd ended up in Malachai's prison. Katelyn interrupted with some colorful descriptions.

"American and Irish," the woman noted. "What about the silent one?"

"My sister," said Henry. He expected Brianna to come back with an I-can-speak-for-myself retort. When she didn't speak up, he turned toward her. She was rooted in place. Her body leaned slightly forward in a drooping posture. Her eyes were glassy and unfocused and her mouth agape.

"Brianna!" Katelyn said sharply.

Gradually, Brianna straightened and shook her head as if coming out of a trance. "Well, that was different," she remarked. "Don't ask me why or how, but I feel like I need to try something." She took the old woman's hands in her own and squeezed gently. Brianna dipped her head and closed her eyes in deep concentration.

At first, nothing happened. Then, suddenly, the woman's body jerked as if hit with an electric shock. Her body stiffened. She gasped—a cross between pain and wonder. Brianna turned her head toward Henry and opened her eyes.

Henry could tell a stranger was looking at him through his sister's eyes.

"No! How is this possible?" The woman tore her hands away from Brianna. "Witch!" she hissed.

Brianna gently touched the woman's arm. "Not a witch. An Enabler," she explained calmly. "My brother and Katelyn have special powers like your wizard. Mine are different and I'm still learning about them. I can amplify their power with my voice. I can understand mice and rats. And now—apparently—I can help a blind woman see."

The old woman's forehead creased in deep lines of thought. "You say you have power like *him*? Can you defeat him?"

Henry paused before answering. He wanted to show strength and confidence, but seeing what the woman had been through, he decided to speak from the heart. "Honestly? We don't know. We've been separated from our group and we were counting on strength in numbers. Our leader, Coralis, has power that is a match for Malachai, but he has also been captured and we don't know where he is or how to find him. So right now, we're flying by the seat of our pants. But we're not giving up. And if we should fail, at least Malachai will know he's been in one heckuva battle."

The old woman breathed deeply as she relaxed. "That is good enough for me. By the way, my name is Natalia. I have waited a long time to find another willing to stand up to him. I will do what I can to help." She reached her hands out.

Brianna took a deep breath to brace herself and reconnected with Natalia, who led them through the maze of alleys until they arrived at the back door of her home. Brianna found a mirror in the tiny bedroom so that Natalia could meet her face-to-face. She had been careful to avoid looking directly at Natalia to save her from seeing what had become of her beautiful face. But she had the wrong angle on the mirror. Natalia squeezed her hand tightly but did not flinch. Instead she asked Katelyn to remove the babushka from her head and tie it like a blindfold around her eyes.

"I am the Lone Ranger, eh?" she joked. "I have been thinking. I know the woman who cares for his twisted zoo. She might be able to tell us where your Coralis is. She works now. We will go to her soon. But first . . . we eat."

THIRTY-FOUR

Navigating their way through the forest was easier than they'd expected. Once they knew what to look for, the vine traps were easily avoided. The forest gave them plenty of cover, and the dried blood on the Wandmaker coats provided an extra layer of camouflage.

The forest was eerily quiet, as if even the insects knew there was something unnatural in the works. Only once did they see any signs of animal life. A massive wild boar that must have weighed in at well over two hundred kilograms had come upon them suddenly. It charged at them, razor-sharp tusks still glistening with the remains of a recent meal.

Luis whipped out a small blowgun he had designed for short-range accuracy and fired a dart that hit the beast square in the chest. The sting had been just enough to confuse the boar, which skidded to an abrupt halt. The three Wandmakers packed tightly together. Serena decided to take emergency action and stepped in front of the group to blast the creature with a stiff wind burst.

But before she could act, the boar ambled up to her, took a healthy sniff, sneezed in disgust, and trotted off into the forest. A dozen meters later, it froze in its tracks and keeled over on its side.

"Did you kill it?" Serena asked Luis.

"Nope. That dart was meant to stun a human. It probably got a good whiff of your smelly feet." He laughed as Serena took a swing at him.

From a clearing at the crest of a rolling hill, they got their first good look at the village. "If I didn't know any better, I'd swear we went back in time," said Serena.

"Yeah, I think our friend Malachai likes living in the past," Luis replied. "Now, who remembers where to go from here? That old man's sketch was okay, but—"

Bryndis interrupted him. "I don't understand. How did he do all this without Coralis knowing about it? We're not that far from the castle. Wouldn't he sense that forces of nature were being manipulated?"

Serena winced. Gretchen had once told her something in confidence. Given the circumstances, she decided she had to share. "There was a time when Coralis had given up. He and Malachai were the last of a golden era of Wand Masters and he was led to believe Malachai was dead. Imagine if you were the last of a species—eventually you'd wither away. Fortunately, he found Henry." She smiled at the thought. "Actually, Henry found him."

"Henry, Henry, Henry," Luis scoffed. "What makes him so special anyway?"

"Coralis once told Gretchen he knows the goods when he sees the goods," Serena replied. "Henry has no clue as to how great his potential is—and neither do any of us. But before today is over, we are going to have to start tapping deep into our abilities. Each of us will have a role to play in victory . . . or defeat. And if Coralis is right, Henry might well be the weight that tips the scales in our favor. Now then"— she winked—"let's go stir up some trouble."

The village's most striking feature was its compactness. The buildings had been constructed so tightly together that they seemed to be connected—like a house that a family outgrows, so they add on and on, section after section. But they knew from the old man's sketch that this was not the case. Between all the buildings ran a complex series of alleyways, most of which were no more than two meters wide.

The village itself was nestled into the side of what was either a small mountain or a large hill—something Luis and Bryndis argued over at length. So while all the buildings were a single story in height, the ones farther up the slope appeared taller. Only one building stood out from the rest, and it was in the direct center of the village. Rising several stories and topped with five conical spires, it had been built to impress. This was Malachai's home—or as the old man had put it, his chamber of horrors.

One by one, the apprentices sprinted to the house closest to the edge of the tree line. The farm couple had filled in as much background as they could. While they had been there at least forty years, the village had been operating under

Malachai's rule for hundreds. Therefore, much of the knowledge had been handed down from one generation of prisoners to the next.

They knew that the population of the village was maintained at one hundred captives, but didn't know if that number had any significance. Most of the people would do anything to help them, but several were known spies and were to be given a wide berth. Every villager had an assigned task that had to be carried out within specific time frames.

Malachai also enforced a strict curfew. At four o'clock, everyone was expected to be off the streets and tucked safely in their homes for the night. Which was why they had waited several hours in the forest before making their move. They skirted along the back side of a few homes before arriving at an alley. According to the old man, this provided the safest passage to the village square—an open area that was used for gatherings that ranged from sermons to public torture, all delivered by Malachai.

The day had started cool but had grown warm and sticky by noon. As the afternoon stretched toward evening, an advancing storm moved in on a cold wind. A light mist began to fall. As it changed to rain, the blood on their coats rinsed off and left a trail of red on the cleanly swept cobblestones. And because they walked in single file, hugging the buildings, the red trail became a red stream that ran downhill in the gutter.

The village baker had a simple routine that he followed religiously. He provided daily bread of a consistent quality that kept him in Malachai's good graces. And he was also a snitch who ratted on even the slightest transgression by other villagers. He was often rewarded with a decent cut of meat—not the leftover gristle Malachai typically provided. But Malachai's demands had become increasingly odd, which was why he had to vary his routine—which placed him outside past the curfew and into an alley where a stream of red flowed in a narrow rivulet.

His stomach growled in anticipation of a good meal as he followed the trail. He spotted the three strangers and silently retreated to the bakery, where he used a century-old telegraph to send a message to his master. Then he put his feet up and smiled, visions of a decent meal dancing in his head.

Malachai had been in a semiconscious state of warped bliss when he heard a tapping sound from the next room.

Half a minute later, Puteo burst into the room. His normal stench doubled when he felt threatened or got excited. And he was *very* excited! He knew to expect the wrath of his master in situations like this, and in some weird way he looked forward to it. Malachai was more than a master. He was to Puteo as Zeus was to the ancient Greeks. He was all-powerful and would soon control the world—and he would take Puteo with him.

Whatever punishment Malachai inflicted on him only made him stronger. He endured the torture as a training exercise and after each one he received a token from his master—like a dog getting a treat for learning to roll over.

Lately, as Malachai descended further into madness, the treats had become more valuable. Puteo took this as a sign that perhaps Malachai was ready to share the secrets of his almighty power.

"Look, master!" He eagerly waved a piece of paper with the baker's message, fanning waves of foulness throughout the room. For the first time, he almost couldn't stand his own stench, and he hoped this would result in an extremely rigorous training session. He stopped short and frowned as he saw the Pangaea Particle. Malachai had been spending too much time with it, which made Puteo jealous.

Malachai observed the change in his assistant's demeanor. "What's the matter, my foul friend? Do you wish to touch it? Do you want to experience the joy and pain it brings?" He held the sphere out, an invitation to touch. But as Puteo reached for it, Malachai jerked it back and clutched it to his chest. "How dare you think you are worthy?" he screamed. "It belongs to me and no one—NO ONE—will ever touch it but ME! Now get out, you wretched beast!"

Puteo stumbled backward under the verbal assault. All his hopes that this would be a special day were dashed to bits.

"Can you not hear? I said get out of my sight!" Malachai bellowed.

As Malachai turned swiftly away and returned to the window with the message, an egg-shaped rock fell from his cloak and rolled across the floor. Puteo immediately recognized it as the remains of the Strix that had been turned to ash. He grabbed it, tucked it into his pocket, and ran from the room.

Malachai waited until the stench lessened. He carefully secured the Particle in its lead box and read the message. He laughed, high and shrill, and clapped giddily as he danced around the room. He didn't understand how they could have escaped his arachnid army, but it didn't matter. What mattered was that Coralis's pathetic band had come to him.

He attempted to rush down several flights of stairs, when a wave of dizziness washed over him. He tripped and tumbled headlong to the bottom. A sharp crack should have worried him, but between the adrenaline and euphoria, he didn't give his badly broken wrist a second thought. Instead he skipped like a schoolboy down the hall and threw open the door to the room where the apprentices had been held captive.

In a split second his extreme happiness transformed into vengeful anger. He screamed a torrent of obscenities as he threw his body at the empty cages. His foot made contact with something that clattered against the wall. *A key!* His eyes blazed red with rage.

In his fury, he abandoned his plan to turn the apprentices to his side and ran to another room. He pointed his wand at the ceiling, unleashing a powerful bolt of energy that dissolved the solid blocks of stone into dust. An earsplitting shriek erupted as hundreds of Strix acknowledged their freedom and took to the skies.

"What was that?" Henry heard the explosion, rushed to a window, and peeked through the shutters. A writhing black cloud rose into the gloomy sky. As wave after wave of four-taloned monstrosities gathered over the village, a pit settled in his stomach.

"He knows we've escaped." Katelyn had come up behind him.

"Quickly!" Natalia ushered them out the back door and barged into the house next door. "Ileana!" she called out urgently.

Seconds later, the woman from the prison who had left the key for them barreled through the front door and bolted it shut, unaware that anyone was in her home. "No!" she yelled when she turned and saw them. "Natalia, you should not be here with them." Her voice trembled with fright.

"Ileana, they can help us," Natalia pleaded.

"No one can help us," she scolded. "He has lost his senses. His mind is mush! And now we are all doomed."

"Ileana!" Brianna used a powerful inflection of Voice to calm her. It had an immediate effect, as Ileana slumped into a simple wooden chair and stared helplessly at her neighbor. "Does he know we've escaped?" Brianna asked, taking the edge off her power.

"Yes." Ileana nodded grimly. "He has released the monsters. But not only for you. Puteo read it on the telegraph, and he told me." She pinched her nose and spat on the floor, showing her disdain for the man. "Others have arrived."

"Others?" Katelyn asked hopefully.

"He called them pesky kids." She doubled over and sobbed.

"Molly must have found a way in." Henry paced the room and threw caution to the wind by fully opening the shutters. The black cloud continued to grow as the Strix amassed for the kill. He knew they were awaiting a final command from Malachai to attack. Anger built up inside him, as did something else. Something he had not felt since he had helped to defeat Malachai's son.

The Roc's feather pulsed in sync with his rapidly beating heart. Their friends needed their help. They would never be able to hold off, much less defeat, the number of Strix Malachai was sending their way.

He turned, bumped into a table, and caught the old telegraph machine just before it fell. His eyes lit up with hope. "I need you to send a message to Malachai."

THIRTY-FIVE

Brianna clutched tightly to Natalia's hand to allow the sightless woman to direct her and Katelyn through the rain-slicked maze. As much as they did not want to drag Natalia into the fight, she had insisted vehemently. And in the end, they knew they could not find the others without her help.

They entered another home, startling a young man. Brianna immediately silenced him. "Sorry," she said. "No time for explanations."

The front of his home faced the village square. Katelyn peered through the window at the open area and tried to imagine what course of action she would take if she were Molly. Natalia had told her that eight alleys converged onto the square. From her vantage point, she could see only five of them, and one of those was obscured by a fountain. But at least the rain had turned down the volume to a light drizzle.

Katelyn mentally ticked off the minutes since they had left Henry. His plan, if one could call it that, was a nebulous mess of maybes. She watched the turbulent skies. She had begun to have second thoughts when suddenly a large flock of Strix broke off from the main body and veered south. Ileana's telegraphed message had told Malachai there was another group emerging from the forest to attack on a second front. Henry hoped that Malachai would be too agitated in his damaged frame of mind to realize all the apprentices had already been accounted for.

So far, their luck had held. Katelyn anxiously scanned the square again. Still no sign of the others, but the plan called for her to assume they were nearby.

Brianna took Katelyn's hand and squeezed with gentle reassurance. "We can do this."

"Where's a four-leaf clover when you need one?" Katelyn opened the door and steadied herself with a deep breath as she focused on her wand. The air high above the fountain shimmered with heat waves as she summoned the fire element. Air molecules bombarded against one another, faster and faster. She squeezed the molecules, compressing them until the stored energy was at the bursting point.

Sensing the moment was right, Brianna placed her hand on Katelyn's shoulder, adding her power as an Enabler. They had practiced this technique before, but never with so much at stake. Amped up with adrenaline, their combined power hit with devastating effect—but in the wrong direction.

A fireball ten meters in diameter materialized above the fountain, but instead of rising up to take on the birds, it rocketed downward. Katelyn lost control of it as it slammed into the fountain, disintegrating it and scorching the entire square. The blast of heat was so intense it flash-dried the muddy earth and created a layer of steam that hovered like a thick fog.

But the level of energy Katelyn had expended also knocked her unconscious, and tossed Brianna across the room, where she sat in a mind-numbing daze. A horrendous shriek filled the air as the horde of Strix attacked—and she knew they had failed.

Henry carefully retraced his steps through the halls of Malachai's zoo prison. If Ileana had guessed correctly, Coralis was being held in a specially prepared room inside one of the five spires that topped the fortress. Fortunately, the building had been constructed with servant staircases—hidden behind walls so that peasant housemaids could go from one floor to another without being seen by their masters. Ileana had told him they were not monitored, but Henry proceeded with extreme caution, using the heightened senses granted him by the Roc feather to stay on guard. He moved silently up three flights of stairs and emerged into a small foyer, where he was assaulted with an eye-watering, acrid smell.

Puteo stood in front of a formidable door, his arms crossed. "Who do you think you are?"

Henry blinked rapidly. His eyes watered as if he had been slicing onions. He struggled to see through his tears. Whoever this man was, his superpower was apparently being able to stink someone to death. If Coralis's life wasn't at stake, he might have laughed. But he had to think of something quick. He didn't have the time to battle a human stink bomb.

Suddenly he thought of a way to use the truth to his advantage. "I am Markhor's son."

"You did not come to rescue the prisoner?"

Henry sensed doubt in the man's voice. "No. Malachai sent me to guard the door. He . . . he sent me to relieve you. He needs you to help fight the intruders."

Puteo dropped his hands to his side. A flash of joy appeared upon his face before he quashed it. "It's about time. Why are you just standing there? Get over here! No one goes in or out. Understand?"

Before Henry could gag out a yes, Puteo raced past him and down the staircase. The residual smell was bearable. Henry wiped his eyes to clear his vision and examined the door. He had seen the locking mechanism before—at the entrance to Coralis's Cryptoporticus. He pursed his lips in frustration. The special key needed to release the locks had to be with Malachai. Unless . . .

No, it can't be this easy, he thought as he remembered a trick his parents always used. He stood on tiptoe and stretched his arm as high as he could to reach the top of the doorjamb, but came up short. He knew that if he used his wand power, Malachai would know he was there, but he was out of options and short on time.

He pointed his wand toward the ceiling, creating a mini-tornado the way Serena had shown him; then he sent it crawling along the top of the door. A circular stone key was knocked loose. Henry snatched it out of the air before it hit the floor, impressing himself with the sudden display of athleticism. He quickly pressed the stone into the locks, hoping the sequence was the same as at the castle.

The door popped open with a hiss, as if he had broken the seal on a vacuum chamber. As he stepped inside, he could feel whatever spell Malachai had employed. He tried to illuminate his wand but something blocked it. There was just enough light spilling in from the foyer to see. He hurried to the chair in the center of the room.

"Coralis!" he whispered urgently. As the slumped figure of the Wand Master raised his head, Henry nearly fell backward. The old man had visibly aged to a point that frightened Henry. "What has he done to you?"

Coralis blinked until he finally seemed to recognize his apprentice. "Henry," he croaked through parched lips. "How . . ." He grimaced in pain as he pulled himself upright.

"Save your breath," Henry said worriedly.

"My boy, you are a sight for sore eyes." Coralis chuckled weakly. He suddenly looked puzzled. "I sense great power." Henry withdrew the Roc feather, which reacted to Malachai's spell like a sparkler on the Fourth of July. The Wand Master smiled. "Do you remember how I once told you that every victory relies on an element of luck? Well, I believe you've found some."

Henry managed to drag the chair into the foyer, where his wand power could function. Coralis gave him explicit instructions to release the binding spell. As Henry proceeded, he realized that his power alone would not have been enough and he silently thanked the Roc.

Henry uttered the final words and Coralis fell forward into his arms . . . where he promptly passed out.

"Keep hitting them!" Luis yelled, though he could hardly be heard over the war cries of the Strix. Their original plan had been for Bryndis to take control of the water from the fountain so that Serena could pressurize it and slice the birds to ribbons. But a sudden fireball had vaporized every last drop and the rain wasn't falling hard enough to accumulate.

Luis quickly improvised and used his power to atomize the cobblestones. Serena then pummeled the birds with powerful bursts of tornadic, pebble-strewn wind. She managed to repel them, but their armored shells prevented any lasting harm. They no sooner were blown high into the sky before they regrouped and mounted another attack.

Brianna left Katelyn in the care of Natalia and chose her moment to sprint across the blackened square to join them.

Serena smiled at the sight of her. "Brianna. I knew you'd be okay. Where are the others?"

"They'll be here soon," Brianna said, but couldn't keep the worry from her voice. She explained what had happened to Katelyn and told Serena to be ready for the jolt as she gripped her shoulder and focused on the wind element.

Serena shuddered as a wave of power nearly overwhelmed her, but she steadied herself. She directed the energy from her wand into an ever-increasing funnel of wind. As it widened in diameter, cedar shingles were ripped from rooftops.

Several dive-bombing Strix streaked into the vortex and immediately joined the debris that spun out of control with blinding speed. Unable to control it any longer, Serena pushed the tornado skyward, where it struck the evil horde with deadly force, capturing all but a dozen and whirling them into the stratosphere.

Serena cried out as she collapsed with the effort, pale and drenched with sweat. Brianna, too, doubled over and rested her hands on her knees while she tried to catch her breath.

A dozen Strix was still a lot to contend with. Bryndis created a series of small fire clusters that she hurled at them like a child in a snowball fight. As the softball-sized spheres of fire raced toward their targets, she uttered a spell. She hadn't mastered the fire element and knew she could not generate enough heat to destroy them. Instead, the fire clusters wrapped around them and sealed them in with a series of loud pops. Unable to flap their wings, they plummeted to the ground, where they thrashed wildly. The fiery cages held firm, but no sooner did the apprentices stop to rest than the other half of the horde screeched in the distance to announce their return.

Katelyn staggered through the doorway and tripped her way toward Serena, totally exhausted. "I don't understand," she panted. "Why can't I recover my strength?" She suddenly realized someone was missing. "Where's Molly?"

"She was injured." Bryndis frowned. Katelyn was right. They shouldn't be losing their strength so quickly. She thought back to their lessons, then put her nose to Katelyn's hair and sniffed. She did the same to Serena and cursed under her breath. Their hair had a slightly smoky scent with subtle notes of exotic spices. "A parasite spell," she said ominously. "As we expend our power, the energy is siphoned off. The more power we use, the faster it is depleted. Which means we are going to have to be smarter about how we fight these things."

Brianna squinted as the black cloud drew nearer. "And hope that Henry finds Coralis. Very soon."

"Can you walk?" Henry helped Coralis stand and slung one of the Wand Master's arms over his shoulder for support. The Wand Master's face was bleached of color. His breathing was labored to the point of wheezing. Henry had seen a class-mate suffer from an asthma attack, but that was different. It almost looked like Coralis didn't have the energy to breathe. "Coralis!" he whispered urgently. "What happened to you? What should I do?"

"Malachai." Coralis attempted to take a deep breath. "Draining my aura."

Henry's eyes widened in shock. "But that's your life-force. How is that even possible?"

"Should not be," Coralis wheezed. "Must be something with the Pangaea . . ." He slid down against the wall to sit. "Energy stabilizing now. But I'm useless."

"Well, we have to do something! The others are out there facing a horde of Strix."

Coralis closed his eyes to gather strength. When he opened them, they burned with fury. "Where is the Roc?" Henry explained the invisible chains that held the giant bird captive. "You must release her. The way you released me."

Coralis grunted and arched his back in pain. Henry remembered all too well what it had felt like when Coralis tried to remove the evil moonbeam that had attacked his aura. He could not imagine the agony of having his entire aura stripped from him. It had to be like a slow, painful . . .

"Death." Coralis silently projected the word into Henry's mind.

"No!" he screamed. "You can't die! We need you!"

"They need YOU!" Coralis forced the words upon Henry with as much Voice as he could muster. "Go . . . before it's too late."

"Promise me you won't die!" Henry cried. "Promise or I'm not leaving."

Coralis reached a withered hand up to tousle Henry's hair. "Bahtzen bizzle," he said with a warm smile. "You are one stubborn young man. But I cannot make a promise I cannot keep. However, I will try to stay alive." The Wand Master closed his eyes until he heard Henry's feet pounding down the stairs.

When he opened them, he was barely breathing.

THIRTY-SIX

Katelyn, Serena, Brianna, and Luis moved like toys with their batteries run down. Between the four of them, they had been able to destroy a handful of Strix, which left Bryndis to try to stave off hundreds. But the Strix had gotten smarter and managed to penetrate their defenses. Each of them wore battle wounds where the terrifying birds' claws and beaks had left them battered and bruised. Most of the damage occurred to their hands and forearms as they instinctively used them to shield their faces.

Bryndis felt momentum shifting against them and had to take charge. She used a break in their attacks to create a small dome of protection—a disorientation spell that muddled the birds' sense of direction. As they approached it, they suddenly found themselves veering away from their targets and had to flap wildly to regain their equilibrium.

Then Lady Luck intervened in the form of a dark storm cloud and renewed rain. Streams of water cascaded from gutters and downspouts on homes, giving Bryndis some much-needed ammunition. She came up with a few clever water formations that Serena blasted with enough pressure to take out dozens of birds at a time. But their power was draining quickly.

In a last-gasp effort to destroy as many as possible, Serena urged Bryndis to erect a wall of water that looked like an enormous shield. She had Luis add all the earth elements he could muster. Brianna placed a hand on Serena's shoulder and used every ounce of reserve strength she had left. The effect was devastating on two fronts.

Strix exploded en masse. Their black blood erupted into a mural that looked as if a mad artist had thrown a bucket of paint at a dirty canvas. The blood rained down upon the ground, where it mingled with the scorched earth and created a field of toxic sludge.

But this also left the five apprentices completely spent. They collapsed in a heap and stared upward with blank eyes. And as most of the black blood mist cleared, the worst of their nightmares still filled the skies.

They were doomed and they knew it. In a last-ditch effort to protect them, Serena held her coat out like a winged bat and threw herself on top of their prone bodies. A sudden gust of wind swept across her with tremendous force. She screamed in anger and frustration at her failure until Bryndis shoved her off.

"Look!" she cried.

Serena's eyes fluttered open; she was prepared to face her fate. She weakly swiped at the rain to clear her vision . . . and laughed. Each of the other apprentices in turn propped themselves up by their elbows to watch.

"What is that?" Luis asked.

"It's a Roc," Katelyn said as she squeezed Brianna's hand. "Henry did it."

The gigantic bird swooped over them like a low-flying jumbo jet. Her wings filled the skies as she glided upward with majestic grace and confronted the Strix with a shriek so loud it shattered windows throughout the village.

While the Strix of lore knew the Roc as their greatest enemy, the new breed that Malachai had created was clueless. But they did know that they had to attack such a humongous foe in force. Just as a school of fish will move as one, so did the Strix. Their remaining numbers gathered into a tight wedge and streaked toward the Roc as a solid mass.

The Roc made an enormous roller coaster loop in the air. With her head pointed skyward and her wings fully outstretched, she awaited the onslaught. The Strix came at her with their vicious claws extended. The Roc not only absorbed every impact; she began to glow.

As the last of the Strix made contact, the Roc snapped her wings shut in front of her body and trapped them against her. Her glow grew in intensity until it was too bright to look at. She opened her mouth and a noxious black vapor spewed forth and hovered above the bird like a soot-laden cloud. She clamped her wings even tighter, somehow remaining aloft as she did it.

The air around her shimmered. Remarkably, the raindrops solidified into hail, for it wasn't heat the bird was generating, but intense cold. The Roc suddenly snapped her wings open. Her light flashed out. And the brittle skeletons of hundreds of Strix tumbled to the ground, where they shattered upon impact.

The great bird floated gently downward and landed at the edge of the square. She faced one of the intersecting alleys, where Henry emerged and walked toward her. He held the feather out for her to take back, but she refused and turned her head toward the place where Malachai had held her captive.

The earth shook as the Roc began to tremble violently. Then she let out a mighty roar of victory that shattered the remaining windows. She thrust herself upward and, with two powerful flaps, cleared the rooftops and glided out of sight.

"Henry!" Serena shouted.

Henry waved to her from across the square. But instead of joining them, he cocked his head as if he had forgotten something and sprinted back down the alley as the apprentices gazed helplessly at his retreating form.

Henry's legs had never moved so fast in his life. Even through the cacophony of noise at the battle scene, he had clearly heard Coralis calling to him for help. He had sounded so weak. Henry knew he didn't have much time. He had barely freed the Roc in time to save his friends. Now he hoped he'd be in time to save Coralis.

He pressed the Roc feather against his chest, where it still tingled with power. He knew their paths would cross again—hopefully under better circumstances.

Henry sliced through the alleys like an Olympic sprinter, then skidded to a jarring halt. He had entered the street directly across from Malachai's home. The evil Wand Master—or what was left of him—stood outside his front door. He held the Pangaea Particle as if it were a sacred object. There was no skin left on his hands—only exposed muscle tissue. A dozen tendrils from the Particle were attached to his decomposing face. Several of them wove in and out of his exposed facial muscles like a needle and thread, creating some kind of demonic quilt. Off to the side lay the unconscious body of the human stink machine.

"Hello, Henry." Malachai spoke, but it was an exact imitation of Coralis.

Henry swallowed his fear. "Where is Coralis? What have you done to him?" His voice projected loud and clear and with authority born of anger.

"You are not afraid of me? First poor, misguided Puteo tries to steal my particle of power. Now you—the underachieving son of a failed Wandbearer—seek to challenge me," Malachai said mockingly. "What's the world coming to? Let's see if we can fix that."

Malachai's hand moved like a blur as he whipped out a wand and zapped two lightning bolts at Henry's feet. The blast tossed him backward, where he slammed against a stone wall, whacking the back of his head hard enough to draw blood. He stood shakily and staggered as he attempted to regain his senses.

"Oh, come on, boy," Malachai chided. "This is going to be too easy. Did Coralis teach you nothing? I'll tell you what . . . give me your best shot. See if you can hurt me." He cradled the Particle in one hand and lowered the wand to his side. "Please? Surely you have something."

Henry's head throbbed. White dots floated in front of his eyes. The realization that Malachai could destroy him with a flick of his wrist was horrifying. He was suffocating under the pressure. Coralis was the only one who could defeat Malachai, and he was . . . where?

"Coralis!" He reached out with his mind.

"Coralis can no longer hear you," Malachai silently answered. He sneered.

Henry wiped his sweaty palms on his pants before taking his wand out and leveling it at Malachai. If he was being given a free shot at the Wand Master, he would make it count. He shut down access to his thoughts.

He felt Malachai prodding unsuccessfully at his mind. "Impressive," Malachai sneered.

Henry concentrated on all four elements at once. Coralis had shown him a technique in which the elements would actually decide the correct course of action for him. He had practiced and improved but was far from mastering it. He was about to give up when he sensed an opportunity.

If Henry were to succeed in somehow separating Malachai from the Particle, perhaps it would confuse the Wand Master long enough to give him an advantage. He closed his eyes and raised his arms out perpendicular to the ground. He called upon the air molecules to levitate him off the street— an imitation of what he had just seen the Roc do.

Malachai continued to jab at Henry's mind, but he couldn't get through. Henry leveled a steely gaze at the Wand Master, whose puzzled expression told him his plan might just work.

Henry held himself steady at a meter off the ground, then began to assemble the rainwater on the roof over Malachai's head. Within seconds, he had gathered hundreds of liters of water and pooled it into a cylindrical column. Appearing as though he had failed, he lowered himself to the ground. He summoned enough heat to form a fireball, which he purposely threw short of his target, and he looked helplessly at Malachai, who smiled wickedly.

"Oh dear. Coralis is worse than I thought. Couldn't even teach the simpl—" Malachai never finished his taunt, as Henry suddenly whipped his wand in a downward motion. The cylinder leapt from the rooftop and pummeled into Malachai like a giant fist.

But the evil Wand Master was too quick. A nanosecond before impact, he erected a narrow, invisible dome over himself. The deluge of water split into two frothing rivers that temporarily flooded the streets. Malachai laughed at Henry's attempt as he waved away the protective dome.

But Henry wasn't finished. He subtly flicked his wrist and brought another thirty-liter fist of water that hammered Malachai squarely on the head. Caught completely by surprise, Malachai fell to the ground. He used his hands to brace his fall.

The Particle rolled from his grip.

Henry surged forward to kick the Particle out of Malachai's reach, but stopped and watched, horrified, as the tendrils held tight to the Wand Master's ruined face. One detached and whipped at Henry. He ducked and nearly avoided contact, but a tiny barb on the end of the tendril nicked the base of his palm and broke the skin. He cried out. The pain was excruciating, as if his hand had been dipped in a caustic acid.

He arched his back and screamed, but it wasn't from the pain. The tendril had given him direct contact with Malachai's hideously twisted mind and revealed his vision for Earth's future. Just before the vision ended, something else came into focus—no, someone.

"Dad! Are you there? Help me!"

Slowly Malachai stood and wiped the water from his face. He quickly reclaimed the Particle. "Now look at what you've done," he growled. "But then again, I did offer you a free shot. And now . . . it's my turn."

THIRTY-SEVEN

L eonardo had been in his workshop putting the finishing touches on the tranquillityite net when a primal scream echoed across the courtyard of Sforza Castle. His head snapped up. The falcon screeched from the rafters.

"It is time." He grabbed a large satchel and packed the neatly folded net, along with carefully wrapped vials of the mandrake solution. Thunder rumbled overhead as a storm blew in on wind gusts that tore flags from their posts and sent them soaring. As Leonardo opened the door, a sheet of rain greeted and immediately soaked him. He called to the falcon and allowed it to crawl into his bag; then he leaned into the wind and forced his way across the courtyard.

He entered the dungeon to the sounds of Henry's father wailing as if he were being tortured. And in a way, he was.

"Leonardo!" Markhor shouted. "My son! Help me!" He squeezed his head, not to block out the vision but to try to maintain contact. His only son was in trouble and the mind-link was the only way he could try to help.

"Leach!" Leonardo yelled. "Cover your eyes!" Leonardo pulled out the net and tested the weight in his hands. Tossing

a fishing net took skill born from years of experience—
something he didn't possess. But in his head he had worked
out trajectories, weight balance, velocity, and force of impact.
He knew he had only one shot at breaking the spell. Through
another dream with the falcon, he also knew the fate of mankind rested in him getting it right.

No pressure.

Leonardo balanced the net and began to spin it over his
head, allowing it to extend to its full diameter. When he knew
he had it just right, he tossed it at the opening. The tranquillityite rocks caught the outer edges of the spell and ripped
them from their moorings. The net captured the spell as it
fell to the floor. Leonardo looked upon the scene, fascinated.
The net crawled along the ground as the spell tried to break
free, until it finally exhausted itself. With a whimpering puff
of smoke, it was gone.

He rushed to the nearest cell. The spell had been broken,
which allowed the cell doors to open easily. The nearly mummified person in the cell could have been either a man or a
woman. Its skin cracked and flaked as Leonardo lifted its head
to administer the mandrake. No sooner did the first drops of
solution enter its mouth than the entire body collapsed into
dust. "What have I done?" he gasped.

Leonardo turned on the falcon. "No . . . what have *we*
done?"

The falcon answered with a deafening shriek as it hopped
through the bars into the next cell. Leonardo frowned. "I
must be a fool for listening to a confounded bird!"

The same thing happened in the next eight cells. But in the ninth, the solution placed the man into a deathlike stasis. Leonardo rapidly continued down the row of prisoners until he arrived at Markhor.

Henry's father was crouched in a corner, moaning in madness-induced anger. "Leach," Leonardo said gently. "You must trust us."

Henry's father looked up. His pupils rolled back into his head as he jerked with a seizurelike spasm. "My son," he gurgled. "Must help."

Leonardo sensed the man's urgency. "Drink this," he insisted. "It will help your son." As Leonardo had hoped, the madness made Markhor's mind pliable enough to listen without questioning.

Markhor swiped the vial from Leonardo's hand and gulped eagerly. For a brief second, his eyes returned to normal, and he managed to transmit one final silent message to Malachai before the drug took effect. *"Time's up, pal."*

He fell heavily to the floor. Leonardo rushed to his side. He felt for a pulse in Markhor's neck and wrist. There was no sign of life. He stood and gazed suspiciously at the falcon. "I hope you know what you're doing."

Henry's body was numb and his mind had retreated to a place that blocked some of the pain. Another trick Coralis had taught him. *"Coralis,"* he reached out feebly.

"Henry, I am sorry." Coralis's response was just as weak.

"What are we going to do?" Anguish crept into Henry's voice.

"There is no we, my son." Coralis's voice was barely audible. *"I am sorry."*

Henry's mind reeled as he lost the connection. He curled up on the ground and sobbed openly as he realized Coralis had left him. Defeat engulfed him. It ate through his confidence and filled him with despair. *Coralis is dead!* Grief overwhelmed him and his mind block slipped.

"Oh, poor young Henry," Malachai leered. *"Is your master gone? You should be glad. He was weak—just like your father. He no longer deserved the title of Wand Master. Now if you will just roll over and allow me to complete your torture, perhaps I will be merci—"*

Malachai twitched, his head jerking to one side. "What . . ." Seconds later he twitched again, more violently.

Henry sensed a change in the air. He uncurled and glanced about, confused. He thought perhaps Puteo had risen to join the fight, but his body was gone. Malachai reached out to touch Henry and recoiled with a vicious backlash. Henry focused on the Wand Master's aura. It was changing. The glowing darkness began to fester and crack. Every few seconds another convulsion racked his body and caused the aura to weaken even further.

Henry was at a loss to explain it. There was no way for him to know that his father and the other prisoners lapsing into a deathlike state had weakened his enemy, but he seized the opportunity. This was the man who had given birth to a monstrous son, taken his father, and killed Coralis. Rage at all the injustice Malachai had caused began to swell within him. He stared angrily at the killer before him and knew what he had to do. He smiled cruelly as he raised his wand and spoke the words to invoke a binding spell.

Strands of unbreakable, invisible cords began to wrap around Malachai's feet and legs, rooting him to the ground. From a place he hadn't known existed, Henry recalled another spell that added strength to the first one. Then he added another layer on top of that. He twirled his wand, providing silent instructions to the cords as they worked their way up Malachai's body, which continued to convulse with pain from an unseen source. He pinned the Wand Master's hands to his body and the Particle fell to the ground once more.

Henry no longer cared about it. He squeezed the spell tighter as he sought revenge.

Malachai's eyes glowed red as the cords began to strangle him. Yet he sneered at Henry. "You cannot kill me," he rasped.

Henry was about to prove him wrong when a sudden idea came to him. He lowered his wand and stepped up to the now harmless Wand Master. "There are much worse fates than death."

THIRTY-EIGHT

Once the villagers saw that Malachai had been defeated, they slowly emerged from their homes like frightened puppies. But their joy at being liberated quickly turned to anger. Henry got his first look at a hostile mob.

He directed his sister to use Voice to quell their fury while Natalia stood by her side to validate her authority. Bryndis and Luis assembled a makeshift stretcher from a piece of canvas and two wooden poles and carried Malachai inside, out of the mob's sight.

Once everything was under control, Henry's emotions began to waver. There was only one thing left to do, and it filled him with dread. He didn't think he could bear to face the lifeless figure of Coralis, and he hadn't told the others for fear of breaking down in front of them. He was not ready to assume the role of a leader, but he couldn't let Coralis down. The Wand Master would have expected him to provide some sort of guidance to the other apprentices.

"We're all behind you, Henry." Serena had sensed his apprehension, if not its cause.

Suddenly, all the emotion of the past few days seemed to catch up to her at once. She ran to Henry and kissed him lightly, wrapping him in an embrace that spoke to the love she felt for him.

Henry squeezed her tightly in return, knowing he needed her by his side to keep going. And he had to let her know the truth.

She gasped as he sent her an image of Coralis—a snapshot burned into his memory. He took a deep breath to steady himself. He detached himself from his emotions as he filled in the apprentices on what had transpired and clenched his teeth to keep from weeping as he watched their reactions.

He asked Brianna and Katelyn to remain behind to guard Malachai as he led the others to the foyer in the spire. After the first set of stairs, he gained speed and sprinted up the next three. His fear was that if he slowed down he would not have the courage to keep going. He burst through the door with Bryndis and Luis close behind.

The foyer was empty.

"Are you sure you have the right spire?" asked Bryndis.

Henry sensed the remnants of Malachai's spells within Coralis's former prison. And the overturned chair was right where he'd left it. "I don't understand."

"Maybe he went looking for you," said Luis.

A glimmer of hope lifted Henry's spirits, but only for a brief moment. He recalled how Coralis had looked so old and frail—too weak to even stand. And the damage Malachai had inflicted to his aura.

Bryndis placed a hand on his shoulder. "Whatever secrets there are about the death of a Wand Master died with him," she said grimly.

They arrived back outside to a minor commotion. A small but heavily armed contingent of Hutsul mountain men and women on horseback were the first outsiders to arrive. The horses huffed heavily, on the verge of exhaustion after their breakneck gallop to the village. Unlike the earlier Hutsuls they had met, these looked battle-hardened. Henry thought their faces might crack if they smiled.

"Dumitru sent us." The leader, a large man with the build of a professional wrestler and the demeanor of a marine sergeant, extended his hand toward Henry. The man's grip was firm but soft. "I am sorry we are late. We tried to get here sooner but could not get through."

"The dome must have broken when Henry captured Malachai," Bryndis said proudly.

"Which must be why our powers are returning," Katelyn added.

Luis punched Henry's arm with a firm jab. "You did it."

Henry gazed at the sky, which had begun to clear. It was like a sign that brighter days were on the horizon. "You're wrong," he said thoughtfully. "*We* did it."

The Hutsuls worked in teams to carry the stretcher. Malachai did not go quietly. He ranted and raved incessantly, delivering idle threats and ineffective curses. Once she'd rejoined them, Molly tried several spells to shut him up, but the Wand Master had just enough strength to break through them.

Finally the leader had had enough. He nodded a silent command to one of his men, who pulled out a roll of bright yellow duct tape imprinted with smiley faces and wrapped it tightly across Malachai's mouth. "Is funny, yes?"

Malachai stared at Henry with fury in his eyes. Henry felt a pang of pity. But Luis snorted and Katelyn giggled, which broke through the dam of sadness. They all burst out in laughter. "Yes." Henry smiled. "Is very funny."

Serena had used her foot to roll the Pangaea Particle onto a piece of canvas. Without Malachai's influence, it appeared to have gone dormant. Taking no chances, she quickly wrapped it with several more layers, then made a second, smaller stretcher, which she and Bryndis carried—always keeping a wary eye on it for any signs of life.

They stopped only once—to deliver Natalia back to a joyful reunion with her sister. Then they continued to a rendezvous point and met up with another train that would take them back toward Castle Coralis.

The Hutsuls remained behind to deal with the warped menagerie of animals Malachai had created. They promised to show compassion and save the ones they could. As for the creatures already in the wild, they would have to be dealt with later.

Once they had settled down on the train, they each retreated into their own private thoughts and wondered what would become of them. The journey back seemed twice as long as the ride out. Foremost among Henry's thoughts was how he was going to break the news to Gretchen. He grinned as he recalled the first time Coralis had mentioned her. How the Wand Master had blushed when Brianna asked if they were married. Henry was certain Gretchen would be devastated—which was why he was stunned when her reply was, "Ach . . . well, life goes on."

Long after a hearty dinner, Henry lay in his bed. Sleep eluded him. He tossed fitfully until he finally gave up and quietly decided to raid the kitchen for a snack. A mouse crawled up his leg onto his lap and pleaded for a morsel of bread. Henry laughed and handed a piece over. The mouse nibbled happily as Henry stroked its tiny head. "What are we going to do now, my friend?"

"Henry."

Henry jumped up! The mouse scampered into a hole in the wall. Something like laughter reverberated in his mind. *The Particle got to me. I'm going crazy!*

"You are not crazy, my son."

"Coralis!" Henry shouted.

"You didn't really think that moron Malachai could kill me, did you?"

"But how . . . ?"

"Your friend, the Roc. She was quite grateful. She flew me back to the castle, where I retrieved my Forever Wand. I am now resting comfortably in the warm springs of Shangri-la, regaining my strength. You really must try it sometime. They—"

"You're alive?"

"Bahtzen bizzle! Of course I'm alive."

Henry jumped around the kitchen, giddy with joy. *"I have to tell the others!"*

"Not yet! You must take Malachai and the Pangaea Particle to the hot spring in the mountains. Bring Serena with you. The Earth Mother trusts her. Place them in the springs. The Earth Mother will do what needs to be done."

Henry thought back to the vision he'd had when he'd fought Malachai. This must be what the Earth Mother had attempted to communicate. She had plans for the evil Wand Master.

"Yes! Yes! I can do that!" Henry pumped a fist in the air. He waited for more but was met with silence. *"Coralis?"*

"There is more," Coralis said grimly. *"The entrance to the Tethys Ocean has been breached. I do not know what has come out."*

This time it was Henry's turn to be silent. Had they won another battle only to lose the war?

"The responsibilities of the Guild never end," Coralis said sternly. *"Are you up to the challenge?"*

Henry never hesitated. *"You bet I am!"*

EPILOGUE

————◆————

"Where am I?" Markhor rubbed his eyes and tried to sit, but a stabbing pain in his neck forced him back down.

"You are with me." Leonardo entered the room, removed his cap, and sat on the edge of the bed. "And you are where no one can find you."

"How long have I been asleep?" Markhor surveyed the sparsely furnished room. A short chest of drawers, a nightstand with an oil-burning lamp on top, and . . . a falcon perched on the bed's footboard.

"You have not been asleep. You have been near death for three months." Leonardo saw the reaction on Markhor's face when he spotted the falcon. "You know this bird?"

Markhor's brow furrowed with deep creases. "It is familiar . . . from somewhere."

"That is good enough for me," Leonardo said with relief. "When you go, take it with you. It is a nuisance." He stood and arranged his cap neatly on his head.

"Can I get back to my family?" The pain in Markhor's

neck was far surpassed by the ache in his heart. He had so many wrongs to set right.

Leonardo worked his jaw as if he were chewing on something inedible. "I cannot answer that. The portal was damaged in order to create the net that saved you. There are others, but they will not be easy to find." Leonardo helped Markhor to his feet and led him to a workroom covered in maps and scrolls. "My secret library. I will show you the way to the nearest portal, but perhaps you should forget about going back. Make this world your home."

"No," Markhor said with finality.

"Have it your way. The odds are not in your favor." Leonardo looked from Markhor to the falcon. "Then again, who knows? Nothing is impossible."

ACKNOWLEDGMENTS

Some people write by starting with an outline of the story. I'm not one of them. The best I can do is start with a vague idea of where I want my characters to end up. I derive great pleasure from watching the story flow from the tip of my pen, never really knowing what's going to happen until it does. And I hope that you, the reader, feel that same sense of excitement about this book.

There is a lot of me in Henry. My love of reading and inquisitive nature as a child provided the foundation for Henry's character. I hope through Henry's curiosity I've piqued your own. This book is an invitation to continue your exploration of science, nature, and history. The supercontinent Pangaea; the Tethys Ocean; insects and animals of the Amazon rain forest; life and customs of indigenous people in Greenland, South America, and the United States; rocks and minerals; ancient fortresses; and especially Leonardo da Vinci, a true genius—all of this is real and is out there for you to discover.

My heartfelt thanks to all who made this book possible. To my editor, Nick Eliopulos, without whose guidance and encouragement my story would never make it into print. To my agent, Marcia Wernick, who knows all the right buttons to push. To Dominic Harman, Carol Ly, and Baily Crawford, whose collaboration on the book cover creates a sense of wonder and gives the book life before you even begin reading. To Kerianne Okie, Jessica White, and Jackie Hornberger, my extraordinary copy editors and proofreaders. In a time of mass misinformation, it is important to be as accurate as possible. Their fact-checking skills and eye for detail are incredible. To Eric Compton, Janet Speakman, Robin Hoffman, and everyone at Scholastic Book Fairs for believing in me. To Tracy van Straaten, Lizette Serrano, Jennifer Abbots, and the rest of the Scholastic team for beating the drum to draw attention to our books. And to my wife, Barbara, whose wit and wisdom always kick-start my imagination when I begin to stall.

ABOUT THE AUTHOR

Born in nineteen something, Ed Masessa is the second oldest of ten children. He was raised in the small town of Middlesex, New Jersey, where he lived until moving to the sweltering swamp known as Florida. He has undergraduate and graduate degrees from Rutgers University—neither of which pertains to his current career.

Ed has been a child all his life, subscribing to the Chili Davis philosophy that "growing old is mandatory, growing up is optional." Formerly employed as a grease monkey, office cleaner, fast-food manager, forklift operator, truck driver, warehouse supervisor, sales rep, and automotive purchasing manager, he found his calling at Scholastic Book Fairs, where he was devoted to finding books that would turn every child into a lifelong reader. Now retired, he is pursuing the same mission as an author.

After reading many, many, *many* books, Ed began to write himself. He is the author of the #1 *New York Times* bestseller, *The Wandmaker's Guidebook*; the well-reviewed picture book, *Scarecrow Magic*; several works of nonfiction; and, most recently, the Wandmaker novels.

Learn more about Ed on his website, www.edmasessa.com.